FIREHORSE

Also by Diane Lee Wilson

Black Storm Comin'
Margaret K. McElderry Books

FIREHORSE

DIANE LEE WILSON

Margaret K. McElderry Books

NEW YORK * LONDON * TORONTO * SYDNEY

Margaret K. McElderry Books
An imprint of Simon & Schuster Children's Publishing Division
1230 Avenue of the Americas, New York, New York 10020

Book design by Michael McCartney
The text for this book is set in Old Times American.

Manufactured in the United States of America

10 9 8 7 6 5 4 3 2 1

Library of Congress Cataloging-in-Publication Data

Wilson, Diane L.
Firehorse / Diane Lee Wilson.—1st ed.

p.   cm.

Summary: Spirited fifteen-year-old horse lover Rachel Selby
determines to become a veterinarian, despite the opposition of
her rigid father, her proper mother, and the norms of Boston
in 1872, while that city faces a serial arsonist and an epidemic
spreading through its firehorse population.

ISBN-13: 978-1-4169-4874-2
ISBN-10: 1-4169-4874-0 (hardcover)

[1. Veterinary medicine—Fiction. 2. Sex role—Fiction. 3. Horses—
Fiction. 4. Arson—Fiction. 5. Family life—Massachusetts—Fiction.
6. Boston (Mass.)—History—1865—Fiction.] I. Title.

PZ7.W69059Fir 2006
[Fic]—dc22
2005030785

FIRST
EDITION

FOR BAILEY, NOW AND ALWAYS

⚙️ ONE

I'VE ALWAYS BEEN RUNNING, IT SEEMS. OR GALLOPING. YES, that's it: galloping! It's not very ladylike and it drives Mother to distraction—not to mention what it does to Father. But I believe it's a way of drinking every last drop out of the glass life offers you.

In Wesleydale, my hometown in Illinois, my horse Peaches and I tore around the countryside like a pair of wildlings. Saturdays, especially, we'd ride out early, make our usual stops, and be waiting in the oak grove past the Murdock farm by mid-morning. When the nine thirty train whistled in the distance, the townspeople thought it was announcing its approach. But I knew otherwise. I knew it was calling *me*. And the challenge it presented kindled a fire in me as hot as the locomotive's furnace.

One Saturday morning—June 15, 1872, to be exact—was already hot and muggy, and my skirt was bunching around my knees. The sidesaddle would have kept it cleaner, but who can run a race with one leg tied up high? Or while wearing a corset, for that matter? I'd left both behind.

Eagerly I gathered the reins up tight, my heart chattering with the *clickety-clack* of the onrushing train. I plaited my fingers through Peaches' mane, and she began dancing. Then, for mind-shatteringly long seconds, we waited. When the train was just around the bend, I eased Peaches onto the road and huddled down, watching over my shoulder. The instant the locomotive came into view, I thrust my arms forward and Peaches bolted.

Belly to the ground, she shot out of the oak grove and raced alongside the railroad tracks. The locomotive charged up behind us. Glancing over my shoulder, I saw the engineer lean out the window. He tried to look grim, but I knew he was fighting a smile. Two short whistle blasts nearly split my ears and then the locomotive was right up next to us!

I crouched so close over Peaches' neck that her mane whipped my cheek. When I drummed my bare heels against her sides, she doubled her speed. The pebbled dirt road melted into a blur. My heart pounded through my skin.

Again the locomotive rumbled at our flanks. It pulled up beside us, then past us, and the engineer, tasting triumph, leaned out the window and waved. I grabbed a hank of mane with one hand and shook the reins at Peaches with the other. I hollered like a heathen. And, bless her heart, she pulled even. We were almost there! For breathless moments we ran side by side: the black machine and the red mare. The panting and the chugging and the pounding swallowed up my world and spit me out anew, free as a winged bird.

The finish line was the brick tunnel near the Evans Dairy, where Jericho Road dipped, curved sharply, and passed beneath the tracks. Taking the turn at such speed was pure danger, but I wouldn't have had it any other way. Seeing it ahead, I clutched Peaches' mane with both hands, centered myself on her bare back, and put my trust in her. She pricked her ears and hunched lower, then suddenly scrambled out of rhythm. Bits of gravel flew into the air as she lost her footing, and for one sickeningly empty beat we were falling. The ground rushed up at us. But somehow she planted a foot and stopped it, heaving us forward in the same instant. And we managed to dash into the dark tunnel just as the locomotive thundered over it.

The whistle sounded once as we shot out the other side, a shrill good-bye. I thought I heard the engineer's laugh carried on its pitch. Before the entire train passed, I spun Peaches around and dived back into the tunnel. Reining her to a standstill, I savored the deliciously frightening roar directly over our heads. The vibrations shook our very bones. And then the train was gone and I was left smiling.

Satisfied, we headed for home. Mundane chores were waiting: The same old weeds, it seemed, were always sprouting up just to be dug up; the same old hens had to be nudged aside to gather the same old eggs. A chemise that never seemed to get properly mended required yet more stitches. The civilized world was impatient to fasten its buttons around us. But we still had a little time. We weren't captured yet. Peaches nodded contentedly as she shuffled, trailing little clouds of dust with each hoof fall. I swung my legs freely and hummed a favorite hymn.

Galloping, I know for a fact, washes you cleaner than any scrubbing. It sends air rushing into your darkest corners and chases the cobwebs out. Every Saturday after our race I felt as clean as a swept porch. Light and happy. And hungry. As usual, I'd slipped out to the barn without any breakfast, and my stomach was noisily reminding me. So when I looked up to find us passing Mr. Jude's apple orchard, I have to confess I was sorely tempted. A new rail fence ran along the side of it, the splintery boards gleaming a pinkish yellow in the sunlight. It was four feet high if it was an inch, and put there, I was certain, simply to make those apples look all the sweeter. My mouth watered.

I knew that orchard. A few months before we'd wandered into it from another direction, and Mr. Jude had chased us out with his dogs. Then he'd gone straight down and told Father about it, adding that Peaches and I had trampled his newly tilled garden, which was a lie. He'd accused me of something else, too, something that I still didn't quite understand.

From my bedroom over the porch, I'd tried to hear what they were saying, but I couldn't make out the words. The front door slamming was plain enough, though. I'd peeked out my window to see Mr. Jude stalking down the drive. Inside, I heard Father's clipped and carefully measured voice, the one he used when explaining his wishes to little children or the elderly. Like a muffled echo, it was followed by Mother's even footsteps skimming the stairs. Father was sending her.

It wasn't the first time she'd served as his messenger. While Father could talk to me rationally about the weather, or the condition of the surrounding corn crop, or sometimes—*sometimes*—about the columns he wrote for his newspaper, he couldn't and wouldn't discuss my many instances of "unbridled behavior," as I once heard him describe it to Mother. I was *her* daughter then. That was *her* job. Funny thing was, I was nothing like my mother.

She came into my room and began darting about, tidying this and smoothing that. She moved as lightly and noiselessly as a butterfly. "Next Saturday morning," she said, "let's invite Mary Grace over and we'll bake up some gingersnaps. Or we could look through flower catalogs; I've just received a new one." I murmured something evasive and left my bed to straddle the chair in front of my dressing table. Fingering its chipped green paint, I waited for her to tell me what she'd really come to say.

She fluttered some more. Then, reaching for the brush, she gave out a little sigh and motioned me to turn around. With her first stroke, the brush caught in my windblown hair and our eyes caught in the mirror. One pair was the color of faded hyacinths, the other was as green as the fields and unnaturally defiant. Two more dissimilar faces you could not have found, yet somehow we'd been planted in the same family.

She petted my shoulder. I knew it was coming: her message. "Your Father thinks, Rachel dear," she said, "that perhaps it's time you give up your horse?"

"No!" I jumped up and shouted the word so vehemently that she actually blanched a shade paler, which I instantly felt bad about. After all, she was merely the messenger.

She reached the brush toward my hair. I took a step back, shaking my head.

"Well, if you'd promise to use the sidesaddle," she cajoled, "maybe your father would consider letting ... and if you'd promise to wear shoes and gloves, too. Why, just look at what those leather reins are doing to your hands." She lifted them by their stained fingertips and made a face. "Honestly, Rachel, you're fifteen years old. Can't you *please* ride like a lady," she begged, "because . . . well, there's really no other way to put it: The way you're tearing around—astride," she whispered the word dramatically, "with your limbs showing—well, people are calling it indecent."

Indecent.

That plopped me back down on the chair. I'd always thought that indecent was the way Mrs. Winnow flirted with our minister, whose wife was deathly ill but not yet passed. Or the way two of our church elders raised their hands and swore not to let alcohol pass their lips, yet were happy to pass the cider jug at the fall plowing match. I thought indecent was leaving a dog tied to a tree day in and day out, for its whole miserable life. But just like that, she threw me into the same sinful category. She sewed a scarlet letter onto me. She and Father and Mr. Jude. When all I'd done was gallop.

That had been three months ago, but the word still rang in my ears: *indecent.* So as I was sitting there on Peaches with my stomach rumbling, I got to thinking about eating an apple—just one—to spite Mr. Jude and his lies.

That's when I heard them coming: the boys. Farther on past the orchard, I saw them, four abreast. Riding into town and to their summer work at the granary and the livery and the slaughterhouse. Riding with their hard boots and their harsh words and their heavy hands. We'd met before.

The road was narrow along this stretch and fenced on both sides. I had no choice if I wanted to avoid them. Angling Peaches toward the orchard gate, which was slightly lower than its fence and situated between us and the approaching boys, I pressed my heels into her sides. She understood at once. With her ears pointed toward the top rail, she picked up a canter. I felt her hindquarters gather beneath me and, with each powerful stride, her withers lifted higher. The boys hooted with glee, thinking we were mounting a foolhardy charge at them. I gritted my teeth and focused on the hurdle ahead. At the critical moment, when there was only freedom or crashing failure, Peaches left the ground and we were flying. For one breathless instant the earth couldn't hold us.

As we swooped down inside, the boys came galloping up to the gate to hurl some jeers over it. I ignored them, as I always had. They had nothing I wanted or needed.

Peaches kept cantering smoothly between the tidy rows. I stroked her neck with gratitude. The coarse voices behind us faded, then fragmented in a sudden flurry of hoofbeats. And we were left alone.

Pulling Peaches to a walk, I let myself fall under the

orchard's spell. It was so quiet among the trees—a private, sun-dappled world that locked out the injustices of everyday life. A low humming lulled us as we ambled along. The ground gently sank and swelled, and I could swear I heard it breathing. Lacy white flowers arced in abundance, their honeyed fragrance seeming to grow sweeter in the warming sun. I reined Peaches down a different row, and then another and another, just wandering. My mouth watered at the thousands of hard, glossy green orbs, but the apples weren't ripe yet and there was no use in biting into even one.

After a time, we found ourselves back at the gate. No need to risk our necks again, so I slid off and led Peaches through, then climbed onto the fence and onto her back. The sun was even higher in the sky, and I knew the chickens wouldn't be the only ones squawking at home.

Sweat had glued my dress to my skin by then, and it was all I could do to keep from wading into the shallows of the Gilead River for a quick dip. The waters sparkled invitation, but I kept Peaches pointed straight and we clip-clopped across the planked bridge.

Turning onto Bell Road, we hurried into a trot to get past the Stokeses' farm. Not only because we were late, but because I couldn't bear to look at their slatted barn with its string of orange fox pelts nailed in cruciform beneath the eaves. It seemed there was always a price to pay for crossing someone's boundaries. Always a price. But what place did death have on a morning as glorious as this?

꧁ TWO

A S SOON AS I RODE ONTO OUR PLACE, I SLID OFF PEACHES and tied her in the barn. I didn't see Mother anywhere, so I rushed into the chicken pen, slowing just enough to keep them from squawking alarm, and quickly gathered up a dozen eggs in the waiting basket. I realized I was holding my breath. I ran to the house, opened the back door, and peeked inside. The kitchen was empty. I set the basket on the table and hurried back to the barn. I gulped another breath. Pausing at the doorway, I yanked up some handfuls of thick-stemmed weeds and heaved them into a conspicuous pile in the sunlight. I glanced around again, then dived into the cool barn and exhaled in a whoosh. My chest heaved. Finally I could breathe.

In Mr. Moore's science class we'd learned that all of Earth's creatures need oxygen to survive. In a process called respiration, we breathe in oxygen and breathe out carbon dioxide. Creatures that live on land get their oxygen from the air. Creatures that live underwater get theirs from dissolved oxygen. Well, I got my oxygen from horses. From riding them and touching them and listening to them and learning from them.

Having bought a little time, I belatedly began grooming Peaches, my fleet-footed racehorse, my winner. I pulled the burrs out of her fetlock hairs and scratched her underbelly and combed her mane until it lay as smooth and silky as the fringe on Grandmother's shawl. I gently traced the whorled hairs on her forehead and wiped the dust from the velvet plain beneath her eyes. She consented to my fussing for only so long before shaking her head free and snorting with the force of the west wind.

Coated in a sticky mist, I laughed and snorted myself. "Oh, thank you. Thank you so very much. Well, if you've had enough grooming, your ladyship, let's have a look at your feet."

Trading the brush for a hoof pick, I sidled up to her near foreleg. Peaches responded to my pinch by agreeably lifting her foot, which I balanced across my knee. She'd had a bout with thrush the past few weeks, but as I bent close and sniffed, I couldn't smell any of the black rot. I couldn't see any either. I scraped each side of the V-shaped crevice and went on to the other three hooves, finding lingering signs of thrush in only the off hind one. Dutifully I soaked a small rag in the turpentine I'd bought at the hardware store and packed it into the questionable hoof. Then I led Peaches to the rain barrel for a long, slobbery drink and returned her to her stall. While she munched her hay, I took up a pitchfork and combed through the straw bedding until it was clean and dry enough for any human guest.

When she was finished, Peaches gave a good shake and cocked one hip in preparation for a nap. I didn't want to leave, not yet, and rested my forehead against hers. "Tell me what you're thinking," I whispered.

That I love you, I imagined her nickered response. *That you bring me everything I need.*

I stroked her cheeks and tugged on her nostrils and braided and unbraided her thin red forelock. With swallows flitting in and out of the wide door, swirling the dust motes suspended in the golden air, Peaches and I shared the silence and each other's company.

There's no better place than a stable, I've found. It's the only place with solid footing. When I'm standing beside a horse, I feel that I'm neither girl nor boy, child nor adult, strong nor weak. I'm accepted just as I am. And there, and only there, I can breathe.

For the rest of the day I tore through enough chores to keep Mother from heaving any of her sighs, at least in front of me. I even managed to mend and wash out my chemise, and I ironed my sash for church. The day was clear blue sailing. Until supper brought a rumbling of thunder.

James had returned from making deliveries for Mr. Hubbard's feed store, taking his seat just before we said grace. Even though he'd stopped to wash up at the kitchen sink, he still smelled warmly of sweat and dust and hay. A burnt redness tinged his nose and cheekbones. His easy, lopsided smile spilled across his face like sunshine. One eyebrow rose with mischief. "Did you have a good ride this morning?" he asked.

I took the plate of boiled carrots he was passing me. His expression said he knew something. Was it my tardiness? Or my trespassing into Mr. Jude's orchard? And why was he raising the subject in Father's presence? "Yes, we did," I answered cautiously. "We rode out past the Murdocks' and came home by way of Gilead Creek." I sneaked a glance at Father. He'd not mentioned my riding in the past months, even after Mr. Jude's visit. To be honest, I don't think he had any idea how often I rode, or how far.

"Some of the Murdocks' cows got out night before last," was all Father said. His eyes, neatly framed by the gold rims of his spectacles, narrowed to black pinpoints of disapproval. "She's not keeping the place up." What he wasn't saying was that Mrs. Murdock, a recent widow, should have sold her husband's farm and moved in with her sister's family. Father didn't hold with female self-reliance. It wasn't natural.

"Well, it doesn't look like rain," Mother said with an effort at cheeriness. "There'll be some nice weather for getting fences mended. Or for traveling."

Traveling? My ears pricked. Who'd said anything about traveling?

She poked at the fricasseed chicken on her plate, her face smooth and emotionless.

"I almost forgot," James said, still addressing me. "William asked about you today. And Nathaniel did as well."

What was he up to?

"Something about . . . apples." He gazed at the ceiling,

tapping his chin with feigned thoughtfulness. "Oh, that's it. They wanted to know if you'll be *sharing* any of your apples."

I would have kicked him if I'd been able to reach him. Instead I impulsively tossed my napkin, hitting him square in the face.

"Rachel!" Mother exclaimed.

"That'll be enough of that!" Father warned.

James wadded the napkin in his fist and laughed. "Don't blame her. You can see she's a sorrel-top through and through, and you know how temperamental they are."

It was another poke in the ribs, but I couldn't help grinning. Unlike most girls with copper-colored hair, I took pride in mine. That's because horses with red coats—be they chestnuts or sorrels or roans—were known to be high-spirited. Dangerous. Some people even refused to own them. How often I'd imagined someone trying to smash a bit against my teeth and my striking out in refusal. No one was going to own me.

Still, I changed the subject. In an effort to placate Mother, I asked, "Isn't Grandmother feeling well?"

Her mother ate with us most evenings, but tonight, for some reason, she'd stayed in town. Mother shot an inscrutable look at Father before fixing her gaze on her plate and softly replying, "I think she's feeling a little uprooted is all." Somehow that put a damper on things. The atmosphere in the dining room took on that peculiar itchy quality you feel on hot summer evenings when the sky is empty but the air is so thick and heavy you just know a storm's on the horizon. I glanced from face to face, finding them all veiled with secrets. James stopped his teasing and spooned food into his mouth with a voraciousness unusual even for him. Father cleared his throat and reached for the bread. I self-consciously drained my goblet of milk, trying not to gurgle under Mother's pensive gaze. We finished our meal to the sound of scraping forks and the weighty silence of something left unsaid. Really, the air pressed on us—or on me, anyway—like an iron. So as soon as the table was cleared, and the leftovers returned to the icebox, and the dishes washed, dried, and stacked, I hurried upstairs. Each of us, in fact, settled in solitude into some part of the house: Father to pore over his newspapers (he was editor of the local one, the *Plowman's Dispatch*); Mother to embroider her apron; James to black his boots; and I to curl up with my favorite book of the past six months, *The Reliable Horse Care Manual for American Owners*. They could have their secrets; I had some of my own.

"Rapturous" was the only word to describe my horse care manual. It was two inches thick, its gilt-edged pages bound in mahogany leather and embossed with three Arabian horse heads in brilliant gold, not the least bit dulled for the fingering they'd endured since last Christmas. That's when James had given the book to me. It was an extravagant present and must have cost him nearly a week's wages. My pulse quickened each time I lifted it onto my lap.

With the crickets humming and the light fading, I turned up the flame on my lamp, settled against the bed pillows, and began reading. After horses, that was my most pleasurable way to spend time.

Over the past six months, I'd worked my way through selecting a horse (already had one, thank you), structure of the perfect horse (that would be Peaches), and diseases of the bones, the glands, the muscles and tendons. Now I was up to page 293 and struggling through diseases of the chest and lungs and their horrific cures. Thank the Lord I hadn't had to attempt any of those on Peaches. The only time I'd been able to apply any practical knowledge at all from the manual was in treating her thrush. And for that I'd had to skip ahead to the chapter on diseases of the feet.

Turning the pages in chunks, I located the spot where I'd left off and dived into the sea of tiny type. I was soon finding it hard to swallow, as I waded through paragraph after paragraph on coughs and consumption and corrosive liniments.

I suppose I was so immersed in my book that I didn't notice the house going to sleep around me. Only when the mantel clock chimed in the parlor below did I look up to check the oil in the lamp. I realized then that James had gone to bed, and Father and Mother were in their bedroom next door. The uneven rise and fall of voices on the other side of the wall sounded as if they were quarreling. Or rather, as if Father was speechifying and Mother was listening, pale-faced and mute for the most part.

A drawer slammed shut and I heard Father mutter something about "backward thinking" and "small potatoes." Another drawer opened and closed. Some shoes hit the wall, low and in the corner. ". . . thinking they could fire *me*," he said with heavy sarcasm. "There are bigger newspapers." My stomach pitched a little and landed unsettled.

I struggled to focus on my book. *Any disease that affects the respiratory organs*, I read over for the second time, *can give rise to inflammation and fever, and in consequence to cough.* Father's grumblings faded into the background. *Should the inflammation and fever be neglected and thus become chronic—*

"What about her horse?" It was Mother's voice this time, quiet as a breeze riffling through her lace curtains, yet clear as a jangling alarm to me. I sat up fast, straining to hear Father's response.

"Time we all made changes," is what I thought I heard, along with some less than flattering comments about "willfulness" and "a disturbing lack of propriety." But then, "For God's sake," he said, loudly enough for the neighbors down the road to hear, "she doesn't even wear shoes." My face burned.

For a while, a silence as heavy as a roar enveloped our house. I remained rigidly upright in my bed, imagining it a small boat on a storm-tossed sea. I braced for the wave that would drown me.

There was more talk, more planning, which I only made out in syllables and phrases. My heart beat faster and faster. Right on the other side of the wall, my life was being decided and all I could do was grip the sheets and listen. *What about Peaches?* I wanted to scream. I heard Father climb into bed, heard him punch his pillow into place. There was more silence.

Out by the garden, an owl hooted. I kept listening. Before long Father's snoring took up a steady rhythm.

Then I heard Mother. Her voice sounded pinched and achingly sad. "She won't understand."

"What?" Father had been startled awake.

"I said, she won't understand."

The bedsprings creaked as Father harrumphed and rolled over. "It's just a horse," he said all too clearly. "And she's just a girl. She'll forget about it the minute we get to Boston. Now, good night."

The next day dawned clear and sunny, with no trace of a storm, though one had surely blown through. And one of their secrets was revealed: It was a plan to change me—to tie me to a tomato stake, as it were, and fasten me up tight and make me grow a certain way. Father had ordered it and, in compliance, Mother had quietly paired my shoes and set them by the nightstand before I awoke. She'd laid my corset on my bed too, where I couldn't miss it. She always complied. Much earlier in her life, someone had tied her to a stake, and while she'd grown tall and rigid, there wasn't much color to her. She hadn't had enough oxygen.

THREE ❦

I T ALL HAPPENED SO FAST, I WENT COMPLETELY NUMB. One minute, it seemed, I was brushing Peaches in the warm, sweet-smelling air of a stable and the next I was imprisoned in a damp tower. In reality it was the stoop-shouldered attic room of a narrow brick townhouse that gasped between dozens of other identical brick townhouses along a cobblestone street in Boston. Father had taken a job as managing editor of a small newspaper there. A shroud of sea fog pressed against the room's one tiny window. The wallpaper curled away from the seams, and odors of stale smoke and wet potatoes clung so heavily to the walls that my throat clamped shut. Just one day after moving there I could no longer smell Peaches on my clothes. I could barely breathe.

I'd thrown a fit when Peaches was sold and led away—childish, I admit, because it was a pure, raving-berserker fit. That had only added to what appeared to be Father's growing disdain for me. Stonily peering through the gold rims of his spectacles, he'd said, "You've none but yourself to blame.

Time's overdue for some changes." And then, with his judgment passed and, I suppose, while waiting for me to make those changes, he'd stopped speaking to me. Other than the necessary civilities of "Pardon me" and "Please pass the salt," our wordless battle had marched across the country.

All during the packing, all during the wagon ride to the station and the long train ride and the carriage ride at the opposite end, I sat motionless and numb. Mother petted my shoulder. "When God closes a door, he opens a window," she said, and I wanted to scream, *Is that what you're calling Father now?* James threw his arm around me and tried to point out scenes of interest. Grandmother was the only one who didn't try to console me. She sat clutching her Bible and staring at the receding horizon, lost in her own misery.

For two whole days after we arrived I lay in my attic bedroom and watched the colorless ceiling shift from morning's gloom to evening's shadows. I watched a spider take hours to spin an intricate web and then cling to its outer edge, hungry and alone, waiting for something to happen. I lay so still that a mouse ran across my foot, pausing to sample a button on my shoe with his sharp teeth before lifting his head to sniff in my direction, whiskers atwitch, and scampering on.

For two whole days I stayed like that. Thinking and wondering. Remembering and wanting. On the third day I rose.

It was terribly early; the sky was black as pitch. The house, this strange house in a strange city, where we were all crammed together, was still. Yet I knew something was about to happen. I could sense it. Sitting upright and wadding the coverlet between my fingers, I held my breath and listened. Down the street came the heavy *clop-clop* of a tired horse pulling a delivery wagon. A wash of silence spilled in behind him. I waited. The mouse and what sounded like thirty of his friends thumped between the walls. Somewhere out in the harbor, a ship moaned. Then more silence. Under the eaves outside my window, the pigeons began chittering uneasily. Stiff tail feathers scraped along the bricks as the birds shuffled nervously back and forth. My leg twitched once, then again. The hairs on my arms rose to attention. Something was definitely going to happen.

That's one of *my* secrets. Ever since I was a little girl, my legs have gotten a strange, twitchy feeling right before something important happens. The feeling isn't frequent. And Father would call it girlish nonsense, especially when nothing at all happens afterward. But, often enough to raise the gooseflesh on my arms, when my legs begin twitching my life is about to take a sudden turn.

Two floors below me, the mantel clock began chiming the hour and I counted along with it. Before I could whisper "four," I was jolted right out of my bed by the raucous jangling of a fire alarm. Dogs barked, men shouted. And even though our house was around the corner and down the street from the neighborhood fire station, the noisy clatter of hooves seemed to charge right through my room. My heart banged wildly. Swept up in the frenzy, I leaped back onto my bed. I twisted the sheets until they were near to ropy reins and hung on every sound. The choppy hoofbeats turned rhythmic: The firehorses were coming together under harness. There was a shrill whinny from one and an answering call from another. The men shouted orders. My breath came faster. The staccato quickened as the horses leaned into their work, then built to a seamless thunder as they turned the corner and raced past our house toward the fire. Like a summer storm, they were here and gone, leaving me panting.

It's a powerful tonic, listening to horses gallop. Clutching the pillow to my chest, I played the hoofbeats over and over in my head, until the silence subdued them. In the emptiness of the ordinary, and as my breathing eased, I began to wonder about the twitching. What did it mean?

The alarm must have awakened Grandmother, too, because in the room directly below me, I heard her talking to herself. Cocking an ear, I could tell she was quoting Scripture. It's funny how you can hear something and instantly smell something, when the two don't seem at all related. At that moment, in the darkness of my room, I smelled bacon. And I remembered a Sunday back in Wesleydale, after church, when Grandmother and I had been working in the kitchen together. I'd promised her to secrecy, then haltingly sought her opinion of my twitching legs.

Grandmother, a woman who was dependably unperturbed, didn't so much as bat an eye. "God has given you a gift," she replied brightly. She tapped my nose with a finger that still smelled of breakfast: butter and flour and bacon grease.

We were rolling out biscuit dough, and I'd been cogitating on the sermon that morning, which had been about Adam and

Eve in the Garden and how it was a sin to try to know too much. "Do you think Reverend Wyeth would call it a gift?" I asked.

Grandmother snorted, dismissing my question as easily as a horse swishes away a bothersome fly. "No, I don't expect that he would. That's because he's a man, and men don't like what they don't understand." She slammed the biscuit cutter hard into the dough and twisted it sharply. "And I expect that's why God gave this gift to you, a girl, or young woman, I should say, since you're taller than me now. At any rate, Rachel dear, don't you ignore those twitchy feelings. They're heaven-sent, I'm sure of it. Use them as your compass to the world around you." She deftly twisted a few more circles out of the dough, plopping them onto the baking sheet, then looked at me. There was a twinkle in her eyes. "And let me know if you get a feeling for which horse is going to win the mile at this year's fair. I'll place a large bet with that know-it-all Mr. Schmidt."

She'd laughed back then and popped a pinch of dough into my mouth. But that laugh, like that scene, had taken place half a nation away from here. She didn't laugh much anymore, ever since Father insisted she move with us to Boston. She'd left her husband buried there; she'd left her beloved garden; and, it seemed, she'd left her laughter.

There was a time when she quoted the Psalms, the verses of joy and praise. But now she was stuck in the last book of the Bible, the Revelation of St. John. It seemed she was just waiting to die. "Fear God, and give glory to him," she recited now, "for the hour of his judgment is come. . . ."

☙ FOUR

EFORE IT WAS FULL LIGHT, I WAS DRESSED. I WAITED, listening, as one by one the other members of my family rose, performed their toiletries, and passed over the hall's creaking floorboards and down the stairs. I thought I heard Grandmother mention my name, but there was only silence afterward, during which I imagined a shaking head. I was grateful they'd stopped pestering me to join them. When the upstairs was empty, I tiptoed down from my attic bedroom and stood in the hall, gazing out one of the tall, narrow windows there.

Fog clouded the small, rectangular courtyard attached to our townhouse, but I knew what was hidden there: a broken-roofed, thoroughly disheveled carriage shed. I'd poked through it on our arrival, halfheartedly expecting to find a horse inside. The lone stall was empty, of course, and stacked with rubbish, its rough planks thick with dust and cobwebs. When I'd stepped onto the desiccated bedding, a rat had scurried up and over one of the planks. But the lingering smells! I closed my eyes and drew them again to mind: a haze of horse sweat, a dried sweetness that spoke of grain, even a hint of oiled leather. The abandoned place was, all in all, completely splendid. And though I didn't have a plan yet, I knew that that carriage shed—and what went in it—was going to be my salvation.

Maybe life in Boston wasn't going to be so terribly awful. It was Saturday; something good had always happened on Saturdays. My heart gave a hopeful buck and I sucked in a deep breath. The unforgiving corset squelched such whimsy. Like a rabbit being squeezed between the jaws of a trap, I started to panic. I couldn't breathe. Holding onto the sill, I fought for one shallow breath after another, the corset all the while grimly clutching me with its bony stays. Almost a full minute passed until I'd gotten enough air to forcibly slow my heaving ribs. How was I ever going to get used to wearing such an uncomfortable contraption?

With a last longing look outside, I continued on down the stairwell. This was the darkest part of the house, perfect for protecting the delicate colors of Father's butterfly collection. The five frames hung there were the first things he'd unpacked. I tried to ignore them, as I had at home. To me they seemed a celebration of death, of the cruel capture of something once beautiful and vulnerable. I didn't have to turn my head to know that each winged creature was stretched between four pins. Centered below each was a tiny label, somewhat yellowed, listing its Latin name in a small, typeset font. Father hadn't added his own handwriting to his collection; he hadn't even collected them by his own hand. Instead, he'd paid boys back in Wesleydale to bring him butterflies. If he approved, he kept a few select specimens. Shuddering, I hurried past, and for the hundredth time wondered how many butterflies had been killed without ever meeting his approval.

From the bottom stair I could see that Father and James were in the dining room, and I could hear Mother and Grandmother in the kitchen. They were quarreling over tea preparation, their voices easily carrying through the thin walls of this pasteboardy house.

"Don't use my good china if you're just going to make dirty water," Grandmother was scolding.

"Tea isn't supposed to be the color of mud," Mother replied impassively. "I'm steeping it for exactly one and a half minutes. That's the way Mr. Selby takes it."

"But I'm going to be drinking it too!" The wooden joints of the kitchen table groaned as Grandmother leaned her weight against it. "Good Lord. You're sending me to the Pearly Gates with a belly full of backwash."

"I wish you wouldn't talk that way, Mother. You're not going to die."

"Well, then, I have a news item for you, Nora: We're all going to die. And I the sooner because—"

"—you're older?"

"No, because I can't get a decent cup of tea in this house. Since you've dragged me across the nation to die, the least you could do is brew me a decent cup of tea."

The door to the dining room swung open and Mother, carrying the tea tray, entered. She was followed by Grandmother, who plopped into her chair with a loud sigh of distress. To distract them from their argument, I quickly slipped into the room and into my chair.

"Rachel!" Mother set down the tray and gave me a hug. "I'm so pleased that you've joined us. Are you feeling better?" She passed a cool hand across my forehead. "Would you like something to eat? I've some porridge ready, or would you prefer eggs?" Before I could answer, she disappeared into the kitchen. I heard the icebox opened. "There's still some ham from last night," she called, "with a few potatoes?"

"No, the porridge is enough. Thank you."

Father remained hidden behind his newspaper, but James leered across the table with one of his patented grins. "Mrs. Rip Van Winkle, I presume? Or Sleeping Beauty?"

Blushing, I busied myself preparing a cup of tea the way I liked it: equal amounts of milk and the brown stuff, sweetened with two heaping spoonfuls of sugar. Grandmother had already poured hers. I could tell by the way she was briskly stirring her milky brew, clanking the spoon against the china cup with the agitation of an eggbeater, that she was on to one of her prickly days.

"It's a wonder anyone can sleep with those fire alarms sounding at all hours," she grumbled. "That's the second one in three days." She bit into a biscuit, leaving a bead of jam glistening on the fuzz of her upper lip. "Your father's learned," she said after swallowing, "that it was Hansen's Livery that burned last night—burned to the ground. More than thirty horses lost."

Even with the milk, the tea tore a hole through my stomach. Thirty horses! Dead! Horrid images filled my head: panic-stricken horses pawing at their wooden cells, charred and twisted bodies stretched stiff and silent. Mother set a bowl of porridge in front of me and I had to look away.

"Such a shame," she murmured.

"Damned morning papers!" Father exclaimed suddenly. "They—"

"Mr. Selby, please."

"—have all the most timely news." Father thrust his paper aside to stab at the meat and potatoes on his plate, taking in a huge mouthful. Pages from several other newspapers were spread open on the table. Mother seemed to have given up complaining about the ink stains on her linens. "How does one compete with them?" He looked around the table, but knowing he'd provide his own answer, none of us said a word. "My only consolation," he went on shortly, "is that the *Argus*, being an evening paper, can provide what they can't. And do you know what that is?" Again, we remained mute, our audience of faces turned toward his. "Editorial examination. Thoughtful, complete, and direct. Helps people know how they should think. That's where you get your money's worth. Facts *and* insight." He waved his fork in the air. "Not a cursed speck of insight in the morning papers! Take a look for yourselves. Just one ridiculous recipe after another for face cream or foot powder or . . . or . . . Professor Flint's horse tonic."

Mother had taken her place at the opposite end of the table. She was pushing at the wrinkles in the tablecloth, a habit of hers when she was bordering on being upset. "Mr. Selby," she began in a whisper-soft voice, "your language. I really wish that you—"

"And that's why this livery fire could prove serendipitous."

"Serendipitous!" Grandmother countered, angling for a fight. "What makes you think it was an accident?"

Father peered over his spectacles. To a stranger, it might seem he was sizing her up, but he well knew this opponent. Secretly, I think he lived for these debates; maybe they both did. I also think that's why he insisted Grandmother move to Boston with us. She was the only one who challenged him. "There are not yet *facts*," he emphasized his favorite word, "to prove that it was an accident or that it wasn't. I use the term serendipitous as it applies to *my* good fortune. In the past two days I have been searching for some topic, some problem here in Boston that needs solving. Something to hang my hat on, so to speak—or to light a fire under the readers of the *Argus*. And it just may be Boston's readiness—or lack thereof—to fight fires. With the Great Chicago Fire having wreaked its devastation just last year, the public needs to examine the state of asbestos in Boston. So that's why this livery fire may be quite convenient."

My toes curled at the thought of thirty dead horses being "convenient" for Father.

Grandmother snorted and leaned forward. "*Your* good

fortune, is it? Did you stop to consider that last night's fire has nothing to do with serendipity but everything to do with the Almighty's displeasure?" Quite the opposite of her own daughter, Grandmother relished fanning the flames. "I remind you of Reverend Wyeth's last sermon: 'For behold'"—she rapped her knife on the table for emphasis—"'the Lord will come with fire and with his chariots like a whirlwind.'"

Father made a showy pretense of curbing his smirk. "I do hope he's not coming today," he retorted, one hand in the air. "I have a newspaper to get out."

"That's blasphemy!" Grandmother rapped her knife again.

"That's business!"

James, always the peacemaker in our family, interrupted. "Speaking of fire," he said, "I heard that the chief at the station around the corner is hiring. I thought about going over there this morning."

"Oh, James," Mother murmured, "you're not old enough for such dangerous work."

"A smoke-eater!" Father tore into the idea as readily as his meat. "Of course you're old enough. You're nineteen . . . ?"

"Next year. Eighteen now, but that's good enough for polishing brass."

"Polishing brass! Ha! You'll be a driver and nothing less. After some of those wild-eyed broomtails you drove for Elbert Hubbard, these city teams will seem as docile as oxen. Why, I'll match you against any driver they can put up and we'll see who gets to the fire first!"

Mother was pressing the wrinkles with ever more vigor. "I still don't think that—"

Father ran her over. "And say, once you're hired on, maybe you can get me the inside story. You know, talk with the men; see what they think about this city's readiness. I've learned there's been a rash of fires recently. Maybe they're somehow connected."

"I've told you they're connected," Grandmother crowed.

"I think I'll boil some more water for tea," Mother said, leaving her food uneaten. "Would anyone like some more tea?" She looked around futilely before gliding out of the room.

James caught my eye. Something was up. "How about walking over with me? I'm told the firehorses are brought out every morning for exercise and viewing by the public. You'd like to see them, wouldn't you?"

No corset could contain it: My heart bucked hard. "That would be wonderful."

"Good. As soon as you're finished eating, we'll go. It's half past eight already, and I'd like to speak with the chief as soon as possible."

"I'm finished," I said, pushing back the chair. It occurred to me that James still planned amusements for me as if I were a child of five rather than a girl nearly sixteen. And I continued to follow. Oh, well.

Mother returned to the dining room in time to hear our plans. "Oh, I'm sorry, dear," she said to me, "but you can't go. Mr. Selby has made arrangements for your grandmother and you and me to sit for a photograph." She clasped her hands together, maybe for Father's benefit. "Won't that be lovely?"

I wanted to bolt.

"There should be time to do both," James said.

"The appointment is for eleven thirty sharp," Father warned. "It won't reflect well on me if you're late." He folded his newspaper and stood. "Besides," he said, without even glancing in my direction, "I don't think your sister needs to be socializing with horses. We've had quite enough of that in the past." He pulled his watch from his pocket, muttered a calculation to himself, and left the room with a perfunctory nod. Snatching his hat from the hallway, he hurried out the front door.

"Now," Mother was saying cheerily, "I want us all to look especially nice. I was thinking white—"

"I've not worn anything but black since Joseph passed and I'm not about to change," Grandmother interrupted.

"But—"

"I'm wearing black."

"Fine, Mother." She turned to me. "You and I can wear white. I was thinking about your good muslin dress, the one we ordered through Wheaton's. And I'll help you pin up your hair like this." She began gathering my hair in her hands.

James must have seen the look on my face. "Mother," he implored, "it's three hours until your appointment. Surely Rachel and I can walk over to the station and be back in plenty of time for her to dress. Let her visit the horses."

"You heard what her father said."

Here they were, talking about me as if I weren't in the very same room.

"Oh, let her go," Grandmother said. "Do her good to breathe in some fresh air."

Mother let my hair fall. "Oh, all right. I wash my hands of it. But hurry, or it's the Selby name that gets a black mark. We're new here. People will be watching."

"Let them watch!" Grandmother muttered. "The devil's got his own eye on them."

James shot me a conspiratorial look. "Can you hurry, Rachel?"

I nodded and jumped up from the table so abruptly that the cups rattled in their saucers. My legs were aching to hurry.

↩ **FIVE**

AMES COULD BE THE MOST WONDERFUL BROTHER ON ONE day and complete provocation the next. That morning he was beyond wonderful.

It had to be provoking for him, then, that I was at my clumsiest. The stiff new shoes that Mother had bought me, and that she made sure I was wearing before we left the house, were a cobbler's curse. In just stepping over the doorsill, one blocky heel adopted a mind of its own, caught the raised edge, and sent me tumbling into thin air. If James hadn't grabbed me by the arm, I would have landed bottom side up on the pavement below. Such a Boston debut might have killed Mother, I think.

Sheepishly I righted myself and tottered down the stairs, safely supported by both James and the wrought-iron railing. When we reached the pavement with no further mishaps and turned down the street, though, he held his arm rigid, keeping me pulled close. Strangers smiled and glanced away, assuming we were sweethearts. That made my face burn all the more.

Still, I was outside. After two days holed up in my tower, I needed some fresh air, as Grandmother had suggested. Only the air wasn't fresh. Sodden odors of turpentine and coal and cabbage assaulted my nose. A damp, iron gray sky weighed on us and on the maze of buildings surrounding us. For as far as I could see, red brick townhouses just as narrow as ours stood braced together like so many books on a shelf. Bulbous facades and steep stairs spilled onto the pavement as if bursting from the books' seams. Crowding us on the other side was the nonstop traffic. Although we lived on a smallish street, it already bustled that morning with delivery wagons and flashy carriages and pedestrians blithely zigzagging their way through the chaos. I shook my head.

"What?" James asked.

"It's not Wesleydale, is it?"

The hot look that sparked in his eyes caught me by surprise. "It certainly isn't. It's different through and through. It even smells different." He sucked in the manufactured air and exhaled a happy sigh. "Intoxicating!" Lengthening his stride, he rattled on. "Think of it! At this very moment, all around us, businesses are being born, fortunes are being made, women are being wooed, men are—"

"Women are being *wooed*?"

James grinned. "Well, someone has to do it. Now, that's a job I could hire on for."

We rounded the corner and as soon as we did so, he pointed out the fire station, another block and a half down the street. I didn't see any horses on display. Maybe they were still inside. "How many do they keep?" I asked. "Horses, I mean."

He frowned, thinking. "I don't know for sure. Let's see, there'd be three to pull the steam engine, I suppose, and a pair for the ladder, if they have one. At least one more for the hose cart." He was counting on his fingers. "And the chief probably keeps one for his own buggy. That's seven. I guess it all depends on how much equipment they have. There could be more."

"And you'll drive a team?"

"You sound like Father," he responded nonchalantly, though he looked pleased. "I'm just going to see if the chief will take me on as an apprentice. I've heard there's a lot of brass polishing before they hand you any reins."

"Oh, they'll let you drive once they see you go," I replied with confidence, all the while staring at the huge, double-wide entry. I half expected a team to come rushing out of it at any moment, and a delicious shiver of excitement skipped up my spine. "What else do you know about the firehorses? I suppose they're all geldings."

"Of course they are; it's heavy work. And you can't very well use some flighty mare that's going to bolt at the first sight of fire."

I yanked my arm free. "Peaches wouldn't have bolted," I argued. "Why, I could stand her nose-to-nose with any locomotive, even with all the smoke and sparks and—"

"No, you couldn't."

"Yes, I could. And I did."

"Where?"

"At the water tower outside Hinckley."

"Hinckley! What were you doing all the way out there? It's not a safe place. Good Lord, Rachel, that was pure foolishness!"

"It wasn't foolishness. Peaches would never have done anything to hurt me. She was very sensible."

"She was still a mare and you're still a girl and if Father ever found out—"

"You wouldn't dare!"

He grinned like the devil but said, "No, you know I wouldn't. Besides, the topic is immaterial now, since you don't have—" The hurt that must have shown on my face was instantly reflected in his. "I'm sorry. That was stupid of me."

I bit my lip and blinked fast.

"Well, here we are."

Directly across the street from us, the fire station rose up three stories, all orange brick and pale granite. It wasn't particularly grand, but it had an air of solidity and order about it. Four pairs of tall windows lined the second story, each trimmed in black paint and discreetly displaying crisp white curtains. Another set of windows, smaller and unadorned, marked the top story. The one ornamental flourish hung above the ground-floor entry in the form of a long black sign that proudly announced in gilt lettering: ENGINE COMPANY NO. 8.

But . . . there still weren't any company firehorses on display. The only horse in sight, in fact, was a plain-looking bay hitched to a buggy, and he appeared to be sound asleep.

James was going on about something or other—the mechanics behind a steam engine, I think—and only now realized that the reason for my visit was missing. He stopped short, looking about him as if the horses might be hidden somewhere. "I don't understand," he apologized. "I was told that every morning—"

"It's all right." I smiled to hide my disappointment. "You go on in. I'll wait."

"Are you sure you'll be okay alone?"

I gave him my most exasperated look.

"I know, I know—just promise me you'll stay away from locomotives." Dodging a milk wagon, he headed across the street. "I'll be back in a few minutes," he called over his shoulder.

I watched him hesitate at the station's yawning entrance, take a deep breath, and disappear inside. As soon as he was out of sight, I crossed the street too, simply to wait beside the buggy horse.

The gentlemanly bay was so thoroughly asleep that his lower lip hung slack enough to reveal his yellow teeth. Yet even in such an unguarded posture, he maintained a pleasant appearance. His face was rather slim, his lashes long. A white star sat neatly in the middle of his forehead. With a twinge, I noticed that the whorl of hairs there spun exactly like the one Peaches had. I couldn't help but reach out to touch it.

Immediately the horse awoke. His ears shot forward and his lips wriggled, nudging my hand for a treat.

I laughed. "I'm sorry, but I don't have anything," I told him. "I'll bring you some sugar next time." He stopped searching at once, quite as if he understood. Peaches used to do that too. When his dark eyes gazed into mine with the same confident patience, I had to blink back tears. To staunch them, I set about combing his black mane with my fingers, and braiding his fore-lock beneath its brow band. I ran my hand underneath his sur-cingle, scratching away a trace of dried sweat. When he'd been smoothed and groomed to my satisfaction and enjoyment, we just stood, the two of us, enjoying the morning and each other's company. Faint aromas of castile soap and sweet feed and lini-ment wafted from the station, and I inhaled deeply. James could have his city smells; for me, this was heaven on earth.

As the minutes passed and James didn't return, I assumed he was being considered for the job and happily went on waiting. When time stretched on, though, I began to grow restless. I left the bay to pace the pavement, glancing now and again at the empty station entrance and wondering what was taking him so long. On one of my passes I heard men's voices inside, volleying anger. My heartbeat quickened: Was James in danger? I cocked an ear to listen, wondering what, if anything, I should do. I could make out the word "she" as the subject of the argument, which eased my worries some. But then I heard the word "gun" and curiosity tugged me right up to the station entry to peek inside.

The sight was absolutely horrifying—worse than any of the graphic illustrations in my horse care manual. A dozen or so firemen, outfitted in their blood-red shirts, ringed a wretched gray horse. At least the horse *used* to be gray. A patchwork of sausage-colored blisters blanketed the animal's back now, the sores swarming right up the neck and exposing its naked ridge. Only tufts of singed hair spiked where a mane had once fallen. The poor horse's head was mostly hairless, too, and such a swollen, misshapen mess I wasn't sure if any eyes could see through those slits. If ever a creature had been burned alive and still breathed, this was the one.

A sourness stung my throat. The morning's porridge burbled threateningly. Clamping a hand over my mouth, I spun away from the entry and pressed myself against the brick for cool relief.

I'd always thought I had a strong stomach. I could pore over the drawings in my horse care manual for hours, and they showed grinning skeletons and flattened nervous systems and dissected hearts. But now I understood that they were only ink on paper. This horse, this bleeding, blistered, skinned horse, was all too real. Even outside the station, the sharp stench of burnt hair mixed with the dank odor of weeping flesh clung to my nostrils. I closed my eyes as my head swam.

A strangled cry, like that of an infant, broke through my fog. It was the horse. I waited, my heart kicking. The cry came again, a lonesome, desperate call that I knew was meant solely for me. I couldn't have defended that belief, but I knew with complete certainty that it was so, and even before my eyes opened, I was pushing away from the wall. Hand to my stomach, quivering like a jelly, I inched back toward the entry. Helplessly mesmerized, I slipped inside and joined the ring of men, unnoticed.

I saw now that the injured horse had a cotton rope looped over a lone patch of mane behind the ears. It was the only sort of harness to be suffered. The man holding the rope was fidgeting from foot to foot, as if the soles of his feet were burning at that very moment.

Betwixt and between elbows, I saw that there was another man standing beside the disfigured animal. He was tall and clean shaven, with chunks of wavy brown hair sweeping back from features that could only be described as hawklike. The assured air of a judge cloaked his square shoulders. His stained apron, on which he was wiping his hands at that moment, was my first clue that he was the veterinary. The bag at his feet, spewing rolled bandages, hinged metal instruments, and various jars of medicine, confirmed it.

The men had stopped their arguing. It seemed everyone was waiting for some sort of decision. All eyes, including my own, rested upon this silent man as he lifted first one hand and then the other, apparently weighing for himself the horse's options. I realized I was holding my breath, like the others in the room, as we grimly awaited the verdict. When the man shook his head, my own cry was lost among the groans.

A door slammed, and the circle respectfully parted for a wiry, gray-haired man wearing the brass-buttoned suit and severe demeanor of a fire chief. A dalmatian trotted obediently at his side, head cocked, awaiting command.

"Harland!" The man's clipped voice matched his brisk pace. "Here it is." He handed the veterinary what looked, oddly enough, like a sack of flour. Just as he did so, the dalmatian stopped, one paw lifted. His coal black eyes pinpointed me. With a high-pitched bark and a scrabbling of claws, he charged. Everything blurred. I took a step backward, tripped—on my skirt, I think—and fell. The dog snapped viciously at my feet.

"What in the devil's name—?"

"Rachel!"

"What is *she* doing in here?"

Arms were suddenly all around me, pulling me to my feet and hurrying me outside. The dalmatian was yanked by his collar in the opposite direction. There was a great deal of grumbling. I was shaking. Frantic. Scared for myself, but more so for the horse. As I gathered my wits, I realized I'd been left alone on the pavement with James, who was thoroughly irritated.

"You oughtn't to have come in, Rachel," he scolded. "In the first place, the public isn't allowed, and in the second place, it's too horrible, especially for a girl."

"That . . . that horse," I stammered. My stomach heaved and I paused to force a swallow. I knew I was only a breath away from fainting. "What happened to that horse?"

James steered me to the brick wall once more, propped me against it, and stepped away. Crossing his arms, he explained tersely, "A burning timber fell on her last night at the fire. One of the horses in the team broke free, but the other two went down and this one that's in there," he jerked his head toward the station, "she took the brunt of it."

"She?"

He nodded. "I heard her called the Governor's Girl. She was the middle horse in the engine team." His wayward glance told me he wanted to be in with the men rather than out here with his meddlesome little sister. But he continued. "When they arrived at the livery fire last night, the driver left them too close to the building. That's where the timber fell—knocked the horses right off their feet. Took so long to cut the harness that that one"—he jerked his head again—"was burned almost to death."

"What's going to happen to her?"

James shook his head. For one cold instant, my heart stopped.

A lone voice carried from the station: "You can't just shoot her!" There was more shouting, and when James left me to rush back inside, I somehow managed to follow in his wake.

The gray-haired chief was brandishing a pistol and motioning his firemen out of the way. Only the man at the end of the cotton rope was refusing to move. "I won't let you do it!" he bellowed.

"Your concern comes too late, Mr. Lee." The chief laid the pistol to the mare's temple. "As you can plainly see, she's as good as dead already!"

"Now, hold on there, the both of you." At the veterinary's stern command the chief eased down the gun, but the two men glared at each other like snarling dogs with raised hackles. The Governor's Girl, head drooped nearly to the floor, stood motionless between them. I wondered if she realized her very life was being decided.

"The fault for this tragedy lies entirely with you, Mr. Lee," the chief argued. "You should have unhitched your team and—"

"I told you that the livery was fully aflame when we arrived." The man holding the rope gestured emphatically, causing the mare to flinch. "The horses trapped inside were screaming. You had to have heard them. I jumped off the engine and ran inside to see if—"

"—to see if you could get your name in the newspapers again!" the chief spat.

The wild-looking Mr. Lee opened his mouth to retort, thought better of it, and clenched his jaw. My heart flew to him for his heroics in trying to save the burning horses.

Noticing us inside the doorway, the chief vented his anger. "Get that girl away from here!"

James grabbed my elbow and roughly marched me out to the pavement. I was too shocked to struggle. My mind spun crazily. "You have to do something!"

"Really? And just what do you want me to do?"

"Talk to the veterinary. Or the fire chief. You can't just let them kill her!" I was searching frantically for a plan. "You can tell them we'll take her! There's the empty shed. Surely we—"

"Hold on there, Rachel. What would *we* do with a burned horse?"

"Save her, that's what!" I cried. "Or at least try to. She deserves a chance, doesn't she?"

James was as tough as leather on the outside, the face

he showed to the world. But inside, I knew, was a softer place, the soul of a poet. So when he hesitated, just for a second, and looked again toward the station, I knew I had him.

"Please, James." I laid a hand on his arm. "'And have compassion for them . . . pulling them out of the fire . . .'?"

He rolled his eyes and snorted. "You're worse than Grandmother, customizing your sermon for every occasion."

I blushed guiltily, but I knew the power of quoting God's word. "Save her," I said, squeezing his arm. "Please. For me." I was dead serious and my brother knew it. Shaking his head, he reentered the station. I hurried back to the buggy horse and began stroking his neck with a fury that raised a sweat. My insides were churning. I was shaking again, now more with excitement than horror. A door that had once been locked to me was being pushed open. Or maybe it was a window. Either way, it was a chance for freedom, and I was going to gallop through it.

ᴄᴇᴀᴏ SIX

HE REST OF THAT MORNING WAS AGGRAVATION—PURE,
unadulterated aggravation. James burst from the station
only long enough to order me home, responding to my questions
about the mare with an exasperating series of "I don't know's."
I beat my fists against the air and stamped my heel to utterly
no effect. Left alone again on the pavement, I lifted my skirts
and started running. Even in those dreadfully clunky shoes, and
ignoring the stares from passersby, I ran all the way home.

Or almost home. Before I got there, I turned down the
alley behind our row of houses, ran along it until I reached our
small courtyard, veered into it and then into our carriage shed.
Like a madwoman, I began digging through its rubbish, heaving
aside empty barrels and stacked boxes, until I found what I was
looking for: a pitchfork, broken-tined but serviceable. To salve my
worry, I began stabbing viciously at the moldy stall bedding.

As the morning ticked by, I was aware of every slow-as-
molasses minute. I didn't know what was happening to the mare,

to *my* mare, as I already thought of her. I didn't know if she was alive or dead. I didn't know if they'd shot her. I did know I jumped out of my skin at every distant bang, every far-off clap of hammer to nail, every slamming door. Sweat began trickling down my face as slowly as the ticking minutes. Slowly and torturously. I stabbed all the harder at the rotting layers of soiled straw. By the time the bedding was turned over into an uneven mass of small clods, my hands were blistered and aching. But there was no news and no relief.

I threw myself into tidying my horse's new home. I neatly restacked all the rubbish in one corner of the shed: the wooden crates, two barrels, a rusted-through bucket, dozens of empty bottles, stiff, crusted rags by the armful, part of a fence, and a squealing wheelbarrow. Panting, yet reveling in the challenge of my labors, I dashed outside to yank a handful of tall weeds from the ground. I used them as a broom to beat down the cobwebs from the rafters. Sweat was streaming down my neck by then—along with a spider or two, which I had no time to flick away. They could tarry at their own risk. I cleaned like a whirlwind, attacking every corner, even brushing the layers of dust from the stall's planks and leaving them as spotless, I guessed, as any table or sill in my own room.

"Setting up housekeeping?"

I spun. Grandmother.

"Gracious!" she exclaimed. "You're a sight!"

With my chest heaving, I realized for the first time that the shed's improvement had meant the worse for me. My fingernails were blackened half moons. My dress, which Mother had only recently sewn from a very pretty, gray-green muslin, was a muddier hue, and one underarm was actually ripped to the skin. My hair, I could tell, was hanging across my face as heavily as a mustang's forelock. Yet all I could say to her was, "I've found a horse." The sound of those words lingered so sweetly in the dust-clouded air.

"A horse?" she echoed, peering into the carriage shed's dark corners. "Where?"

"At the fire station. She's been badly burned and James is bringing her here. We're going to save her."

"And how are you going to do that?"

On the heels of her question, James barged into the shed, clearly out of breath. "With your prayers," he puffed. A look of triumph showed on his face. "She's coming," he said. "The veterinary said he'd bring her round this afternoon in his ambulance. And I've been given permission by the chief himself to tend to her—under the veterinary's supervision, of course. It seems she's quite valuable, and with no extra stalls at the station just now—or the help—I'm their man."

The wave of envy I felt at James being named the mare's caretaker was squashed by the relief that she was alive. And soon to be living here. I threw my arms around him. "Thank you," I whispered.

"Oh, no! Oh, my goodness, no!" Mother had made her way out to the shed too, stopping just short of the doorway, but she'd seen enough. "You promised you'd be ready," she cried, "and just look at you!"

I should have been repentant, I know, but I was in such a state of bliss. I was soon to have a horse!

"Our appointment is in forty-five minutes. I don't know how we're going to get your hair combed out." She measured me up and down. "There's certainly no time for a bath. Honestly, Rachel, you've disappointed me." Taking a peek inside the shed, she could only scowl. "And if all this . . . this tidying . . . of yours is in hopes of having a horse, I won't be party to it. You'll have to deal with your father's displeasure, I'm afraid . . . alone."

Grandmother spoke up. "Oh, leave them be, Nora. It's just a horse and just a good deed that they're doing." Grumbling something else that was unintelligible, she brushed past James and Mother and headed for the house.

"Father may not mind at all when he learns of the deal I've struck," James proudly told Mother. "As the station's newest apprentice," he paused for effect, "I'm on my way to the feed store for supplies—to be charged on the *chief's* account. Keeping a horse won't cost Rachel, or us, a penny."

She winced. "An apprentice firefighter? I'd prayed you were too young. Don't you think you're too young for this?"

"I'll be nineteen in January. The chief thinks it's old enough."

"Well," she said, brushing her sleeves of imaginary dust, "I suppose that's something that will please your father. Never mind what I think. Come along, Rachel." She extended her hand, expecting me to grab hold of it as a child would. Sighing, and rolling my eyes at James, I did.

"Take care of her until I get back. Promise?"

"I promise," he replied. "We'll be waiting for you."

Mother didn't ask about that exchange, though I was certain she'd heard it. She heard everything. So it was hardly fair, I suppose, that I didn't hear her as she scolded and needled and begged me to hurry. How could I? I'd found a horse!

Squealing like a steam whistle, I slipped free of her hand the minute we were inside the house. I stampeded through the kitchen and up the stairs and past the lifeless butterflies, pausing only long enough to glance out the hall windows. To my way of thinking, the old carriage shed was standing straighter already. I rushed on, taking the attic stairs two at a time, and nearly breaking my neck when those awful heels clipped a step and sent me tumbling chin first. But I scrambled to my feet, hardly caring.

Mother had already been to my room, I saw, because my white dress, the one intended for school exhibition ceremonies, was laid out on the bed. Beside it was a matching hair ribbon. Hurriedly, I unbuttoned. It wasn't easy, with my sweat-dampened skin, to climb into the dress's starched stiffness. The high lace collar itched horribly. At least it hid my grime-streaked neck, saving me from having to scrub it.

Mary Grace, my best friend in Wesleydale, who was a year older and who lived in town, would have liked it. Actually, she would have said that she liked it, and then she would have told me everything that was wrong with it. She was always one for frills and ruffles and the latest styles in *Godey's*. According to Mary Grace, your waist couldn't be too small, your bustle couldn't be too big, and your hair couldn't be too curly. Mary Grace had her perfume shipped from Chicago. Mary Grace was engaged to be married.

Well, there were no curls showing in my mirror, just a mess of thick, shoulder-length copper hair adorned with a few feathery cobwebs and flecks of something dark. I reached for the hairbrush. My horse care manual lay beneath it. Temptation struck and my hand passed over the brush. This would only take a minute.

I flipped to the index. To my frustration, the headings there went from Breeding to Bronchial Tubes and straight on to the Cs with no entry for Burns. Quickly, I paged through the chapter on "Diseases of the Skin and Ears." Treatments were spelled out for warts and sore noses, for mange and swelled ankles. But there wasn't a single sentence about burns.

"*Rachel!*" Mother's stinging call shot up the stairs. "We're going to be *late!*"

I hurriedly dragged the brush through my hair just enough to make it presentable, tied the mass back with the ribbon, and shot down the stairs. Then, with Mother in white on one side of me and Grandmother in black on the other, we set off down the street. We headed in the opposite direction from the fire station.

For a while, the three of us bustled along in silence, though Grandmother gradually lagged behind, huffing. I could tell by her hobble that her knees were bothering her. She'd never complain, though, or seek to slow us. Mother, without actually acknowledging it, did adjust her pace enough to maintain only a slight lead. Her forehead wasn't as creased as it had been when we'd started out, so maybe she was softening.

"I'm glad that you're feeling better," she said to me. "I know that our moving to Boston has been difficult for you."

I nodded absently. My attention had been captured by a beautifully matched pair of flaxen-maned chestnuts harnessed to a phaeton.

"You know, dear," she went on, sidling toward a new topic, "your father is very eager to make a success of himself here. He's already working very long hours at his job. He needs to impress the newspaper's owners. As his family, of course, we're part of that impression. So I'm not sure this is the right time to bring—"

An alarm jangled inside my head. At once I knew where she was going. "I want to save her," I interrupted. "I can't let her die."

"Mmm." She nodded, and for a very brief moment I was lulled into believing that she understood. Until she said, "There's that word again: I." She gave me one of her plaster smiles and grabbed my hand. "Maybe you should set *your* wants aside and consider what your father wants. Or what God wants. If this horse is as badly injured as it sounds, maybe it would be a blessing to allow her to die."

I couldn't believe what she was saying. My hand, clasped inside hers, grew cold.

"Oh, Nora." Grandmother spoke from behind us. She'd

obviously heard the whole conversation and had readied her objection. I'd never known a mother and daughter so dissimilar. On second thought, yes, I had. "God has never yet willed one of his own creatures to die."

Mother stiffened. Over her shoulder she said, "Is that so?"

"Yes, I believe it is so." Hurrying to make up the few steps, and puffing harder, Grandmother said, "And I believe that anyone's eagerness to say 'it's God's will' is little more than laziness, an easy excuse for turning a blind eye to suffering."

"I never said—"

"I heard what you said," Grandmother admonished, "and that's not how you were raised—to just stand by and let others suffer. And that's not how I want my grandchildren raised. I don't want them to just sit on their hands and nod to the sermon; I want them to act—"

"All I was saying was—"

"—to act for the good, to change things if necessary. I want them to heed their callings. So if James and Rachel want to heal this firehorse, then let them try." As proudly as one of the soldiers from her hymns, Grandmother marched onward and ahead. Mother set her jaw and passed her. For once it was I who was dragged along in tow.

We weren't more than a few blocks farther along when a dog's urgent barking made us pause and look back. I was surprised to see the fire chief's dalmatian zigzagging down the street. He was chasing shoppers toward the pavement and nipping at the heels of carriage horses to move them aside. In the path that he was clearing came the fire engine, though the driver didn't seem to be in any great hurry. The three horses were only coming at a trot, with the one in the middle, a narrow-chested gray gelding, looking quite unsettled.

"Breaking in a new horse, I see." A man in a sack jacket and matching vest who was standing beside us spoke knowledge-ably to his companion. "Looks like a goer. Bet you a dollar there's some racing blood in that one."

"Keep it," the other responded. "You're probably right." We all watched the steam engine go past, its silver boiler shin-ing so brightly in the sun that we had to shield our eyes from the glare.

"Won't be easy, though. There's quite a set of shoes to fill, with their best horse dying."

"The big gray mare? Did she die now? I heard she'd been badly burned. That's a right shame." He sounded truly hurt. I swayed on my feet, reaching out for a lamppost to steady myself. "But you know, I've always been the first to say that a fireman's harness is no place for a hot-tempered mare. Remember the time when she plowed straight through that load of barrels on the way to a house fire?"

"I most certainly do," the friend concurred. "Shattered them to splinters."

Blood pounded through my veins and my head throbbed. The Governor's Girl was dead? It couldn't be! James had said she was coming. I couldn't go on to our appointment; I needed to run back to our house to learn the truth.

"Come along," Mother said, taking my arm again, "we really have to hurry." In a state of shock, I was half-dragged along the crowded pavement, then through the maze of carriages and horsecars, past the long green stretch of the Common, and into Patterson's Photography Gallery. Dazed, I followed the photographer's directions to sit straight, turn sideways, fold my hands, drop my chin. I was numb. The window had been slammed shut in my face. I felt like a hapless butterfly being stretched against a white cotton background. My wings ached.

After the sitting, Mother and Grandmother insisted on stopping into C. F. Hovey's dry goods store to marvel at the vast array of dress materials and ready-made garments. To my infinite torture, they examined the handiwork on each and every mantle, whispering about stitching quality and shaking their heads in disbelief at the pricing.

The trip home was longer, it seemed, and with the fog having lifted, hotter. Only Mother and Grandmother talked now, idle conversation about what to cook for dinner, the late hours kept by our neighbors, the need to empty the ashes from the stove. It was all so absolutely unimportant when those words kept ringing in my ears: "Did she die now? Did she die now?"

By the time we were turning the corner onto our street, the day was stewingly hot. The blisters on my heels were oozing. Mopping the perspiration from my face for the hundredth time, I noticed an odd contraption in front of our house. It was a wide, low-slung wagon with a canopy and a boldly lettered sign that read HORSE AMBULANCE. Hardly daring to hope, I gathered up my skirt. Mother gripped my arm yet again. "Ladies don't run," she scolded.

"Mother, please," I begged, but she shook her head firmly. Her fingers tightened. I fretted and pranced the remainder of the way, as uncomfortable as the new gray horse in his harness. Until we reached the front steps. That's when I pulled free and went tearing around to the back of the house. All the way to the carriage shed I ran, plunging through the doorway, breathless with imminent euphoria.

James was there. And the same veterinary I'd seen at the fire station that morning. And, yes, so was the Governor's Girl.

But, oh my Lord, the hours must have washed the horror of her from my mind. Up close, she wasn't so much a horse as some wretched, half-slaughtered cow. Her swollen tongue hung from her mouth and though she was bracing shakily on spread legs, she looked as if she could drop over dead at any second. She must have just arrived, because the rope was still dangling from her neck. Fresh, golden straw bristled across the stall's floor, and an old rain tub had been dragged to the corner and filled. God bless James. Something must have been thrown in the trough, too, because a sparrow was hopping cautiously along its rim, cocking his head with interest.

The Governor's Girl showed none. Her face and lips were so badly swollen from the burns that I didn't see how she could eat. She looked so miserable, so cast off from the world. I had to go to her. I had to whisper to her that she'd be all right, that I was going to take care of her.

"Here now, miss. You'll get yourself hurt." Just as I started to duck under the bar, the veterinary grabbed my elbow. Why was everyone trying to hold me back today? He looked at James as I struggled, quite unladylike, to get free. "Really, Miss . . . Miss . . . ?"

"Selby," James answered. "Rachel Selby, my sister. Rachel, this is Mr. Harland Stead, Boston's finest veterinary, I'm told."

I nodded acknowledgment but pulled my arm free. I was suddenly focused on the mare. I couldn't see her breathing. Couldn't they see that she wasn't breathing?

"Well, how much money would you lay on her?" James asked, as blithely as if they were betting on a game of croquet.

"How's that?"

"Is she going to pull through?"

The veterinary cleared his throat. "Interesting choice of words. Have you ever seen this mare pull?"

James shook his head. The mare finally took a shallow breath and I took one myself before turning to the veterinary with new curiosity.

"There are firehorses that pull when the driver speaks to them," he was saying, "and there are firehorses that begin to pull when the alarm rings. And then there's this mare. Seems as if she's pulling toward something all the time."

"What do you mean?"

"I've been at the station when it's quiet. The other horses, they're just chewing on their hay. But this one? I've seen her lift her head and wait, all twitchy, like she knows something's going to happen even before it does. Then she starts leaning her chest into the stall rope and bang! The very next instant the alarm rings, the rope drops, and she's first in front of the engine, dancing and snorting and waiting for the harness to drop."

"The harness to drop?"

"You'll see soon enough, if you're going to work there. But to answer your question, this one's a puller. The bad news is that some of these burns that looked to be class two last night are actually threes. She's bordering on shock. Surviving the night, and half this day, are good signs, but–" He shrugged, pulled a tangled bandage from his satchel and began rolling it. "At least she's alive; better off, I guess, than those thirty others that went down with the livery itself."

My stomach upended. Dead horses, dying horses. But not this one. I wasn't going to let it happen.

"Are you all right, Miss Selby? Perhaps you'd like to return to the house?" Mr. Stead looked closely at me, concern clouding his face, and then at James.

I shook my head, determined to stay. "No, I'll be fine." For several minutes we all watched the mare; I counted her every breath. I got the eeriest feeling that the spirits of thirty dead horses were hovering about her unseen, inviting her to join them. I mouthed the words clearly: *"Don't go!"*

"Does anyone know how the fire started?" James asked.

When I turned to hear the veterinary this time, I was surprised to realize that he didn't have all that many years on

James. It was his sharp features that made him seem older and perhaps more serious. But his hazel eyes were definitely those of a young man, and heartwarmingly gentle.

"It could have been about anything," he replied. "Livery stables, as you know, with their lofts full of hay and their wooden wagons by the dozen, and more often than not bales of cotton and rags, are in simple terms nothing more than a fire in need of a spark."

"But I'm sure that everyone working in a livery knows to exercise caution," James said.

"Yes, well, it happens nonetheless, and more frequently than I like to think about. There are rumors, though, that this fire was no accident."

I got a chill as Grandmother's words were echoed. "You don't mean that someone deliberately started the fire . . . with all those horses trapped in their stalls . . . and no way to . . ."

The veterinary glanced at me, then concentrated on his bandage. "Firebugs . . . or arsonists . . . aren't like the rest of us with feelings. There's such as will burn down an entire city to prove their point, with no thought to the cost in lives."

"So where's the point in this?" James angrily gestured toward the Governor's Girl.

Mr. Stead shrugged again. "Sometimes answers are where we least expect to find them. The Good Book, for example, says that there are certain things that are never satisfied, and one of them is fire. I'll add another: the man who sees an imperfect world and takes it upon himself to set things right."

✣ SEVEN

HE MEN FINALLY LEFT, BUT BEFORE THEY DID, THEY propped open the shed's sagging double doors. The air that drifted in was hot, hardly a comfort to the Governor's Girl, who'd been slathered in linseed oil and wrapped in bandages like some mummy from Egypt. Abandoned to her sea of straw.

I refused to leave. For some reason, this mare mesmerized me. She was different from any horse I'd ever laid eyes upon. Even though the shed was stifling, and clouded with annoying black gnats that kept entangling themselves in my eyelashes, I settled myself on an upturned crate and prepared to pass the afternoon with her. There was truly no place in the world I'd rather have been.

A meditative silence settled over us. Sitting in a stable could be very much like sitting in a church, I'd always thought. On that afternoon I sensed God's presence in the weightless motes drifting in a slant of light. And as always when I quieted myself, I became distinctly aware of the many other lives unfolding around me. At my feet a black beetle clambered across the freshly turned dirt, tumbling and righting itself again and again to keep on course. Atop the pimpled rust of an old hoe, a pale wisp of a spider balanced against the new breeze. He was waving one leg. A brown-capped sparrow alit in the frame of the open window before hopping onto the feed trough. Another joined him, then another, and the three chirped their questions and considerations to each other. Completely content, I picked up a stray blade of straw and methodically creased its length under my thumbnail, curling it into a spiral. Holding it up against the window's bright square of light, I studied it. The spiral ran around and around, much like my galloping, I thought. But did it go anywhere? And if it did, where did the journey start? At the center, moving outward, or at the outside, moving in? And was the center truly a destination, or just the abrupt end of all that galloping? Was it death? I shook my head to clear those rambling and unanswerable thoughts. Shredding the spiraled straw, I watched the beetle's progress.

James returned all too soon, unknowingly breaking the harmony. He was balancing a cumbersome packing quilt, along with a plate of cold lunch and a goblet of milk. He narrowly missed squashing the beetle. I jumped up to help.

"Mother's gone out again," he informed me, arranging the food on the upturned crate. "I know she's not happy about . . . this." He nodded toward the Girl. With a heavy snap, he spread the quilt on the dirt floor. "Grandmother's resting in her room."

I couldn't stop smiling. "Isn't she . . . ?" I wanted to say "splendid," but to anyone with two eyes that was lunacy.

James was different, though. He understood. "She's a fine mare," he agreed. Then he crossed his arms in big-brotherly fashion. "You did hear what the veterinary said, didn't you? That she's not to be trusted?" He waited for my nod, but I wasn't going to betray my mare by agreeing. "I've already heard the men at the station say the same: She has a mind of her own; you can't predict what she's going to do. That's dangerous. Are you listening to me, Rachel?"

"Um-hmm."

"You have to promise me you'll stay away from her until we know her better."

"I will." Since he'd started talking, my eyes hadn't left her.

"I mean it. Don't go in there alone."

"I *won't*," I promised, and dropped obediently onto the quilt. "See? I just want to look at her. I want to stay with her."

James's frown lifted into a smile. "All right, then. I'm off to polish some brass—a lot of it. And perhaps," he added in a deep, ghostly sort of voice, "to be Father's informant. I'll see you at supper." His happy whistling sounded all the way down the alley, fading away when he turned the corner. The Girl and I were again alone.

Saying that I wanted to look at her was an exaggeration, of course. The mare's injuries were so ghastly that I had to work to keep my stomach settled. I certainly had no appetite for the lunch at my elbow—cold chicken, bread, and jam. Yet I couldn't *not* look at her. For some reason she kindled a flame inside of me, and I sat there trying to figure out how she was doing that.

The obvious answer would be that, amongst the blisters and bandages and soot, there were remnants of her beauty. Her mane, for instance, or at least the one tuft behind her ears, was as absolutely fine and white as fringed silk. And the dappling on her muscled hindquarters, an area that had escaped the flames, put me in mind of a spring rain on a silvery pond. It must have been something to see her galloping to a fire: nostrils flared, white mane blowing, tail flagged. *She mocketh at fear and is not affrighted.* The Biblical words that leaped from my memory had never seemed more apt. *She swalloweth the ground with her fierceness.*

As I saw past the awful injuries, my stomach calmed and actually began to growl. I'd had little more than a single bowl of porridge in close to three days, so, chasing away the flies, I picked up a chunk of Grandmother's bread and nibbled its crust.

From where I was sitting, staring up at the mare, she seemed taller than Peaches, though I don't think her legs were much longer. I think the deception came in her massive girth; her powerful shoulders and high, rounded withers gave her a certain grandeur. Her knees, in fact, were set lower than Peaches', and there was some feathering around her fetlocks. There must have been some draught blood in her veins. Her hooves were huge. Then there was her face. Even ignoring the hideous blistering, it was so different from Peaches'. While she had had a narrow head, with sweet, almond-shaped eyes, this mare had a forehead as broad and flat as a skillet, and a long, Roman nose. Her eyes, large and liquid, burned like black fire.

My breath caught. That was it. It was something in her eyes, something about her spirit that was kindling my own.

Ever so slowly, she began turning her head. I could almost hear the burnt skin crackling and I tensed. When her gaze fell upon me, I was taken aback. The only way I could describe her look would be critical, and I realized nervously that it was my turn to be appraised. Self-conscious, I straightened, wondering if I'd measure up. The Girl stared hard at me, and through me, not even blinking. It was as disquieting as a surprise examination in Mr. Moore's science class.

At long last she let out a miserable groan and looked away. I had no idea if I'd passed judgment. Just like Mr. Moore, apparently, she was going to keep my grade for the morrow, leaving me to wonder.

There was something else on her mind. I could see that she was gathering all her strength in an effort to move. Shifting one hoof, and then another, she slowly began shuffling toward the rain tub. The procession took several minutes. I held my breath, agonizing every step of the way with her. When she finally reached it, she just stood, her head drooping over the water. It occurred to me that she was staring at her reflection, and while I knew the idea was absurd, I couldn't help but wince at what she must see.

Little by little, with her stout gray legs braced against the tub, she sagged over its rim and stretched toward the water. I heard the double gulp, watched her throat ripple as it delivered the coolness to her massive body. That probably brought no more relief than a drop of water cast upon a raging fire. Nonetheless, swallow followed swallow until, finally, she raised her neck. For an even longer time she stood motionless, and I worried again that she was going to fall over and die right in front of me. It took a slackened hip to show that she was dozing. I didn't dare move for fear of awakening her. I just sat, still as could be, and imagined what it was to be trapped inside a skin caught on fire.

I'm sure that at least an hour passed. When the Girl awoke with a shudder, as if from a bad dream, the first thing she did was turn her head stiffly, looking, I thought, to see if I was still there. I smiled. "Hello," I murmured.

I don't know what I expected her to do, but when she made a great, heaving effort to move closer to me, my heart thumped wildly. This time when she stood looking down at me, she wasn't so much considering me as she was ordering me. As if she'd spoken the very words, I came to realize that she was hungry. That was a wonderful sign! She wanted to live! I jumped to my feet and . . . what? What could *I* do? Everyone had said she was dangerous. And I'd promised James not to go near her.

But she lived by her own rules, it seemed. Unconcerned by my pledge, she stubbornly kept staring at me . . . and staring at me.

There was nothing else I could do. I *had* to go to her.

With my heart beating at a thoroughly guilty tempo, I climbed under the rail.

Standing beside the mare was a little frightening; she was even bigger than I'd thought. All she had to do was snort and I jumped. Second thoughts filled my head. Maybe I'd imagined her command; maybe it would be better if I scrambled right back under that rail. But other, less cautious thoughts prevailed. Schooling myself to calm, I sidled toward the trough. Her black eyes rolled, watching my every move. Slowly I scooped some grain into my hands, crept back beside her, and cupped the offering beneath her mouth.

Her swollen tongue was still pushed past her teeth, and the purplish-red color of her muzzle was only slightly darker than the raw flesh surrounding her eyes. When I looked into the black depths of those eyes I saw a sharp hurt; she thought I was playing a cruel joke. Of course she couldn't eat; she could hardly open her mouth to drink. I should be horsewhipped.

An image of Peaches came to mind. There was a time, last October, when she had been sick and stopped eating. The veterinary had examined her and, finding no specific ailment, had recommended feeding her a warm bran mash. Because it was as soft as porridge, I'd been able to spoon-feed it to her. Maybe, just maybe, I could do the same with this mare. I let the grain dribble through my fingers. "I'll be right back," I promised, and cautiously climbed under the rail. The moment I was outside the shed, I ran to the kitchen to light the stove.

The house was quiet as I set a pot of water to boil. Mother

hadn't yet returned, and Grandmother must have still been resting in her room.

Worried and anxious, I paced. My thoughts wandered soberly from fires to firebugs, to galloping and God, to newspapers and Father. How was I going to tell Father about her? I dreaded doing that. Maybe James could. After all, he was her official caretaker. He'd actually arranged the deal. I conveniently ignored the fact that he'd done it for me.

The water was taking forever. When it finally sent up its first few bubbles, I dumped in two cups of bran, stirred, and waited some more. By the time I was lugging the small iron pot of mash to the shed, the shadows were lengthening across the yard.

The Governor's Girl looked distressed. With shameful pride, I wondered if it was because she'd missed me. The moment I ducked under the bar, however, I was humbled. She pinned her ears and grunted like some wild creature from the woods.

"Easy now," I murmured, as much to myself as to her. "There's no reason to be frightened."

She grunted and squealed and made ghastly, unhorselike sounds. I'd never heard such before, but I understood their warning. My knees began trembling. There were only two choices now: stay or leave. I screwed up my courage and inched toward her.

"This is just a simple old bran mash," I soothed in a singsong voice. "As soft as pudding and as sweet as molasses. Try it and you'll be as good as new in no time." Even I could hear the utter lack of confidence in my voice. The Girl waggled her head menacingly.

My hands shook as I dug the wooden spoon into the pot. Lifting it high, I shoved it in the direction of her mouth. She flung her head defiantly, and the warm, pasty mush splattered across my bodice. Too late, I realized I was still in my good white dress. Mother would howl blue murder for certain.

Well, so be it. I was going to finish this job. Mustering my courage again, I inched closer, eyed the least ulcerated spot on her mouth, and pushed another spoonful of bran at her. Just as deliberately, the Girl swung her head again. Only this time, instead of just knocking away the spoon, she hit me across the cheek. Bone cracked loudly upon bone. I staggered backward. Everything was flooding to blackness as I reeled out of the stall and crawled toward the quilt. The inside of my head felt like a smashed egg, a jellylike confusion of yellow and white.

"Gracious, girl!"

I nearly jumped out of my skin. Grandmother again. Her unexpected appearances were going to be the death of me, if this mare wasn't.

"What's happened? Are you all right?" Not getting an immediate answer, she talked louder. "Rachel! Are you all right?"

"Yes." Queasy and hot-faced, I braced myself against the quilt's undulating support.

"That horse do this?"

I managed a painful nod, which set the yellow, eggy bits to dancing.

"Your mother's going to raise the roof when she gets a sight of your dress."

I knew she was right. "She can't eat her grain," I explained, gingerly testing my jaw. "I was trying to give her a bran mash."

"Doesn't appear that she wanted it." Grandmother actually chuckled. "You know, you do have a tendency to add too much salt."

An unplanned laugh burst out of me, making my head shriek.

"Come along to the kitchen," she said. "If you're having trouble with her appetite, I'll show you how to stir up a wondrous tonic. She'll lap it up like a kitten does a bowl of cream."

"Maybe we should wait for the veterinary," I cautioned. "Or James."

"Nonsense." She was already on her way back to the house. "Men don't know a thimbleful about how to treat people or animals. That's up to the women. Are you sure you're all right?" she called over her shoulder.

"Yes, I'm fine." A lie. My head was throbbing fiercely. Steadying it between my palms, I studied the mare. She was still staring at me, her eyes burning with emotion. Had I misunderstood what she wanted? She'd just taught me a lesson, I knew. A lesson about us. But did it mean that our relationship had ended . . . or just begun?

⤔ EIGHT

GRANDMOTHER CALLED FROM THE CELLAR AS SOON AS THE screen door slammed shut. "Rachel? Find the funnel if you can and an empty bottle—no, don't bother with that, I see one here."

The kitchen wasn't fully unpacked yet. Mother hadn't had the time to find a suitable servant girl, and she'd concentrated on putting the front rooms in order first, anticipating the critical eyes of new neighbors. So it wasn't easy finding anything, let alone a small tin funnel, amidst the haphazardness that was the pantry and the kitchen table and even the floor. To make my task harder, the cramped room, being on the back of the house and having no window of its own, was already shrouded in dusk. I set about lighting the two gas lamps, as well as a lantern, and began my search. Grandmother was climbing the cellar stairs, each wheezy grunt echoed by a squeaky step, before I found the funnel rattling around inside a dented sieve. I plucked it out reluctantly, still unsure about taking the mare's medication into our own hands.

"I don't know what's keeping your mother," Grandmother said upon making it to the top. She gripped the doorjamb with her knobby knuckles, swaying as if holding the mast of a rocking ship. "I hope she's not lost in this big city."

Her armful of clinking jars and bottles was loosed onto the kitchen table, accompanied by several packets of spices. With a wistful smile, she held up one sealed, blue-green jar. "Look at this," she said. "Last year's tomato preserves. I didn't know anybody had cared enough to pack them." She set the jar down, exhaling a sigh, and slid it toward the wall. "The last taste we'll have of the garden, I suppose. I wonder what's become of it." She seemed to have carried an invisible melancholy from the cellar as well, because the sparkle had left her eyes and the pouches of skin beneath them sagged more. "It's probably overgrown with weeds by now. Dead." She balanced the funnel in the neck of a flat-sided brown bottle. "My fate soon enough." Grimly she began mixing the tonic.

Her words smacked me in the face nearly as hard as the mare had. Why was she talking about dying? And doing it as if she looked forward to dying? I should say something, set her right. My mind raced. My mouth opened . . . and closed. And, just as I had proved useless in the carriage shed, I ended up waiting slack-shouldered beside her and only watching her work.

Odd ingredients from the spice packets were carefully shaken into the funnel and down into the bottle: powdered gingerroot, cayenne pepper, licorice. She added five raw eggs, cracking them one after another into the funnel, and then removing it to shake the bottle vigorously. When she held it up to the lamp for inspection, my throat tightened. Surely this was no cure for a horse.

Reciting something to herself, she sprinkled in a bit more pepper and added a pinch of something white and powdery. As the parlor clock began chiming a quarter past six, Grandmother wiped her hands. She gave me a curt nod. "Let's go. You bring the lantern."

It was a short walk, no more than thirty steps, from the kitchen's door to the carriage shed. If it had been longer maybe I could have broached the subject more eloquently. Instead, I charged in with, "Why do you talk so much about dying?"

"Because I'm tired," Grandmother snapped. A bird shot skyward and the crickets in the courtyard damped their evensong. Gathering herself, she laid a hand on my arm. She closed her eyes, took a deep breath, and let it out. In a gentler tone, but purposely looking away from me, she said, "And I miss your grandfather. It's been too long."

"Oh." The two of us proceeded into the shadowy quiet of the carriage shed. The Girl lifted her head to watch. "Boston's a big city," I offered, clumsily trying to bandage her ache. "Maybe you'll make friends here, meet someone new."

No, completely wrong. Even I had to groan at such an empty bromide.

Grandmother was more generous. "Thank you, Rachel," she replied, patting my hand. "You've a kind heart. But that's not likely to happen. Boston's as hardened a place as any in the world—and it's a world I no longer want to be a part of."

The Governor's Girl listened to us, one ear flicking forward and back. The lantern's flame was reflected in her suspicious eyes, and I wondered if she was more concerned with our approach or with that slim bit of fire coming so near her.

"And from reading the newspapers," Grandmother continued, "it's also a wicked place." She was at her pulpit now and there was no stopping her. "Why, right on the front page—including the front page of your father's newspaper—are sordid accounts of murder and thievery and all manner of uncleanness." She shook her head wearily. "I'm too old for such and I'm too *tired*. I know my days are numbered and . . . well, I'm ready. I'm ready for my wings." With a stubborn upturn of her jaw, she shocked me by adding, "And if the good Lord can't see fit to give them to me soon, I'm prepared to get them myself."

"I must be late." Mr. Stead, satchel in hand, surprised us by stepping into the carriage shed. Politely he doffed his bowler hat. "Didn't know the sermon had started," he apologized, "and me not even in my pew." He hung his head in mock shame.

Grandmother put on her welcoming smile, though I knew she'd been caught off guard. I made the introductions, suddenly wishing I'd had the forethought to change into a clean dress. Odd, since I never thought about my appearance. Mr. Stead didn't seem to notice. In his calm manner, he pulled his apron over his head, took the cotton rope from its hook and ducked under the stall's bar. The Girl pinned her ears but he ignored them, smoothly slipping the loop over her head and adjusting it to rest on an area that wasn't burned. When she tried to pull away, he simply held the loop tight. With his free hand, he lifted her lip and pressed a thumb against her gum. After motioning for me to hold the lantern high, he released his thumb and we silently watched the gum hold pale a second before flushing pink.

"By the way," he asked, moving his examination to the Girl's eyes, "what's the topic?"

"The sins of this world," Grandmother stated defiantly.

"The end of this world," I muttered under my breath.

"One will bring about the other," she warned. "Are you a believer, Mr. Stead?"

He glanced over his shoulder, grinning shyly. "I'm a believer in avoiding the topics of religion and politics." Noticing the bottle in Grandmother's hands, he asked, "What do you have there?"

"The nation's best tonic." There was a challenge in her voice. "Ginger, cayenne, licorice, and eggs. Made by my father before me and his father before him. Guaranteed to restore condition to any sick or injured animal."

The veterinary started shaking his head and I, for one, was thankful. "I'll have to disagree with you there, Mrs. Boon. Medicine *is* a topic I'm not shy to discuss, and while there's bushels I don't know about it, I do have a certificate from the state of Massachusetts."

She made no attempt to hide her disdain. "A certificate is no replacement for experience, young man."

"I agree," he replied equitably. "But it does have a certain value in today's world, and with all due respect for your family's recipes, I'll need to insist on my own tonics for this mare."

"Then you can insist on them by your lonesome," she cried irritably. Shoving the bottle into my hand, she said, "I'm tired of ignorance. Proverbs One, verse . . . something or other: 'Wisdom cries aloud in the street,' but no one is listening." All in a lather, Grandmother gathered her skirt and stormed back to the house.

Mr. Stead's mouth hung open. His eyes practically bulged in astonishment. "I'm sorry," he said to me, "I didn't mean to—"

"No, *I'm* sorry," I interrupted, flushing with embarrassment. "That's just the nature of my family. Someone's always feverish about something: My grandmother has her Bible; my father, his newspaper; my brother . . . young ladies, I suppose." I laughed nervously.

He'd dropped the rope and pulled some scissors from his apron pocket. Patiently he began rubbing a wad of gauze along the blades and listened to me, as if he had all evening to do no more than that. "And you, Miss Selby?" he asked. "What brings out the fever in you?"

I blushed again. So many answers came rushing through my mind: horses, of course . . . and the kind of book you could lose a whole afternoon to . . . and the freedom to gallop down a dirt road with no one watching . . . and the thrill of trying something hard, even scary, and doing it . . . and learning, always learning. Yet I found myself stumbling for an answer: When was the last time anyone had bothered to ask *my* opinion?

"Come on, now," he cajoled. "There must be something that lights a fire in you."

That made it easy. "Her," I murmured, nodding toward the Governor's Girl. I noticed she was watching me now.

"Mmmm." Mr. Stead pulled some rolled bandaging from his satchel, cut it into long ribbons, and tucked them and the scissors into his apron pocket. "A lover of lost causes, eh?"

My breath caught. "You don't mean—"

"There, there," he stopped me. "It's back to my turn to apologize. You'll be next, I suppose." His smile was genial. "I don't mean that she's going to die; she's still standing, which, in her condition, is a lot to be thankful for. What I do mean is: Don't pin your heart on something that you can't . . . er . . . perhaps you should set your sights upon something more . . . oh, confound it! Oratory is not a skill required in veterinary classes." He gazed through the shed's open door, as if wishing for an escape. "Is your brother, by chance, in the house?"

"No, I think he's still at the fire station."

"Oh." Disappointment sounded in his voice.

"Do you need him for some reason?"

"No, no, I guess I can manage without. You see, like your grandmother, I'm planning on getting my own tonic down this mare. I've already mixed up the ingredients. But she's been known to dispense a black eye or two with that hammerhead of hers. She's got a streak of cussedness, to be sure, so I was hoping for an extra hand."

Gingerly I touched my bruised cheek. I knew what he meant.

"I don't suppose you would consider assisting me?"

The shock must have shown on my face, because Mr. Stead immediately withdrew the proposition. "I'm sorry," he said. "I shouldn't have—"

"I'll try, if you'd like," I answered quickly.

He looked at the Girl, then at me, and the frown creasing his forehead suggested he was having second thoughts. I was once again struck by his angular good looks; the serious air that he pulled on like a coat when he was thinking gave him the demeanor of a professor. Then he smiled. It was a smile so warm and confident that I would readily have attested to its power to heal from across a room. "I *would* like that," he said. "What's more," he lowered his voice, "I think *she* would like it." He indicated the mare, who was watching both of us now with heightened suspicion.

I didn't want to tell him that she probably would *not* like it, and decided to keep our earlier clash a secret.

"Of course she'd never admit to liking it," he was going on, "being the strong-minded creature that she is, but I'm thinking that a feminine hand might just be the key to winning her over. That, and a peppermint candy or two." He dug into his pocket and rustled some paper. One of the mare's ears came forward. When a hard white candy appeared in Mr. Stead's palm, the other ear came forward. He quickly slipped the treat inside the corner of the mare's mouth, then stood back and folded his arms. There was a noticeable softening in the Girl's eyes.

"I didn't know horses liked peppermints!"

He winked. "What girl doesn't like a gentleman caller to bring her sweets?"

I laughed. And blushed again.

"Now that we've made a good impression," he whispered conspiratorially, "let's move on to the real business. You do exactly as I tell you, and we'll just see if we can't get this old girl tonic'd and rebandaged before she can finish her candy."

I followed his instructions to hang the lantern from a convenient nail and join him in the stall. A thrill rushed through me. This was dangerous ground, yet I felt rock solid on it. Mr. Stead motioned me closer. He stood near the mare's haunches, then slid his hand down her back leg, past her hock and almost to her ankle. When he pinched her fetlock, she obediently lifted that leg.

"Standing on three legs will keep her mind on her balance," he explained. "Do you think you're strong enough to hold this one up?"

I nodded and took his place. Even in her weakened condition, the mare's power was evident. My heart beat faster.

Stay calm, I schooled myself. This was no different from cleaning one of Peaches' back hooves. Hold the leg straight out behind, and she can't kick. Lacing my fingers through the long white hairs, I cradled the bent ankle in my hands. But the instant and brutal reality was that holding up the Girl's leg was akin to supporting an elephant's. My back was already straining.

"Here," the veterinary said, handing me a cloth, "put this across your dress so you don't get it dirty."

Wondering how he missed the splatter of mash across my bodice, I shoved the cloth between my white skirt and the thick, feathered ankle. The Girl took advantage of my distraction by trying to jerk her leg away. I gripped her ankle tighter and struggled to hold her leg in place. For a moment there was a seesawing tug-of-war. It took all my strength to keep her iron-rimmed hoof from becoming a weapon.

"Good girl," Mr. Stead said. My back was to him, so I wasn't certain if he was talking to the mare or to me, but I warmed with pride anyway. I couldn't see what he was doing, so over the next several minutes my understanding of it was related through the mare's grunts, her sudden shifting of weight, and her repeated struggles to free her leg.

"Okay, that's it," he said at last. "You can let her go."

The freed leg dropped with a thud. I straightened slowly, my back uncoiling like a rusty spring.

Mr. Stead was nodding with satisfaction, only this time I knew the approval was for me. "Well done," he said. "You've spent some time around horses, I see."

I nodded, happy.

He dropped some utensils into his open satchel and took out a rolled cloth. "Most of her bandages seem to be in good condition. I'm just going to change the one along her chest. It's almost impossible to keep anything in place there. Too much movement."

I winced as he ripped the old bandage from the sticky wounds. The Girl grunted and started swinging her head menacingly, but he worked quickly, dodging this way and that, and the new bandage was well in place before she could carry out her threat.

Afterward, we stood outside the stall looking at her. "Such a pity," he said softly. "She's a good horse, the last one that deserves this."

"But you just said she had a streak of cussedness."

He chuckled. "That I did, and she does. But she's honest about her cussedness and she's honest about her work. I value that. I'd have her on my team any day." As he bent to get his satchel, his pocket crackled. He pulled out the peppermints, popped one into his mouth, and handed me the bag. "You'd better keep these," he said with a smile. "Bribes. Maybe next time you can get more bran in her instead of on you. I'll look forward to seeing the both of you tomorrow, Miss Selby." Winking, he picked up his satchel, stepped into the night, and was gone.

NINE ✌

FULL TO BURSTING WITH PRIDE, I RAN TOWARD THE HOUSE.
I had to tell someone how I'd helped the veterinary.

Mother's voice inside stopped me short. There was something else I had to do: get out of my soiled dress and into a clean
one—my third of the day!—before she saw me. Luckily, she and
Grandmother were in the parlor, examining the room's dingy
curtains, so I was able to race up the stairs undiscovered. "I'll
be right down for supper," I shouted.

"It's 'dinner' now that we're in Boston," Mother called
after me. "You don't want people to think we've stepped straight
out of the backwoods."

The image in my bureau mirror could have been a wild
creature out of the backwoods—I was that rumpled and dirty,
with limp twists of hair pasted to my smudged face—but it
was a thoroughly happy creature. I couldn't stop smiling.
I set about scrubbing and brushing and smoothing, even to
Mother's standards, and dashed down the stairs. Composing

myself, I slid into my chair at the dining room table.

Mother and Grandmother were already seated, and for some reason, servings of boiled fish and beets and chopped cucumber salad had been heaped onto each of our plates. The men's plates sat empty, their untouched goblets of milk beading and running with sweat. Assuming grace had been said, I grabbed my fork.

"It's only polite that we wait," Mother said, halting a morsel halfway to my mouth.

In stubborn response, Grandmother picked up her fork. "Nonsense. There's nothing worse than room-temperature fish. They know what time supper is served."

"*Dinner,* Mother. That's what they call it here."

Grandmother lifted a flaky chunk to her mouth and brazenly spoke while chewing. "I'm not from here. And I've been calling it *supper* for more than sixty years. I'm too old to change."

Mother's lips tightened ever so slightly. She turned her attention to the painted metal vase in the center of the table. A modest bouquet of violets drooped over its rim, and she concentrated on rearranging them to her satisfaction. I quietly relinquished my fork and returned my hands to my lap. I stared at the bouquet too, my discomfort measured aloud by the stern ticking of the parlor clock. And by my growling stomach.

"I helped the veterinary today." Anything to break the silence.

"What veterinary?" Mother asked.

"The one that came to treat the burned mare. Grandmother met him. His name is Mr. Stead."

"He's a cocksure young fool," Grandmother snorted. "I'll say that about him." Her tongue parted her lips and she plucked a fish bone from it.

Mother shifted her glance to me. "I don't think I like the idea of you being in a barn with a strange man. And I know your father wouldn't. It's not seemly. Besides, isn't it your brother's job to . . . do whatever it is you're doing to that poor horse?"

"He wasn't there," I explained, surprised to find myself on the defensive. Why was I being pelted with shame? "Mr. Stead asked me to help and I helped."

"I'm afraid that won't do," Mother replied. Such an authoritative tone, I'd learned, was used only in Father's absence. "You'll not tarnish your reputation when we're so recently arrived in Boston. Kindly allow James to assist the veterinary from now on."

"But he wasn't there."

"Then Mr. Stead should not have been there either." Closing the book on the subject, she picked up her fork and turned to Grandmother. "I think I've decided on the bone-colored lace for the parlor curtains." She slipped a small bite into her mouth.

"With the scalloped edging or without?"

"With."

"They're too ornamental," Grandmother stated flatly. "They'll overwhelm such a small room. I prefer the cream ones with the straight edging, the ones that were on the next display over." With that, the two of them entered into a tedious discussion of every set of curtains they'd seen that morning, weighing the merits of scalloped edging over plain, and the nuances that visitors might infer from hanging white versus ivory versus bone. Mother went on eating, little by little, as she talked, and I took that as permission to start eating as well.

Neither James nor Father had appeared by the time tea was served, so we cleared the table of all but their plates. I didn't know if that was so Mother could feed them when they did arrive, or leave them served with a blank portion of guilt for not having arrived on time. Afterward, she insisted we all retire to the parlor. She lit the lamps and arranged the three of us near the bay window, where evening passersby could observe us. Grandmother opened her Bible and began reading and rocking. Mother then insisted I dig out my stitchery sampler, which I hadn't held in my lap for over a month. She stifled my pained sigh with a tilt of her head and one dark look.

Sewing of any kind was such excruciatingly boring work. And at the rate I was going, I'd still be embroidering tiny veined leaves onto long-limbed trees when I was thirty. Or older. Especially when Mother shook her head in disapproval and had me rip out an entire evening's progress. Over the past year I'd satisfactorily completed relatively little. I'd done the alphabet twice in a royal blue stem stitch; the two sets ran along the bottom of the sampler. Above them were two sets of numerals in a green running stitch that, if you didn't examine the eights too closely, were rather good. And there was my name, Rachel Selby, and age, fifteen. The date had yet to be stitched in. If I finished this year it would read 1872, though I could just as easily picture myself sewing an 1882 and then dropping over dead from exhaustion. Mother fitted a needle with some modest brown thread and pointed to a gnarled garden limb that arched around the top right corner. Dutifully I began embroidering.

All I could think about, though, was the Governor's Girl. I wondered how she was faring on her first night in the carriage shed. Alone. I wondered if Mr. Stead's tonic was giving her any comfort. With a flush of warmth, I remembered his "Good girl" and "Well done." I let those words echo pleasurably in my mind, over and over, until I lost my concentration and the thread knotted on itself and caught.

"Rachel," Mother cautioned, "you're going too fast."

"I'm sorry." A lie, really. "I suppose I'm tired." There was the truth. "May I be excused to bed?"

"Of course, dear. But no reading. You need your sleep."

I couldn't promise that but didn't say as much. After kissing each of them good night, I stowed the sampler in its basket and climbed the stairs to the attic.

I *was* tired. It was just that, as I changed into my nightclothes, I couldn't help noticing how the lamp's flame was playing across my horse care manual. The gilt-edged pages glowed almost magically and, if I squinted, the three embossed horses on the cover could be seen to toss their heads in grandeur. My heartbeat quickened. That book *was* magical to me, full of potions and instructions and detailed drawings for healing horses. Of course I was going to read it.

I climbed into bed and pulled the book onto my lap. It was nearly as heavy as a sack of flour and creased my stomach with its weight. To my mind, that only served to underscore its value.

There was nothing on burns, I knew, but I thumbed through the pages anyway. The next chapter I was due to read was "Diseases of the Brain," but I wasn't up to such a heavy task tonight, so I skipped ahead and browsed a few pages on foals and foaling. Not reading in any particular order, I learned that autumn colts should always be allowed mother's milk until the spring grass arrives. And that when they're teething, wood ashes mixed with salt will cure the inevitable indigestion.

My mind strayed back to the Girl. None of this had anything to do with healing her. Restlessly I riffled through some more of the manual's 652 pages. An essay entitled "General Principles in Treating the Horse" caught my eye. Its author certainly began with an authoritative trumpet.

First, and foremost, I was instructed, *you must remember that the horse is more like unto Man than any other animal. In his natural state, he is happy and free from disorders, but kept in cramped quarters against his will he suffers. The practitioner of healing must always remember to work with, and not against, the horse's true Nature.*

Concern immediately overtook me. Was the carriage shed's stall too cramped for a horse the size of the Girl? Maybe I could make it larger. I pondered that possibility. Maybe I could knock out the rails on one side—I'd found a hammer in the shed—and take some of the old boards there and . . . my hand slipped across the page as my head nodded. The tumultuous day was catching up to me. Shaking myself awake, I found my place on the page. *Because the horse is so closely associated with Man, he has been cursed with his same diseases—the sure and sudden consequence of sin.* My head buzzed. That sentence and the next ran together so that I lost their entire meaning and had to start over. But before I could latch onto one coherent thought, the ornate bits of type began floating off the page, swimming dizzily past my eyes and through my brain. The heavy book sagged lower on my stomach and I gave in to sleep.

It was sometime during the thick of the night that the fog's damp chill or the book's sharp edge awoke me. I shoved the book aside, rolled over, and pulled the covers to my chin. There was a faint glow in the darkness. Dully I struggled to make sense of what I was seeing. It had a yellowish cast, a sort of shimmer as it moved. Like a flame.

At once I awoke. My skin prickled with the awful realization that I'd fallen asleep with the lamp still burning. And there was just a small lick of kerosene left. Oh, good Lord! With trembling fingers, I reached over and turned off the flame. A cavelike blackness enveloped the room.

Go back to sleep, I told myself. *It's all right now. Everyone in the house is asleep, the street below is quiet. Just lay your head on your pillow, close your eyes, and sleep.*

Except that my blood was roaring through my body so

hard and so fast that it swept away the very notion of sleep. Ghastly thoughts kept flashing through my mind. What if the lamp had burned dry and cracked the glass? Or what if the kerosene had exploded? I'd have incinerated this house and all my family with it. We would have died like the horses in the livery fire, screaming for help that would come too late.

I heaved myself over the other way and the book fell to the floor with a thud, making me jump. Mice skittered behind the wall. My mouth was as dry as dust, and for some reason I thought of Mr. Stead's peppermints. Immediately Mother's stricture pounded in my ears: *You'll not tarnish your reputation, you'll not tarnish your reputation.* I rolled back. The room seemed suddenly hot. The sheets twisted around my legs and I kicked at them until they were a knotted mess. I punched my pillow once, twice. *Sleep,* I schooled myself. *Sleep.* But aggravating student that I was, I tossed and turned for more than an hour. Sometime between when the clock chimed three and a quarter past, I finally dozed fitfully, then woke again with a start.

The night air was thicker and heavier than before. Smoke. I was sure of it. My throat clamped shut; I couldn't breathe. Panicked, I clawed my way out of the bedcovers and hurtled down the stairs. Only I couldn't seem to get anywhere. The stairs went on and on endlessly, circling past the landing and Father's dead butterflies and then opening onto more stairs and more butterflies. I kept tumbling down them, falling, it seemed, straight into everlasting doom. When I thought I'd never escape the house, I was no longer in it; I was in the carriage shed. The air was just as still and heavy there, but more damp than smoky, more like a cave. Or a tomb. I could barely see the Girl. She was nothing more than a gray, ghostly image wrapped in her bandages. And she was making a queer noise, sort of a choking sound. To my sudden horror, I realized that someone had bandaged her too tightly. She'd been wrapped up completely: her neck, her mouth, her nose. Only her eyes were uncovered and they were frantic, rolling to white, begging me to help. I ran to her at once, lifting my arms—but found that I was as neatly wrapped in bandages as she was. I was helpless too. The Girl rocked back and forth in suffocating agony, and I could only watch. In a final spasm, she went still as stone. There was a moment of emptiness and then, as I reached out to touch her, the bandages began crumbling away, she with them, only so much dust.

"Earth to earth," I heard Grandmother solemnly intone somewhere in the distance below me, "ashes to ashes, and dust to dust."

⌘ TEN

WHAT A HORRIBLE NIGHT. WHEN BLESSED SUNDAY DAWN finally crept into my room, I threw the bedclothes back and dressed with the haste of a prisoner granted release. I had to get to the Girl. I had to make sure that she'd survived the night, that my dream was truly just a dream. Shoes in hand, I tiptoed down the stairs.

Noises from the kitchen—the clank of a skillet and repeated thuds of the icebox—told that Mother was up, and probably Grandmother, too, so I'd have to slip out the front door if I could. A newspaper rattled in the dining room. Father was up as well. That was going to make it harder. As I reached the newel post at the bottom of the stairs, I heard him preaching his own Sunday sermon, loud enough to reach his congregation in the kitchen.

"They're overly taken with calling themselves 'journalists,' in my opinion," he said. "Especially the female one."

The kitchen door scraped open on its worn hinges, and

I heard china cups clink against their saucers. A heavy platter was set on the table. "You didn't tell us you had a woman writing for you," Mother said.

A woman worked on Father's newspaper? That held me in place.

"She doesn't write for *me*," Father corrected. "And if I have my say, she won't be writing for the *Argus* much longer. She was already on the staff when I accepted the managerial position. I can only surmise that the editor before me had some different opinions on the ability of women to contribute serious news."

"Mmm." Mother murmured a response that avoided commitment.

"I don't want to appear behind the age," Father said, and I couldn't help but roll my eyes. "Women, I suppose, can take employment in a restaurant or a mercantile, if they must. At least they know how to cook and to shop." His newspaper snapped open as he chuckled at his own joke.

The hairs on the back of my neck stiffened, but I didn't hear a response from Mother. Was she still in the room or had she returned to the kitchen? No matter, Father went on speech-ifying loudly. "Do you know what aggravates me all the more about this female would-be writer?" he prodded. "Who's feeding her husband? Who's taking care of her children?"

"Does she *have* a husband and children?" Grandmother now. I heard her drop into her chair so heavily that an unlady-like belch escaped her. Father ignored that; he was more inter-ested in having an adversary.

"Of course," he responded confidently. "Do you think I've neglected the facts?"

"How about some nice tomato preserves with your hash, Mr. Selby?" Mother's remedy for argument was always a forkful of food. To be quickly followed by another.

Maybe he nodded, I don't know, but he didn't speak to her. He wouldn't now. "What I wonder is," he charged on, "just what sort of a man it takes to let his wife—and a pretty wife, I might add, quite attractive—spend her days in a printing office surrounded by men? Not all of whom are married." He mumbled through a mouthful, "It's too distracting, really. It's scandalous."

"Scandalous that they aren't married?" Grandmother asked in an innocent tone.

"No, scandalous that this woman insists on working among these poor fellows. And without the decency to wear a corset!"

Mother gasped. I think she dropped into her own chair. "Oh, my goodness gracious!"

"Oh, well, that's another matter altogether." Grandmother sounded equally astonished. "Are you quite certain about it?"

"I have eyes, don't I?" Father exclaimed.

"I'll have some of those preserves, please," Mother interrupted. "Would you pass them?" There was a brief pause, followed by a thank-you. "Dear, dear," she chided, "such talk for a Sunday morning." Steering the conversation in another direction, she asked, "Have you decided on a church to attend today?" She could have gotten the same response from the wall. She cleared her throat and tried again. "Mr. Selby?"

"Yes?"

"Have you decided on a church for us to attend? I saw a nice-looking one yesterday on Tremont Street, across from that lovely Boston Common. It's Episcopalian, I believe."

"That church?" Grandmother snorted. "It doesn't even have a proper steeple."

"King's Chapel. That's the place to be seen," Father stated. He fought with his newspaper rather loudly.

"King's Chapel," Mother echoed. "It sounds nice. Do you know what kind of a church that is? I'm only asking because—"

"Yes," Father cut her off, "it's the kind of a church where the Selby family belongs. Are you questioning my competence?" He said it with a smile, I was sure, because I knew that smile. It was challenging, icy, and heavy with disdain. It was the kind of a smile that brought you to your knees and closed your mouth.

"No, of course not," Mother murmured, then immediately asked Grandmother to pass the biscuits. There was yet another rattling of newspaper, a triumphant exclamation point. I seized the opportunity to dart for the door and escape.

Outside, an early morning fog had our entire row of red brick houses packed in cotton. Everything was hushed, a balm after my sleepless night. Happy to be out of the house, I hurried around to the courtyard.

Instantly I knew something was amiss. Voices were coming from the carriage shed, one of them spewing oaths. "Damn it all!

Stop that!" A horse's body thudded against a wall. There was an anxious squeal. I lifted my skirts and ran as if my life depended on it. Rushing into the shed, I found James and another man trying to corner the Girl. She was lashing out at them with both hind feet. Torn bandages dangled from her body.

"It's no use," James said. "We'd better wait."

"No, let me try again." The other man feinted one way, then rushed along the mare's other side, grabbing for the rope that was hanging around her neck. But she was too quick for him. Dodging his hand, she spun and kicked, grazing his thigh. "Ow!" the man cried. He doubled over, pressing a hand to his leg.

"You're on your own," James said as he escaped under the bar. "Stand clear," he told me. He spread his arms as a barrier.

The man in the stall—I was sure now that I'd seen him at the fire station; he'd been the one arguing for the mare's life—wouldn't give up. Still hunched over, he eyed an opportunity and lunged for the rope again. The Girl pulled out of reach, screaming in pain or fury or both, and swung her huge head at him. He ducked, narrowly avoiding a good whack. But before he could recover, she was on top of him, attacking with bared teeth. I thought he was going to be killed for certain, but he nimbly dived under the bar, rolled once, and jumped to his feet. Grinning, he shook his fist at the infuriated horse. "You're Satan's own daughter, you are."

I was trembling with rage. "What are you doing to her?"

"Just changing her bandages, miss, though she's not of a mind to have it done."

James appeared equally shaken. "Rachel," he said, by way of explanation and introduction, "this is Mr. Benton Lee. He came over to help me with the Governor's Girl. Benton, this is my sister, Rachel."

"Good morning." Mr. Lee's greeting was accompanied by more than a hint of a leer. He boldly looked me up and down, full length. I didn't know whether to laugh at the absurdity or cringe at the impropriety. His shock of black hair and the thick beard framing his olive-skinned face gave him a rather sinister, though certainly not an ugly, appearance. What truly caught my attention, though, were his eyes. They were so dark as to blend iris and pupil, and they wouldn't fix on anything, but kept hunting, piercing each subject on which they landed. When they kept returning to me, I instinctively made an escape: into the Girl's stall.

"Here now," Mr. Lee shouted. His lunge was too late and too short. "James, she shouldn't—!"

I paid them no mind. I couldn't. I had to get to the Girl. She was heaving herself back and forth in a tormented—and dangerous—frenzy. Praying that she'd remember, I walked right up to her and slipped her a peppermint. To my relief, she took it, eyeing me with what I thought was new respect. I lifted the rope from her head and we stood unfettered, facing my brother and Mr. Lee.

"Seems as though you've made a friend," James said.

Mr. Lee spluttered. He looked like a boiler ready to explode. "I still don't think—"

"Save your breath." James laughed. "My sister is half horse and more at home in a barn than a parlor. I'll be responsible for her. Besides, I think it'll take Mr. Stead to change these bandages. You can go on back to the station for some sleep."

A foul word escaped Mr. Lee's lips. "I won't be sleeping there for a while, didn't you hear? The chief suspended me—without pay—for 'reckless conduct while on duty.' You probably just got yourself promoted to driver."

James's expression balanced between friendly sympathy and selfish hope. "Did he suspend you for leaving the team?"

"For trying to save some horses' lives is the way I see it."

"How long?" James asked.

"One week."

"What are you going to do?"

The way he was pacing back and forth reminded me of a black cat on the wrong side of a door. "Oh, I'll find something to do," he said, a decided air of mystery cloaking his words. He nodded toward our house. "I heard your father was a newspaperman."

Instantly the chief's accusation came to mind—"to see if you could get your name in the newspapers again"—and I listened to Mr. Lee with growing distrust.

"He is," James replied. "He's the managing editor of the *Argus*."

"Never heard of it."

"It's one of Boston's smaller papers."

"Your family moved all the way here so your father could be a little fish in a big pond?"

James laughed again. "Yes, well, he'll find a way to make a splash, mark my words."

The dark-haired man stared at our house, deep in his own thoughts.

"I've heard there have been quite a few fires in the past month," James said, and I could almost hear Father prompting him.

"Have you?" Mr. Lee spun and that crazy, leering grin of his took hold. "I don't think there have been any more than usual, but do you know what? My ears have been ringing all morning." He tapped one, still grinning. "And the ringing sounds just like a fire alarm, so I'm betting there's going to be another one soon. I've just got a way with these things, you know?" He glanced at the house again before announcing, "Well, I'll be off now. You two take good care of my girl." And he bolted through the door as if someone had struck a match under him.

James and I exchanged bewildered looks. He shook his head and then, referring to my friendship with the mare, asked, "How did you manage this?" For the next several minutes I poured out all my excitement and satisfaction at having helped the veterinary. I included the peppermints.

Oddly enough, James seemed less than pleased. "Father doesn't know yet, does he?"

I shook my head.

"Did he see you leave?"

"I don't think so. When did you get home last night?"

"After eleven. I'm done in."

"Then why did you get up so early?"

"Benton told me he'd meet me here to help with changing the Girl's bandages. I got out of the house by telling Father I had to go to the station." He wadded up some of the bandages at his feet and moodily tossed them into the corner. "I don't know how much help I'm going to be in treating her, though; I can't even get close to her." He put his hands on his hips and sighed. "We're going to have to tell him about her today," he said. "Otherwise, he's bound to find out."

I looked up to find the Girl watching me, which gave me a chill. "I won't let him take her away," I said, as much to myself as to him. "Not this time."

James looked at me quizzically but chose not to question. "We'd better get back into the house. How about if I go in the front door with a bit of a racket, and you sneak past me and up the stairs. Then you can come down again, all right?"

The plan worked without a hitch, and soon we were all seated at breakfast, with no one the wiser. The air was still uncomfortably heavy with the secret we were all keeping from Father, but he was back to blustering about women in the workplace, so of course he didn't notice.

Soon afterward we were hurrying off to our first church service in Boston. Father marched us briskly to King's Chapel, and we strode straight into its blazingly white interior, marveling at the magnificent columns and arches and high, suspended pulpit. To our collective humiliation, however, but most especially Father's, it was pointed out that the sanctuary was partitioned into private boxes rather than pews and that these boxes bore the names of Boston's most prominent families. Not a one said Selby. It was a stiffer figure that we followed back down the street to St. Paul's, a plainer church that, as Grandmother noted again, didn't even have a steeple.

Father put us on display nevertheless. As he'd always done at home, he led us down the aisle and sat us in the front pew. I think it was his way of proving, on a weekly basis, that he was aligned with might and right; that he and God, as it were, wrote for the same newspaper. I clasped my hands in my lap, giving the appearance of prayer and hiding, I hoped, my embarrassment.

The church grew quite crowded, and hot. As we waited, I began stealing peeks this way and that. The interior wasn't nearly as ornate as King's Chapel, though it used a lot of stone in a grand manner. The altar was impressive, the congregation well dressed. Hand-held fans fluttered like so many panting butterflies. At long last a man in a frilly black robe appeared at the front of the sanctuary and took his time turning the onionskin pages of a prayer book. He led some singing and some recitations and made some announcements that had nothing to do with me. The service dragged on and on. When the minister finally took the pulpit and began speaking, I had to pinch off an exasperated sigh. His chosen topic was one of my least favorite: predestination.

It was one of those sermons with which I couldn't possibly agree, one of those intolerable lectures that always set me on the back of a horse and sent me galloping. It was a wonder God didn't strike me down right there in that front pew. I'd heard it preached so many times before: Each of us is nothing more than a mindless ant following a path that has long ago been set out for us. We can't choose the path, and we can't leave the path. That would be an insult to one's Maker. The man's voice droned on, but his earnest words were lost amid the rhythm of hoofbeats inside my head.

Surely I was a sinner, the way I was always galloping away from the path. And such a wicked one that I couldn't even see what was wrong with blazing my own trail.

The minister pounded the pulpit with his fist, and I jumped as if it were a lightning bolt straight from the heavens. James slid a bemused glance at me, which I ignored. Flames and reprobation, the man thundered. Hooves beat louder in my head. Sin and salvation. Sweat rolled down my face. I thought of the Girl and incongruously pictured myself on her back galloping through walls of fire. Then a black void stretched before us. Death? I couldn't see what was ahead, but she gathered herself and we leaped and—

"Amen," the minister said. "Amen," the congregation echoed. We rose to leave.

ELEVEN

ALTHOUGH IT WAS SUNDAY, FATHER DECIDED TO GO INTO his newspaper office after church. Mother meekly reminded him of the fourth commandment, the one about abstaining from work on the Sabbath and keeping it holy, but he brushed her away with a wave of his hand. Work *was* Father's religion, I thought. As for the rest of us, we were happy to be freed from it. For me that meant no dishes, no laundry, and especially no sewing! And no having to tell Father—yet—about the burned horse in our carriage shed. I had the whole blessed afternoon to spend with her.

It was going to be an extremely quiet afternoon; I could see that when I tiptoed through the doorway. The Girl was dozing heavily, the early-morning battle with James and Mr. Lee having exhausted her. Some very unholy thoughts went through my head as to what I'd like to do to each of them.

Swarms of blackflies crawled across and through the sores along her back and neck. That made my own skin twitch, but she was beyond noticing, it seemed, or caring. The cramped quarters reeked almost to suffocation with the sickly odor of weeping flesh, and I remembered the warning words I'd read just last night. Was this place too small for her? I shouldered the shed's doors wider, startling her awake. My efforts proved useless, though; there was no breeze to dry the sweat that darkened her chest.

Picking up one of the discarded bandages, I fashioned a sort of rag-tailed fan and began manufacturing my own breeze. At least that chased the flies from her wounds. A small act, but it was something. When Mr. Stead came, he'd do something more for her.

So, as the minutes ticked by and I fought to ignore my aching arms, I eagerly watched for the veterinary's arrival out of the corner of my eye. My heart skipped whenever a sound resembled a footstep, but my arms gave out before he showed.

James came to watch us for a bit. He went through the motions of warning me to be careful, but finding the Girl and I standing agreeably side by side, he gave up and returned to the house. Grandmother came out too, carrying a pot of bran mash that she'd cooked up. "Less salt," she said with a smile. And with her holding the pot and me the spoon, we did manage to get a little sustenance into the mare.

But all too soon the shadows were stretching longer and longer and then the day disappeared and Mr. Stead still hadn't shown. Reluctantly I went in for supper—I mean, dinner—but the food I put into my mouth did nothing to fill my emptiness.

When I climbed the stairs to my room afterward, I was dusty and itchy and feeling strangely unsettled.

That night was as sleepless as the last. Even though I twice checked that the lamp was turned off, I tossed and turned for hours. The parlor clock chimed my wakefulness in fifteen-minute intervals, and somewhere between four thirty and a quarter till five I found myself staring wide-eyed into the darkness. My heart was pumping too fast; it was climbing right up my throat. I swallowed it, tried to breathe slowly, tried to relax. But the blood that was rushing to the ends of my fingers and to the tips of my toes was setting them atingle. The prickly sensation circled my ankles, skipped up my shins, and gave my kneecaps a hard jerk. I wadded the sheets in my fists. Something was about to happen.

Two sudden bangs, like gunshots, split the darkness: hooves striking wood. I recognized the sound at once. That was followed by a frantic staccato of thuds and strangled screams. In the next heartbeat I was out of my bed and tearing down the stairs.

Doors were being flung open in the hallway. Mother was fumbling to light a lantern beside Father, who, without his spectacles, was squinting as blindly as a mole into the dark courtyard below. "What's all that cursed racket?" he shouted.

The flame jumped to life and ensnared me in its yellow glow. Pausing just long enough to reply, "It's a horse," I fled past him.

Mother tried to explain. "We didn't wish to disturb you with the news earlier, so—"

The jangle of a fire alarm cut her short. All over the

neighborhood, dogs began barking. Out in the shed, a board snapped in two.

"What in . . . ?" Father barreled down the stairs, overtaking me in the front hall and shoving his way past. James followed in his wake, his face shot with worry.

In the kitchen we came near to piling one on top of the other because the back door was sticking. Father tugged on the metal knob with one hand and then the other, his temper ratcheting ever higher. Exploding in frustration, he kicked at it with his slippered foot and shouted an oath that made even James wince. With his leg braced on the frame, Father gave the knob a two-fisted yank—and the door began ripping away from its rusted hinges. "Confound it!" he swore as he wrestled with the toppling weight.

A few blocks away I heard the clatter of the firehorses gathering into their harness. *That's* what was wrong with the Governor's Girl: She was trying to go with them. She'd known the alarm was going to ring even before it did, and she'd tried to break out of her stall.

"What's happening?" Grandmother called from upstairs. "Is someone hurt? Hello?" Mother rushed off, carrying the lantern with her and unmindfully plunging us into total darkness.

"Get another light," Father ordered as he struggled to prop the damaged door against the wall. While James began searching out match and lantern, Father kicked open the screen door and stormed into the still-black morning. I was right behind him. We rushed into the shed together.

To my horror, the gray mare was feverishly heaving her weight from side to side like some berserk shuttle on a weaver's loom. Even in the darkness I could see that the bar at the front of her stall was splintered almost in two.

"What in God's name is this animal doing here?" Father demanded. "And what's wrong with it?"

"She's a firehorse," I began, unsure of how much to tell.

James appeared with the lantern. "From the station," he added, somewhat breathlessly. "I've made arrangements with the chief to—"

The mare lashed out with a hind leg, cracking another board.

"Enough!" Father shouted, raising his fist. "That will be enough of that!"

The Girl kicked again. Mother and Grandmother joined us, easing their way into the small carriage shed to stare open-mouthed at the commotion. I was stabbed through with worry.

"Get me a halter!" Father demanded. There was none to be had, of course, so he cast around for himself. Spying the cotton rope looped on its hook, he grabbed it and took the lantern from James. He walked right up to the Girl, raised the light in her face, and shouted, "Stop that!" He slapped at her with the rope. "Stop that!" The mare lunged at him, raked her teeth across his arm, and recoiled.

"Dash that animal!" Father dropped the lantern. "It bit me!"

Flames instantly sprouted from the oil that spilled across

the dirt floor, and, working as one, James snatched up the lantern while I smothered them with an overturned pail.

Father didn't seem to notice. "Have this horse removed from my property at once!" he said. My heart stopped beating. "I want it gone before daylight, and I don't care if you have to raise the dead to do it!" Clasping his free hand over his injured arm, he strode out of the shed. "Mrs. Selby," he called back, "I'll be needing your attention." With a weary *I told you so* look, Mother hurried after him. A moment later Grandmother followed.

The Girl was still weaving from side to side, but she was doing so drunkenly now, near to collapse. I had to do something to keep her from injuring herself further. Even though I'd left the peppermints in my room, I was sure I could—

"You're not going near her," James said, grabbing my arm roughly. "Not this time. She's obviously gone mad." He yanked me toward the door. "There's nothing we can do, so come along."

The Girl came to a dead stop, and I think she looked at me. I was sure of it. She let out a long, exhaling groan and as she did, she seemed to grow fainter, gloomier, just as in my dream. I feared she was going to crumble away.

"James . . ." I begged.

"No." He gripped my arm tighter and pushed me toward the house. Suddenly he was very much like Father. "This was all a mistake. I should never have let you talk me into bringing that horse here." I struggled wildly, blindly: an animal being crushed by a trap. "Stop that!" James ordered. "Stop it now!"

He plowed ahead, dragging me against my will. Resentment boiled inside of me.

The moment we entered the kitchen I shook free of James and he stalked off toward Father's study. That's where Father was, swearing a blue streak while slamming drawers. I assumed Mother was with him. Grandmother turned from the stove to give me a mild look of understanding and sympathy, but she'd obviously chosen to stay out of the fray this time.

Of all things to happen at that hour, an urgent knock sounded on the front door. We both looked toward the hall, but the very oddity froze us to our places. The double knock came again, right away, and more insistent. I, for one, scrambled.

Father got there first, with James in his shadow. He flung open the door and there stood Mr. Stead, his arm poised for another knock. Thank the Lord. I wrapped my arms around myself to stop my trembling.

"Forgive the hour," he said to Father, doffing his hat. "I was just on my way home from seeing to a sick horse when I heard the fire alarm and . . . well, I saw your lamps lit and wondered . . . is the mare all right? Have you seen to her?" His eyes darted past James's to search mine.

"Oh, we've seen to her, all right," Father interjected. "She nearly took my arm off." He held up his bandaged limb for evidence. "And if you're the veterinary, you have my permission to put that horse down this minute. She's a danger to society."

In the orange glow of the hall lamps I could see that Mr. Stead's eyes were rimmed by fatigue. Still, with that endless patience that so entranced me, he asked, "Would you like me to take a look at your arm?"

"I'm not some damned animal," Father cried, holding his arm well out of reach. "Just get that vicious horse off my property!" Mother rushed forward in an attempt to soothe him, but he ignored her. Looking at James, he said sternly, "I want to have a talk with you in my study, alone." Without even excusing themselves, they disappeared into the next room and the door closed behind them.

Mr. Stead didn't appear to take offense. He calmly returned to the matter at hand. "How is she, Miss Selby?"

Whether it was the gentleness in his voice or my utter helplessness or the fear that I was going to lose another horse, I was suddenly and ashamedly so choked with tears that I couldn't answer.

"I'd better go take a look for myself," he said, nodding politely to Mother. "If you'll lead the way, please, Miss Selby?"

Mother drew herself up tall. "I don't think it's proper that—" she began, but Grandmother appeared in the hallway to interrupt her.

"Let her go, dear. There's been nothing about this morning that's proper by any means."

Grabbing the lantern, I led the veterinary in a rush through the kitchen and across the courtyard. With every step I breathed a prayer of thanks that he'd arrived. The Girl would be all right now. He'd take care of her.

But the moment we entered the shed, I found we were too

late: She was down. Only her arching white belly rose like a bloated ghost from the bedding. I gasped.

In one smooth motion Mr. Stead was under the bar and kneeling beside her, his ear pressed to her distended stomach. She flicked an ear. "I'm afraid she's colicked," he said, and my heart skidded to a stop again. Horses could die from colic. The frown on his face made his next words sound like an accusation. "How much has she had to eat?"

I shook my head. "Hardly anything. A few peppermints, some spoonfuls of mash."

"Are you certain she's had nothing else? We must be certain."

The urgency in his voice frightened me further. "I'm certain."

He rose, walked to the water tub, and plunged his hand into it. "Did you give her cold water, after she was heated?"

Fighting the shaking in my knees, I answered, "No . . . no, it's the same water."

"What about her manure?" he asked, kicking at the straw. His movements alarmed the Girl enough that she began struggling. She lunged wildly, as if she'd been shot, but finally clambered to her unsteady feet. "Easy," he murmured distractedly. "What about her manure?" he asked again, still searching the bedding. "What's it looked like?"

I'd read about the subject, but I'd never been asked to discuss it. The words wouldn't come.

"This is no time for delicacies," he said sharply. "If you

want to see this mare live, I need your help. Now, do you remember her passing any manure yesterday, or seeing her do so this morning?"

I tried to recall, but . . . the past two days and nights were all jumbled in my mind. I shook my head; I was just as useless as I'd been in my dream. The veterinary continued kicking through the straw, easing his way around the Girl. She stood with her sides heaving, watching him guardedly.

"If she's impacted," he mused, "I'll have to—wait, here's some." He nudged a clump of straw with his boot, then bent over the dark pile. "See?" he said, as if it were obvious. "Fairly fresh. And moist. That's good. Still . . ." He gave me a severe appraisal. "I need to perform an examination. I know you helped the other day, but this will involve more than bandages . . . and additional indelicacies. Will you run along back to the house and send out your brother?"

I shook my head. "I want to help."

"No," he answered curtly. "While I appreciate your determination, what I need to do isn't going to be pleasant . . . for any of us." He was already donning his apron and rolling up his sleeves, his indifferent attitude dismissing me.

I ducked under the splintered bar and pushed up the sleeves of my robe. "I *have* to help her."

Irritation flickered across his face, but he didn't argue further. He pointed to his satchel. "There's a small tin of grease inside. If you'll find it, please?"

I fell upon the black leather bag, dug through its myriad

supplies, and handed him the tin. He began slathering the grease over his muscular arms. "Do you think you can get the rope around her head?" Hearing the doubt in his voice set my jaw. I picked up the coiled rope from where Father had dropped it and approached the Girl. I looked her straight in the eye, wanting to let her know that I was trying to help her, but her eyes were black with pain. She wouldn't know me from Adam. Or Eve. Carefully, I fit the rope over her head, settling it on the one patch of mane.

"Ready?"

I swallowed and nodded.

Standing at the mare's back end, Mr. Stead tried to nudge her tail aside with his elbow. She clamped it tight. So, grasping the white hairs with his greased fingers, he forcefully pulled the tail out of the way and pinned it with his elbow. I stared. It was bold and indecent, but I couldn't help it. I'd never seen anything like this before. As his slathered arm began passing under her tail and disappearing inside her body, though, I looked away. I tried to think about something else, anything else—the sound of an early delivery wagon out on the street, the square of graying sky that showed through the window—anything except what was happening right beside me. A buzzing filled my head. When Mr. Stead spoke again, he was wiping his arms.

"No impaction," he stated. "Some wind has been released, which will bring a modicum of relief. But I'm going to mix her up a drench and bleed her just to be sure."

"And then she'll be all right?"

He sighed wearily. It suddenly occurred to me that he must hear that same hope-filled question with every sick animal he treated. That wasn't fair; he wasn't God.

"I wish I knew," he replied in a very tired and very human voice. "I think the sound of the fire alarm overexcited her this morning. I should have thought of that; I just wasn't expecting another fire so soon. We'll stuff some cotton in her ears before I leave. But the excitement, I believe, combined with her already compromised condition, caused the contents of her stomach to sour. Although she could have bots or enteritis, either of which could prove far more serious."

"How will we know which it is?"

"We *won't*." The sharpness in his response was immediately reined back by, "At least we won't know for certain. Medicine," he explained in carefully measured words, "even that applied to horses, doesn't provide black-and-white answers. We look for symptoms, we consult our books, we use our experience and God-given abilities, and—for better or worse—we treat the afflicted animal." While he talked, he pulled various small bottles from his bag and poured differing amounts into what looked like a very large bottle of oil. After inserting a stopper, he shook it vigorously. "We'll start with this," he said.

"What is it?"

"Spirit of turpentine, laudanum, and linseed oil." He took an L-shaped metal pipe and a funnel from his satchel. Prying open the Girl's mouth, he quickly shoved the pipe partway down her throat. While she gagged and struggled weakly, the oily concoction was poured and poured and poured through the funnel.

Finally he set those implements aside and pulled a large white cloth from his satchel.

"What's that for?"

"Her own good," he answered emotionlessly. He tossed the cloth over the Girl's face, by necessity covering her sticky wounds, and knotted the ends under her jowl. Returning to his satchel, he withdrew a black leather case, and from it, a sharp silver lancet.

I think my mouth fell open. "What are you going to do?"

"Are you in need of a blindfold as well?"

If that was humor, I was numb to it. He cleared his throat. "I'm going to let some blood from her neck," he explained. "That will take some of the heat from her body. It won't be a lot, and it won't hurt for more than a second. Are you sure you can do this?"

I was still staring at the lancet's deadly point.

"Turn around, Miss Selby."

"Pardon me?"

"Turn around." With his free hand, he gripped my shoulder and spun me the other way. "Now, hold her head as steady as you can." I slid my hand up the rope, took one last look at the blindfolded mare, and closed my own eyes. Mr. Stead took a position at my back, so close that the heat of his body warmed mine. "Ready?" I wasn't, but I nodded anyway. There were two dull thuds, like a fist hitting meat, then silence. The Girl flinched and grunted, and then, after a few moments, I heard fat, wet drops hitting the straw.

Blood-spattered images colored my mind. I felt a little weak, as if I might faint, but I forced my legs to straighten. I breathed in, deeply, and then out. Over and over. I focused only on my breathing.

"That will do, then." Mr. Stead's voice pierced the fog. I opened my eyes, swaying slightly. "Give me a moment to clean up and you can turn around."

The Girl's blindfolded head drooped. Ever so slowly, she began slumping against me. She was sleeping, it seemed. I splayed my feet and pushed back, but I was no match for her weight.

"She's falling," I cried.

Mr. Stead was at my side in an instant, slapping the mare's chest until she startled and stood straighter. He yanked the cloth from her face. "All right now, step out of the way," he ordered me. I ducked under his arm so hastily that I slipped on the bloody straw and nearly went down myself. Anxious, I watched him balance the mare as one does a teetering tower of blocks. He stepped back. The Girl swayed on her feet. Though her glazed eyes were open, she still appeared on the verge of sleep. A silver pin, which had been twisted into the skin of her neck, glinted in the first rays of light streaming into the shed. Fresh blood oozed around the fastening. "She'll be all right now, I think," he said. "We'll just let her rest a while." He smiled that smile of his. "Rather an admirable job, Miss Selby. Not many girls in Boston could match your steady nerves, I'd wager. Thank you."

I smiled back, feeling as if I'd been treated as well, beginning to feel as refreshed as if I'd just awakened from a sound sleep. Until I remembered Father's ranting. "My father won't let us keep her here."

"Yes, I do remember words to that effect," he said. "Maybe I should go talk to him."

I shook my head. "You don't know him. Once he's set his mind, he won't budge."

"Well, I have more peppermints," he said, patting his pocket. "And I'm not planning on wrestling him, just talking to him. Shall we give it a try?"

☙ TWELVE

THE SKY SHIMMERED WITH THE COLORS OF AN OPAL WHEN we stepped out of the shed. The *clip-clop* and rattle of horses pulling morning delivery wagons had doubled. The air was cool and moist and promised new beginnings. Until I noticed a faint odor of smoke. Shivering, I remembered that that was what had started this morning's rumpus: another fire.

"Cold?" Mr. Stead laid a gentle hand on my shoulder.

I shook my head. "Just tired." But it was more than that. What if there were more burned horses out there that needed help? What about the burned one right here? "Are you sure we shouldn't stay with her?" I asked.

His smile showed he understood. "She needs her rest more than she needs us right now."

There was comfort in his voice, and we walked the few steps to the house without speaking further and not the least bit awkward for it. It was nice being with him. His coat smelled of hay and horses and something musky-sweet, so different from the nose-wrinkling tobacco and ink odors embedded in Father's clothes. And he'd complimented me once more: "Admirable job," he'd said. Vain, yes, but if I could press those words into my album, I'd pull them out again and again just to hear them.

Apparently Providence thought I needed some humbling. As we climbed the narrow stairs of the back stoop, Mr. Stead reached past me, in gentlemanly fashion, to open the screen door. I tried edging around it and him, only to lose my footing. Flailing like a whirligig, I teetered toward a bed of withered morning glories. Pride goeth before a fall, indeed.

He pulled me right just in time. "Steady there."

I mumbled an embarrassed thank-you into the collar of my robe. "I'm sure Father's still in his study," I said. "Please come in." Too red-faced to explain the battered door leaning against the wall, I led the way through the kitchen. On the stove was an empty skillet crusted with cornmeal. Beside it, a kettle of hot water simmered just below a whistle. We found Grandmother and Mother huddled over cups of tea in the dining room. A round of cornbread, cut into wedges, sat on a platter.

Mother leaped to her feet. "Mr. Stead! I didn't realize you were still here." She made a close study of my face, searching for evidence of impropriety.

"Yes, well," he cleared his throat, "things took a mite longer than I expected."

"Would you care for some tea?" She said it coolly, making no move to offer him a chair or a cup, or even a cold breakfast of cornbread.

The man who had seemed so confident in the shed unraveled a bit. He cleared his throat again and shook his head. "Thank you . . . but no. It's very kind of you, though, Mrs. Selby," he stammered. "I was hoping to have a word with your husband. Is he . . . ?" Peering hopefully into the parlor, he searched for an escape.

"He's in his study, with our son and a Captain Torrance Gilmore, who says he's the chief at the fire station. If you'll follow me?"

I wanted to roll my eyes at Mother's formality. Our house was so small that she could just about turn in place and, with a good reach, lay her hand on the doorknob to Father's study. But instead, she made a show of guiding the veterinary around the dining chairs and through the corner of the parlor into the narrow hall, where she halted him with an upraised hand. Laying an ear to the door, she tapped on it. "Mr. Selby?" The men's voices fell silent. Footsteps sounded and then the door opened to reveal Father's annoyed face.

"Mr. Selby, Mr. Stead would—"

"Come in, come in," Father interrupted. The veterinary was pulled into the heavily draped room. "We were just discussing the merits of—" The door closed in Mother's face with a decisive *click*.

For the briefest of moments she stood there, pale and silent, and my heart squeezed. I knew how she felt. When she turned, though, her face was completely composed. "Goodness, it's been a busy morning," she said. "Your grandmother and I have brewed some chamomile tea for its calming effects. You could do with a cup, I imagine."

Nothing inside of me wanted to be calmed, but I obediently turned to take my seat.

"What have you been doing all this time?" Mother asked as she set a cup and saucer in front of me. "Dressed only in your robe and alone with a stranger?"

She was trying to pour shame along with the tea, and I wanted neither. "Mr. Stead isn't a stranger; he's a very good veterinary and I was helping him."

"Not helping him with that horse, I hope," Mother exclaimed. "She's a vicious animal. You saw what she did to your father, and . . . oh, Rachel, look at your hands! I hope Mr. Stead didn't see these." She grabbed my hands from the tablecloth, turned them over and back, and shook her head.

Grandmother rattled her empty cup against its saucer. "And what's so wrong with getting a little dirt on your hands, may I ask?"

As if they showed signs of leprosy, Mother let mine drop. "It's more than dirt that she has on her hands." She took a seat and poured herself some tea. "Mr. Selby and I don't think it's seemly for a young woman of Rachel's age to be wrestling horses alongside men. What about her reputation? All she has is her reputation."

"I helped save a *life*," I argued.

Mother got that pinched look. "Saving her life," she said firmly, "will be God's doing, not yours or Mr. Stead's or anyone else's." She pointed toward the stairs. "Now please go put on

something clean, *if* you have any dresses left. And scrub some of that filth from your hands before you return to the table."

I flung myself at the stairs, gritting my teeth. All I had was my *reputation?* I was nothing more than an amorphous cloud of someone's version of "good"? Hah! I was more than that. I had steady nerves; he'd said so. And a way with horses. And . . . knowledge. Mother didn't know what thrush was, or founder, but I certainly did.

As I reached the upstairs hall I heard the door to Father's study open. Something had been decided about the Girl, and I had to know what that was. Spinning round, I clenched my fists and crouched out of sight on the top step.

Father and James came out first, then Mr. Stead and Captain Gilmore, the fire chief, the same slightly built man I'd seen at the station Saturday morning. He did appear to be the impatient sort; he kept frowning at his pocket watch while his white mustache twitched like a rabbit's nose. To my astonishment, the dalmatian also stepped from Father's study to take his place at the chief's side. Father had never been one to allow animals in the house. To my further surprise, the dog immediately sensed my presence. He looked straight up the stairs, found me, and froze; I prepared to scramble.

Father was slapping James on the back and talking in an unusually loud voice to the other men. That was his brand of salesmanship. "I'm telling you again, Captain, he's a good one. I guarantee that if you put the reins in his hands, those firehorses of yours will gallop off their feet."

Captain Gilmore pocketed his watch. He didn't smile. His lined forehead suggested he was a worrier, a man who'd need to devise a plan to smile before risking one. "No doubt, Mr. Selby," he answered, fiddling with the hidden watch and rocking back and forth on his feet. "No doubt. But it takes more than speed to negotiate this city. A good driver has to have a feel for the surface of the street, *and* the weight of the steam engine, *and* the temperament and ability of each horse."

"Then James is your man," Father stubbornly declared. "He can do all that *and* have that burned horse of yours back into harness in no time. You have my word on it."

I clamped my hand over my mouth. The Girl could stay!

The boasting embarrassed James, something the chief was quick to notice. "Confidence is a valuable trait," he said, "until it is carried to the extreme." He looked squarely at Father. "I don't believe Mr. Stead shares your optimism on that last matter."

"You heard him say the horse is doing better—"

Mr. Stead defended himself. "Now, I didn't exactly say 'better'—"

"The horse is on its feet, isn't it?" Father argued.

"But she *wasn't*, just this hour, and—"

"But it's on its feet *now*, isn't it?" Father pressed the point, grinning all the while. He could smell the victory.

"When I left her, she was standing, yes."

"And my son has been treating the animal in between your visits, correct?"

"That's partially—"

"There!" Father clapped his hands. "James is the answer to all your problems, I tell you. He'll have that horse back in harness in no time. And I want you to promise me, Captain, that he'll be the one driving."

The white mustache twitched faster. "Mr. Selby, as I've already told you, it's the law that a fireman be at least twenty-one years of age."

There was a light, rapid knocking on the door. Father ignored it to keep grinning at the chief. The two were nearly face-to-face. He wasn't speaking, yet I knew a message was being sent. "If my son gets to the fires," he finally said, his words so quiet that I had to hold my breath to hear them, "we'll both get what we want."

The watch was practically alive in Mr. Gilmore's pocket. "I have no idea what you mean," he said uncomfortably. "But I do know that I must be going. I've work to do."

"We all do," Father said jovially as he opened the front door. "We all have our work."

A boy in gray knickers and a striped shirt waited anxiously on the steps. "Is the veterinary here?" he asked.

Mr. Stead stepped forward. "Yes, what is it?"

"Mr. Lauber needs your help, sir. His Queenie's having trouble with the baby." The boy's eyes were dark with worry.

"Tell him I'll be right along," Mr. Stead replied. As the boy scurried down the steps, he called after him, "And tell him to leave her be until I get there." Turning back to the men, he glanced up the stairwell. I blushed. He'd known all along that

I'd been sitting there and listening. "It seems the horses of Boston have conspired to keep me from having so much as a catnap today," he said. "So if you'll all excuse me, I have to go deliver a foal. It's the mare's first, and sometimes things can take a wrong turn." He hesitated, as if he was going to say something else, then, thinking better of it, headed out the door.

Mr. Gilmore checked his watch again and shot a warning glare at my brother.

"Understood," James said with a smile. "I'm on my way." They both left at once. The dalmatian paused at the stairs, until a sharp whistle called him outside too.

A wave of relief washed over me. I was in clover. The Girl could stay. Suppressing a squeal of joy, I jumped to my feet.

Just as Father was closing the door, Mr. Stead returned. He looked apologetic and somewhat flustered, and he was talking in such a low voice that now I couldn't hear his words at all. I did hear Father's scornful reply: "What would she want with this?"

My heart skipped. They were talking about me, I knew it. Mother left the dining room to join in, then Grandmother. With a dismissive harrumph, Father returned to his study and closed the door. What *was* it?

Grandmother started up the stairs. Pulling herself along by the railing, she smiled at me. "Ladybug, ladybug, fly away home," she said in a mysterious, singsong voice. "Hurry and get yourself dressed, Rachel. I believe this is *your* work."

◆ THIRTEEN

UNDER PENALTY OF TORTURE I COULD NOT HAVE DESCRIBED one moment of that trip, not one moment. I was so excited that all I could recall was climbing into Mr. Stead's buggy alongside Grandmother, then hearing the word "whoa" and being handed down in front of a mansion the like of which I'd never seen.

My mouth hung open as a servant led us past it and into a carriage house as grand as any church. A full two stories on the inside, it was strikingly clad in alternating ribbons of brick and stone. Thick golden sunlight streamed through a row of high windows, burnishing the wooden posts that divided the stately box stalls. That put me in mind of the boxed pews at King's Chapel. A similar sort of holy hush did blanket the place. Along the central aisle, the horses, notably all black bays or dark chestnuts, pressed against their half doors and craned their necks with interest toward the doubly large stall at the front. That's where the servant pointed us before disappearing.

"Harland!" A man pacing beside that stall broke the silence with his holler. "The foal isn't coming. It's been stuck like this for almost an hour. Why isn't it coming?" He was as well appointed as his stable, even without his black waistcoat, which was neatly folded over the stall door. His linen shirt stood snowy white against a gray silk vest, and his cuffs and collar had been starched to perfection. At the moment, however, that perfect appearance was creased with anxiety. "Look!" he said.

We all peered over the high door to see a round-bellied chestnut mare lying on her side, obviously in distress. A pair of tiny white hooves stuck out past her limp tail.

Mr. Stead responded with his typical calm. "Let's see what we have here," he said as he donned his apron and rolled up his sleeves. In an instant he was kneeling waist deep in the spotless straw bedding. He tugged on the two hooves, testing them a bit, then pushed against them. "I suspect," he said as he leaned his weight into the mare, "that the foal's head is turned back on its body and that's what's blocking the birthing." He grunted with the effort. His knees slid on the straw. "I'm just going to . . . push . . . the front legs back in . . . and . . . maneuver them a bit. Hopefully the head will slip around and come forward like it's supposed to."

The mare, looking as fragile as a deer in this awkward situation, suddenly snorted in alarm. She began scrambling violently, sending straw and dust swirling through the air.

"Here now," Mr. Stead scolded. He threw his arms across her hindquarters in a vain attempt to keep her from flailing. "Mr. Lauber, get in here and sit on her head."

Mr. Lauber rushed into the stall too fast, alarming the mare all the more. She tried to get to her feet. He charged at her head several times, tentatively grabbing for her halter, desperate to avoid the sharp hooves.

"*Hold her down!*" Mr. Stead ordered.

"I'm trying," the man cried.

The mare managed to right her front end. She was about to stand up. "Miss Selby!" Mr. Stead shouted, and I was inside and at the mare's head before he could finish his request: "I need you."

Taking a sure grip on the mare's halter, close to her ears, I leaned my weight against it. She fell back with a soft thud. Before she could arise, I carefully straddled her neck, stroking her cheek and crooning to her at the same time. There was so much fear in her eyes. I wanted to make it go away.

"Well done," Mr. Stead murmured under his breath. He was concentrating on the twisted foal hidden inside the huge belly. "Steady now."

Entranced, I watched him return to his rhythm of pushing, then gently pulling, twisting a little this way and a little that. The strain showed on his face. I glanced at Grandmother, who was watching over the top of the high stall door. Her lips were moving, in prayer, I suppose, but otherwise she was silent. Twenty or even thirty minutes must have passed before Mr. Stead abruptly sat back on his heels and heaved a sigh of despair.

"What? What is it?" Mr. Lauber stood over him, his voice fraught with worry.

"The foal's body is too dry. I can't get it out. I fear it's dead."

"Dead?" the owner echoed. "It can't be. That's a thousand-dollar stud fee I'm out."

"You could be out more," Mr. Stead said wearily, wiping the back of his hand across his brow. "If I can't find a way to get the foal's body out, you'll lose Queenie, too. And even if I *can* get it out, there's no telling what damage has already been done to her, which means you'll lose her anyway."

"That's not acceptable." Mr. Lauber stubbornly crossed his arms as if he were arguing the price of hay, rather than the ebbing life of a fine broodmare. "You're just going to have to keep trying. Keep trying, I say!"

Nodding, Mr. Stead reached back inside the mare. His face grew taut with concentration as his fingers puzzled their way around the foal. The mare had given up struggling, and I slid off her neck. I was afraid she'd given up living. Kneeling beside her, I kept stroking her damp cheek, praying that she'd manage to hang on, praying that her foal somehow managed to be born alive. The stable fell quiet again. Every living thing, human and animal alike, seemed to be focusing on this one birth. The only sounds that disturbed the silence were the determined grunts and groans of Mr. Stead, the accompanying rustle of straw beneath his knees, and the occasional nervous cough of Mr. Lauber. Far, far away in the distance I heard a ship's whistle. It seemed odd that people were traveling elsewhere, going on with their lives, when everything of importance was happening right here.

Mr. Stead's face suddenly broke into a satisfied grin. "Aha!" he shouted. Using both hands, he pulled, long and slowly, on the two little hooves, and this time a small head with a wide white blaze followed. The pale sack that covered the foal ripped at the point of the hooves and, as the tiny bundle continued emerging from the mare, the sack fell around its shoulders in a gauzy shawl. With one final pull, the foal—a colt—plopped into the straw, a motionless lump. Queenie nickered weakly. The small body didn't answer.

Mr. Stead murmured, "I'm sorry."

I looked up to see tears streaming down Mr. Lauber's stricken face.

"You haven't all given up, have you?" Grandmother rapped on the stall door. "Give him a good rub, now. Go on, you'll see." She waggled a finger at us. "And pray."

I repeated my prayer more urgently—*Please, God, please let this colt live*—as Mr. Stead took a towel from his satchel and began rubbing the spindly chest, the ribbed sides, the limp neck. He lifted the head onto his lap and gently wiped out the nostrils and the mouth. Bending over, he blew air into the still body. Nothing. He blew again, and again. Still nothing. He glanced helplessly at Grandmother, who waggled a finger a second time, and he returned to rubbing the foal's sides.

All at once, a shiver rippled the colt's damp body. His eyelids fluttered and he sucked in a little gulp of air. Feebly, he tried to raise his head. Queenie nickered. With an enormous effort, she righted her front end, arced her head toward her tail, and sniffed at her newborn.

Mr. Lauber's face was even wetter now. "You did it!" he exclaimed. "You did it!"

Slowly climbing to his feet, Mr. Stead smiled. "It wasn't all *my* doing," he said humbly. "I don't make claims to raise the dead."

The two men quietly exited the stall and joined Grandmother in admiring the newborn. I eased into the corner, awestruck. The perfectly miniature horse was chestnut, with a silvery muzzle and impossibly long legs. The tips of his fuzzy ears curled toward each other like parentheses.

"What a handsome little fellow," Grandmother said. "I anoint him 'David' for he is 'comely in appearance.'"

To my immense surprise, Mr. Lauber agreed. "I like that," he said. "His mother's Queenie, so it's only fitting she have a king for a son. King David it is, then."

Although she seemed far too weak for it, Queenie managed to stand. Rocking unsteadily, she began inspecting her colt. She nuzzled his damp back, his ears, his face. Her breath ruffled the fringe of curly mane on his neck. Even though she was trembling as much as he was, she licked him from one end to the other, then began nudging him to stand.

Having no more substance than a sprite, David popped to his spindly legs. He tottered a mad step or two and collapsed in a heap. Queenie whinnied. Her concern was immediately echoed by the whinnies of the other horses in the barn. I wanted to rush over to help him, but Mr. Stead, who must have read my mind, kept me to my place by quietly saying, "He'll learn it. You watch and see."

So the four of us kept watching, with me digging my

nails into my palm at each of David's tumbling failures. After a while, it seemed that his mother lost interest. She nosed through her hay a little, then stood with her back to us, splay-legged and dozing. David clambered to his feet again, swayed wildly, and crumpled in the straw.

We had to do something! I looked up at Mr. Stead and found, to my blushing surprise, that he'd been watching me. "Why isn't she helping him?" I asked across the stall.

"Because this is something he has to learn to do on his own," he replied. "God gave him strong legs to stand on; he just has to learn how to use them."

"Father, is anything wrong?" A young female voice sounded from the end of the carriage house. "What are you watching?"

"Shh!" Mr. Lauber hushed his daughter. "Queenie's had her colt." He motioned for her to join us.

She arrived without a sound of footsteps, which oddly reminded me of my mother's silent comings and goings. The girl was strikingly pretty, with the porcelain complexion of a china doll, and maybe a year or two older than me. But with no more than a glance over the stall door, she announced, "Mother wants to know—"

"*Shh!*" Mr. Lauber shot a warning look at her.

The command came because David had again made it to his feet and was managing to keep his balance this time. He bravely took a step, wobbled, took another one, and was still standing. His mother pricked her ears and nickered encouragement. He answered in a high-pitched whinny. With innocent determination, he lifted first one spider leg and then another, rushing the sequence until he was tottering . . . right in front of *me*.

Holding my breath, I slid down the wall to crouch at his level. His bulging eyes tried to follow the motion. I smiled. With his whiskery chin and bobbling head, he reminded me of a little old man who'd been drenched by an unexpected rainstorm. I extended my hand. Inquisitively he stretched his skinny neck. His damp muzzle tickled my palm. When his lips parted, I felt his rubbery gums bumping against my skin. Such a look of surprise came over him that he jumped back, shook his head, and nearly fell over. I had to stifle a laugh. Queenie nickered again, and this time he found his way directly to her side. Almost by accident, though I suspect it was more by God's hand, he found his mother's teat and began suckling.

Mr. Lauber spoke to Mr. Stead. "Thank you, Harland," he said, before returning his misty gaze to the mare and foal.

Mr. Stead nodded. Looking back at the new pair, he smiled and said, "My pleasure."

⌘ FOURTEEN

HE EXCITEMENT IN THE CARRIAGE HOUSE FADED gradually, like the last quavery thrumming of a church organ. The other horses returned to their hay, and we walked back down the aisle in contemplative silence.

The spell was broken when we stepped into the sunshine. "Ew!" squealed Mr. Lauber's daughter. "Look at your hands!"

It was the second time that morning my hands had received critical marks. I'd forgotten to scrub them after helping Mr. Stead with the Girl, so now they were doubly mottled with dried sweat and horsehair, and a drop of dried blood crusted one knuckle. The grimy half-moons tipping each fingernail showed even more darkly. Yet I wasn't the least bit embarrassed. I was proud of my hands and the work they'd done, and answered her horror—that same horror I'd seen on Mother's face—with a broad smile. Perplexed, Miss Lauber gathered her skirts a little closer.

Her father, however, frowned. "Mr. Stead, may I have a word with you?" He motioned for them to move a few steps away. Something in his sudden change of expression pricked my curiosity. Feigning an interest in the manicured bed of roses behind them, I murmured, "How lovely," and left Grandmother and Miss Lauber to sidle nearer the men.

"It's bad enough that you let her upstage me with my own horse," Mr. Lauber was complaining, "but what if things hadn't gone as they did? What if she'd been kicked? Queenie's a hot-blooded mare, you know. The girl could have broken a limb—or worse! I don't think it's right."

"She knows her way around a horse," Mr. Stead countered. He sounded somewhat irritated himself. "I'm sorry if her presence has disturbed you. I just didn't see any harm in it."

Grandmother made her way to my side, interrupting my eavesdropping. Bending over a deep red blossom, she whispered, "I've changed my mind. That veterinary of yours is a good man."

"Um-hmm," I mumbled, moving to another bush, still pretending interest in the roses while trying to listen to the men.

"Perhaps you're too young to realize this," Mr. Lauber went on, "but many people consider it unseemly for a girl to witness a birthing."

I sneaked a glance as Mr. Stead crossed his arms. He was a good head taller than Mr. Lauber and looked down on him with such an unflinching air that, despite his seniority, the older man started rowing backward. "I'm not saying you're not a good veterinary, Harland. You know I have no complaints there." He ventured a laugh and reached up to clap him on the

❦ FOURTEEN

shoulder. "Besides, I was a young man once myself. I remember how it was with the fillies. But take my advice: Consider your reputation and keep them separate from your work." Tipping his head like a bold robin, he took another stab at control. "There's others that will be thinking the way I do," he warned.

Mr. Stead stiffened. It was ever so slightly, but I saw it, even if no one else did. "Then they have my pity, is what I'm thinking," he replied. Spinning on his heel, he picked up his satchel and headed for the buggy. Grandmother and I followed.

Mr. Lauber was quick to entwine his daughter's arm in his own and escort us. "I owe you an apology, ladies." His artificial friendliness reminded me of soured milk; on the surface it seemed all right, but . . . "I didn't properly introduce you to my daughter, Emilyn. Emilyn, this is . . . ?"

"Mrs. Esther Boon," Grandmother replied. "And Rachel Selby, my granddaughter."

"How nice to meet you," Emilyn said coolly.

"I wish I could have shown you both more hospitality than my poor stable has to offer," Mr. Lauber said, "but I wasn't . . . expecting you." He looked pointedly at Mr. Stead's back.

"I've visited homes not nearly as fine as your stable," Grandmother said. "We enjoyed ourselves."

I latched on to the buggy horse like he was an old friend. In a way he was, because he was the same horse I'd seen outside the fire station, the one to whom I'd promised a treat. Now, at my approach, he wriggled his lips hopefully. All I could do was pet his neck and murmur, "I'm sorry. I forgot."

"What's that?" Mr. Stead asked. He nodded for the waiting servant to take hold of the horse's bridle so he could help Grandmother into the buggy.

I blushed; I hadn't planned on human ears hearing me. "I . . . I promised your horse I would bring him a treat."

"That humbug! Has he gone to begging again? Balder!" He rattled the whip in its stand. "You're a second-rate scoundrel, you are," he said to the horse. "Mind your manners." With a smile and a wink, he handed me up into the buggy and climbed in beside. The servant stepped away. Waving crisply to Mr. Lauber and Emilyn, Mr. Stead clucked to the horse. "Now look lively, Balder, or I'll send you down to the docks for some real work." The bay moved off, but not before shaking his head and snorting with what was surely indignation. I hunkered down to keep from laughing out loud.

On the drive homeward I took more notice of my surroundings. We were passing through a particularly well-to-do part of Boston, and the streets were lined with one amazing mansion after another. Mr. Stead entertained us with tidbits of gossip about the wealthy occupants, and I felt rather grand just trotting by such luxury, especially when we passed a public horsecar. It was crowded, with people packed together like herrings, either sitting on benches or standing, suspended from leather straps, all of them looking wilted in the heat. I had little reason for pride, I suppose, because the buggy's one seat was nearly as crowded. Jostled between Grandmother and Mr. Stead, I became uncomfortably aware of his leg pressed thigh to ankle against mine, of his black jacket scratching the fabric of my dress. I tried to pull in my shoulders.

Grandmother leaned across me. "Are you a married man?" she asked bluntly.

That shrunk me some.

"No, Mrs. Selby, I'm not."

"It's Mrs. Boon, if you'll remember," Grandmother said. "I'm the mother of Rachel's mother. I'm *not* a Selby." She flicked a cinder off her skirt. "And why aren't you married?"

Mr. Stead shifted his position, pulling his leg away from mine, though for lack of space it gradually sagged back against it. I sneaked a glance at his face. If he was discomfited by her liberty he didn't show it. He took time clearing his throat, then said, "Well, Mrs. Boon, I'm not married because . . . Here now!" He jerked on the reins as a fancy trotter pulling a basket phaeton came round the corner at such a reckless clip that they nearly collided with us. Balder snorted, more in disgust than alarm, I thought, and once the reins were loosened proceeded calmly. "What were we talking about? Oh, yes." Mr. Stead chuckled. "Well, I suppose it's because I'm very busy and"—as he searched for words, an embarrassed grin widened across his face—"and, well, let's just say that my horse has better luck with the ladies than I do." I shot Grandmother the most injurious of glances, which she blatantly ignored.

"Which church do you attend?"

Mr. Stead looked past us. At first I thought he was seeking escape, until he raised his whip over his head to signal he was turning. We joined with traffic on a busier street, and when we'd settled in, he answered her question. "I rarely have the time," he explained. "You see, most of my patients don't recognize the Sabbath as a day of rest. Or at least their owners don't. So I commune with our good Lord when I can. And that's as likely to be right here in my buggy as in a white steeple church."

That seemed to satisfy Grandmother on that topic, but she was too much the terrier to sit idle for long. Before we'd gone one whole block she had another question. "Did you ever consider becoming a real doctor?"

"Don't I look real?"

"It's a better living."

He shrugged. "Better is a slippery word, Mrs. Boon. I'm a better man for my education. I help animals get better. And, let's see, how does that verse go? 'There's nothing *better* for a man than that he should find enjoyment in his toil.'" It was his turn to lean across me. "Ecclesiastes," he whispered to Grandmother.

A smile tugged at her lips, though she tried to look serious. "I like a man who knows his Bible," she said approvingly.

Enjoyment in his toil. I looked down at my lap. Did that count for *her* toil as well? I had to wonder, because my hands were burning like they'd grabbed hold of stinging nettle. The fiery—and yet somehow thoroughly enjoyable—sensation had sparked when that foal touched his tiny muzzle to them. I closed my eyes, shutting out the city noises and trying to recall his excited, high-pitched whinny. I shut out the smells and tried to breathe in the lingering aroma of his sweet breath. From his very first movement he'd been so full of life, so eager for it. I wanted to race back there and hug him to me.

Before I was ready, we were home again. I didn't want to end the dreamlike morning by climbing out of the buggy and touching ground. I didn't want to go back to holding a needle in my hand, squinting over a circle of stretched linen. I wanted to hold a tiny head in my hands, to hold life. But Mr. Stead climbed out and took Balder's bridle while I helped Grandmother down. She tackled the stairs alone, allowing me to linger. I pretended to check the buggy for anything left behind, when of course we hadn't carried anything with us but our excitement.

"Shall we check on your mare?" Mr. Stead suggested, and I nodded. The dream would last a little longer.

We found the Girl dozing. The silver pin was still in place. Just below it, a drop of blood showed black against a remnant of her light coat. Quietly, Mr. Stead stepped into her stall and pressed his fingers against her throat to check her pulse. I knew my own was racing. He nodded satisfaction, then felt for the cotton he'd stuffed deep into her ears. That was to keep her from hearing a fire alarm, to keep her from hurting herself, but I instinctively recoiled at the dulling of her senses. "She's doing fine," he said in a low voice.

Someone must have stuffed cotton into my own ears, because I was moving in a stupor. I knew we were walking back out to the buggy, but there was a buzzing in my head that brought my world in close. The day had grown so stewingly hot that when a bead of sweat trickled down my arm it seemed like liquid fire. The tingling in my palms was explosive. My hands felt foreign to me, as if someone else's hands had been attached to my body. In a way I felt newly born myself, and as if this new person, not me, was speaking, I heard the words: "Teach me."

"I beg your pardon?"

My breath caught. What was I saying? This was unknown territory.

But there was no use in hesitating; I was galloping. "I want to be a veterinary too. I want to help horses. I want to feel—"

"Hold on there," he said with a laugh. "You're talking faster than my ears can listen. You want to be a *veterinary?*"

I nodded. My heart was pounding so hard inside my chest. I was galloping toward the biggest fence I'd ever faced. It was terrifying and exhilarating at once.

"Girls don't become veterinaries," he said with that same patronizing smile Father often wore, and my chin hit mane as the hooves slid to a stop. Anger flared inside me. He'd suddenly joined all the rest of the men and boys who'd laughingly pushed me away. "Although if any young woman could, I'd lay money on you."

I went as cold as forged iron. "Teach me, then. I want to learn."

"I don't know. . . ." He rubbed his chin, looking doubtful. I suspected he was recalling Mr. Lauber's warning.

"I won't bother your clients, I promise. I'll stay out of the way. And I have a horse care manual that I'm already studying; I've read nearly half of it." I clenched my fists. "You don't understand; you can't, I suppose, but I have to do this. I *know* I have to."

He took note of my fists. "A whole half of a manual, have you? Well, then, answer me this: How would I go about treating a case of thrush?"

That was easy, thanks to Peaches. "Clean the affected hoof well," I recited, "then soak a rag in turpentine and pack it into the hoof."

He withheld his opinion and presented another question. "When do tushes appear?"

"When a horse is between four and five years old." I allowed myself a sly smile. "They're also called 'bridle teeth.'"

He raised an eyebrow and rubbed his jaw again. "True or false: Distemper is most likely to appear in young animals."

I had to think about that one. "Diseases of the Glands" had been a difficult chapter, though I thought I remembered that distemper was akin to smallpox. "False. It's very contagious for every horse."

He finally grinned. "You don't need me," he said. "You already know more than most of the so-called horsemen in this city."

"Then you'll teach me?"

The small gap in our years was nothing compared to the greater one in our gender. "Veterinary medicine is not all bandages and birthings," he said with a laugh, as if I were a little girl asking to play dress-up. "There's a rather ghastly side to it that's just not suitable for young women. Or any women. And it does take a certain amount of strength to wrestle the beasts."

He thought he had me, but he was wrong. "You didn't use your strength to treat the Girl," I argued. "You used your mind, and me, to keep her off balance, and you rewarded her with peppermints."

"Yes, well—"

"And as for the ghastly side of it, what does it matter what an animal looks like or what the treatment requires, when you own the ability to heal it?"

He looked taken aback. "Did you say veterinary or lawyer? You argue your case like the latter."

"Veterinary," I stated firmly. I could feel my fists clenching again.

He paused, studying me. "If it's not too personal, may I ask how old you are?"

"Sixteen in September."

With a guarded nod, he said, "Well, that's on the young side for veterinary school, though age isn't as important as practical experience and, of course, money. It's a three-year course, you know. But, the thing is, I've never heard of any lady veterinaries in the Boston area."

"There are some lady doctors on Warrenton Street; we walked by their offices on our way to the photography gallery. What's the difference?"

"Well, one difference is that their patients can at least say where it hurts." He chuckled at his own joke and I smiled politely, waiting for a more serious answer. The silence made him uncomfortable. Clearing his throat, he adjusted his hat and tugged at his collar. "The Selbys certainly are a determined lot, aren't they?" He had no idea. "Well," he began again, glancing skyward, "I suppose that I could at least teach you some of the basics." And then, as if finally convincing himself of the possibility, he said, "All right, all right, here's what I'll agree to do." He took on a newly stern expression and I stood as tall as I could. "I'll allow you to accompany me when the situation and client are suitable, and we'll see how long your interest holds up."

I opened my mouth to protest his evident doubt. He shut it with a warning finger. "But you have to agree to do a few things as well."

I nodded like a whirligig in a windstorm. I'd do anything.

"You have to keep studying your manual. Which one do you have?"

"*The Reliable Horse Care Manual for American Owners.* My brother gave it to me."

"That's a good one," he replied. "Accurate illustrations. I can warn you that not all the books out there are as reliable as their titles. Let's see . . . you'll have to pass a few more tests of my design. And . . . you'll have to obtain your father's permission."

The utter hopelessness of that last assignment must have shown in my eyes.

"Oh, come now," he said with an all-too-patronizing chuck under the chin. "Just think of him as a stubborn horse and apply your obvious talents. And remember this from someone who's been around five more years than you have: Nothing worth having comes easily."

ᑌᑕᓴ FIFTEEN

THE REST OF THAT DAY MY HEAD BUZZED LIKE I WAS stuck inside a beehive. It had to be exhaustion, yet I didn't feel tired. In fact, I absolutely threw myself into Mother's household chores. Whatever she asked, I did more. I ripped away the dead morning glory vines from the backyard and went on to rake the dirt off its stubbly attempts at grass. I lugged crates down to the cellar and unpacked their contents onto uneven shelving. I scrubbed the hall floor with a tremendous ferocity. All the while I tried to summon the courage to go to battle with Father.

Mr. Stead had simply asked me to get Father's permission, but that was like playing jackstraws: Touching one topic would invariably wiggle others. Permission to learn about veterinary medicine would lead to a discourse on what girls *couldn't* do, which was attain higher education. (He'd written a column once that quoted a professor from Harvard University who believed that grappling with university-level topics caused a woman's organs to wither.) And that would lead to a lecture on what girls *shouldn't* do, which was anything outside the home, anything not corseted, buckled, bound, protected, or otherwise restrained. Certainly nothing as dangerous as treating horses.

I scrubbed so hard the soapsuds went flying.

By late afternoon, the house was spotless. Mother was soaking one of my soiled dresses and mending the sleeve of the other, and Grandmother was slicing cooked potatoes for supper—er, dinner—when James surprised us by coming in the back door. The shocked look on his face stopped my heart cold.

"No, no, she's fine," he said right off. "I picked up a copy of Father's paper on my way home. His first column's in it."

To a one, we stopped what we were doing. Mother held out her hand, prepared, along with the rest of us, for the worst. She carried it into the parlor and sat down. We gathered behind her, making no pretense of not peering over her shoulder. After taking a deep breath, like she was preparing to jump into a pond of cold water, Mother read aloud:

"Esteemed poet and former son of Boston Mr. John Greenleaf Whittier wrote, 'Men said at vespers: "All is well!" In one wild night the city fell.' He was recounting, of course, the innocent trust pervading the city of Chicago on the eve of last year's Great and Terrible Fire.

"Poets, as we know, lament the tragedies in our lives. And while their verse is beautiful to the ear, it is completely ineffectual. Rhymes are mere afterthoughts, wreaths thrown on a coffin. A singular moment of foresight, however, and one well heeded, can prevent the need for these wreaths.

"That is why I repeat Mr. Whittier's words to those men of Boston who, at this very moment, innocently trust their city and ours to the same antiquated firefighting equipment used when President James Buchanan led our nation, when the North and the South worked shoulder by shoulder in harmony, and when fire's presence in our homes was little more than a flame in the hearth.

"And I remind them that this is the year 1872. President Grant resides in the White House, a Great War has been fought, and many of Boston's homes boast their own basement furnaces, which carry warmth, yes, but also the risk of fire throughout our wooden structures. Fireplaces and chimneys are abundant. Every kitchen has a red-hot stove fed by wood or coal. Lamps full of burning fluids teeter on table and mantel. In short, never before has fire been such a permanent visitor within our homes.

"But this visitor, I warn you, is not to be trusted. Having recently arrived from one of the Western states, I can attest to a thorough knowledge of firewood. And I can assure the good citizens of Boston that this city, although one of great sophistication and possessing all the latest in conveniences, is in truthfulness nothing more than a stacked cord of seasoned wood, awaiting the spark from a match head. When this spark is struck—and, trust me, such a spark will be struck—Boston will burn as the grandest campfire which history has had the privilege to witness.

"What can be done, you ask, to avert this imminent tragedy? Collar your elected officials and request, nay, demand new firefighting equipment for every fire station in Boston. Order them to erect additional fire stations. Tell them to release funds for the improvement of water mains and hydrants. Because until our wives and children can sleep soundly in their beds, and until we husbands and laborers can rest assured that our businesses and goods are secure, this editor and this newspaper dutifully warn its readers that, in Boston, most definitely, 'all is not well.'"

Mother folded the paper, ran her hand along its length, and laid it in her lap.

"It sounds as if he's going to strike the match himself," Grandmother said.

"Mother!" her daughter scolded halfheartedly. But it was what we were all thinking. With Father, the end always justified the means.

It generally started simply enough: An editorial suggesting more fire equipment or a new school would appear in the newspaper under Father's name. But it seemed he could never leave the situation at words alone; he took action. Bold action. Just last month, back in Wesleydale, he'd decided that the town's one horsecar should deliver passengers all the way to the new bank at the edge of the business district, even though the rails didn't extend that far. He'd first written a column proposing the change. Then, a week later, he'd boarded the car with the announcement that he had a deposit to make to his account. When the car got to the end of the line, a few blocks shy of the bank, Father refused to get off. "I want to go to the bank," he was heard to shout over and over. "I've paid my dime, why don't you take me there?" The horsecar turned around and rolled back to the other end of the track, with Father still in the front seat, fuming and demanding to be delivered to his destination. The trip was repeated time after time. When the sun went down and the horse was unhitched, Father was still sitting in the car, shouting that he'd paid his money and not received satisfactory service. The police had to be summoned, and Father actually spent the night in a jail cell. When she received the unsettling news, Mother dealt with it the only way she knew how: She cleaned. She calmly took down all the curtains in our house and bleached them, but before she could rehang them Father was fired, Peaches was sold, and we were on our way to Boston. It wasn't tarring and feathering, but a haze of shame still clung to each of us.

Mother leaned toward one of her potted ivies, snapped off a wayward vine, and tucked the shortened offender back in line. Then she rose. "Well, supper isn't going to get itself on the table." No one dared breathe the word "dinner" to her.

For a habitual ghost, Mother could conjure up a respectable backbone. In Father's presence she hung in the shadows, pressing her lips together and smoothing her tablecloth. But in his absence she reclaimed her territory. She'd never challenged him face-to-face, yet when Father went "chasing after one of his dragons," as we called his incendiary campaigns, we instinctively gathered behind her. From experience we knew that the flames he fanned often turned on our family. And while Mother couldn't provide us with protection, she could provide order. Rather than wait glassy-eyed for our world to be upturned, we marched to her orders and numbed our worries in routine.

Like a row of ducklings, we followed her into the kitchen. With only a disapproving look, she gave her first command. She stared at James's gray-coated fingers.

"Sorry," he said. "Brass polish. I'll go wash up."

"Rachel?" I straightened. "There are seeds in the lemonade. Please strain them out." Even Grandmother received instruction. "Your biscuits can go on the basket-weave platter."

We marched. The table was soon set and laden with food, and we three women, echoing Saturday, waited in our chairs for the men. A jumpy sort of silence poked at us, and I had to sit on my hands to keep from wriggling. I knew we were each thinking about Father's column, wondering what it was going to cost us this time.

The stewed kidneys puddled in their blue and white bowl and the lyonnaise potatoes steamed faintly among glistening slivers of onions. We waited. The pitcher of lemonade, free of seeds, sweated on the sideboard. I tried to swallow my thirst. The parlor clock ticked loudly. In double cadence, Grandmother tapped her fingernail against her plate, but she didn't reach for her fork.

James finally came clattering down the stairs in a clean shirt, only to rush into his chair so fast that he pulled the tablecloth with him. Mother gasped as the plates and bowls and silver were tugged out of position, and she slapped her palms on the cloth.

"Sorry," he said, as the settings were carefully rearranged. "I'm famished. After all the work I've done today, I think I could eat a horse. No personal offense intended, Rachel." He pointed his fork at the kidneys. "That all that's left of the beast?"

He was trying to chase away our worries, bless him. Grandmother laughed and I smiled and Mother gave the necessary stern look, but we all breathed easier. Until feet climbed the front steps and the front door slammed. Father blustered into the dining room and, in a wildly weird and happy sort of way, announced, "This city is a veritable tinderbox!"

"Amen!" Grandmother responded.

A faint burnt smell wafted into the room with him, and I wondered just how actively he was already promoting his column. He took his seat at the head of the table and we began passing the dishes to him, then filling our own plates.

"Everyone see my column?" He looked around the table and we nodded in turn. "Do you know that I was actually stopped on the street on my way home? People can't hear enough of this talk, apparently; they've just been waiting for someone to stand up and say this very thing." In one voracious gulp he drained his lemonade. The empty goblet smacked the table with a thud. "Yes, I've found my topic—'my dragon,' as I know you like to call it," he said. He motioned for more lemonade, speared some potatoes, and began chewing away happily. "Did any of you know that this city, population three hundred and fifty thousand, owns no more than twenty-one steam engines? That's only one engine for every fifteen thousand people!"

I did the math in my head, arriving at a figure closer to 17,000, which actually bolstered Father's argument, but chose to keep quiet. This wasn't the argument I wanted to make. I fiddled with my spoon, too nervous to eat.

"It gets worse." Father leaned into his pulpit, much like the reverend does when coming to the meat of his sermon. "There are only seven—I say seven—hook and ladder wagons in the entire city and only eleven hose companies. And this with the buildings getting taller by the day. Why, Summer Street is lined with buildings four and five stories high. You've seen them, haven't you?"

We all nodded again.

"Now, picture a family out shopping with, say, half a dozen children. They're on the top floor of a store when a fire breaks out. Flames surround them, blocking escape by the stairs. How are the firemen going to save them? No ladders reach that high. How are they going to put out the flames? No hose can deliver water that high. So what can the firemen do? Nothing!" He pounded his fist on the table so hard that the butter knife leaped off its dish.

"That was exactly the subject at the station today." James's eyes were glowing to match Father's. "The men were complaining about the outcome of last night's fire—it was a warehouse," he told me, "no horses involved—and while they got there quick enough—"

"Quick-*ly* enough," Father corrected.

"Yes, sir. And while they got there quickly enough, their

one engine wasn't strong enough for the fire. Another station sent a hand pump, but that wasn't much help."

"A hand pump!" Father exclaimed. "A hand pump! With hardly enough water pressure to douse a match, I'll bet." He shook his head, though a sense of satisfaction spread across his face. "City the size of Boston," he mused, "third largest in the nation, and we're so behind the age that we're still using hand pumps?" He shook his head in wonderment, smiling all the while. "Splendid! I'll write another editorial next week that's certain to light a fire under the bloated backsides of—"

"Mr. Selby!" Mother pleaded.

He turned innocent eyes upon her, grinning with mischief.

"There's something else," James said.

"What's that?"

"They're saying this last fire was especially suspicious. Seems it started in a warehouse that wasn't in use and was only storing a few shipping crates. The chief is looking into it."

"So . . . there's a firebug among us, is there?" Father mused. "Even better to lend some urgency to the situation. Pass the biscuits," he abruptly demanded. "I'll be certain to share your information with the good people of this city." He broke open a biscuit and spooned some pear jelly onto it.

"I don't think the chief wants his suspicions made known quite yet."

"Nonsense! Don't Boston's citizens have a right to know that some amoral hooligan is threatening their lives?"

"Well—"

"Of course they do," Father asserted. "Here, have a biscuit." James took one from the platter and reached for the honey. "No, no," Father scolded, "the pear jelly. The honey's too sweet." Without hesitation James extended his hand further, though I knew honey was his favorite. "This is wonderful jelly, Nora. You really do make the best."

Mother nodded but remained mute. Flattery didn't go far with her.

"Oh, by the way, I let that woman in my office go."

"The journalist?" Grandmother asked.

"Hmph! She'd like to call herself that. Yes."

"How did she take it?"

He shrugged his shoulders and gulped some more lemonade. "How was she supposed to take it? She's a woman. She cried and argued . . . and cried some more."

"Did you have cause?" Grandmother asked.

Father lowered his glass. "Cause? What cause would I need? She didn't belong there, isn't that cause enough?" Father looked around the table for support. Although no one openly disagreed with him, none of his family voiced approval, either. Seeing our blank faces, he bellowed, "No female is going to work alongside men where August Selby has a say about it. It's *not right*."

⤲ SIXTEEN

HE NEXT DAY DAWNED TO A GRAY AND UNSETTLED SKY, which certainly matched my mood. I felt as if I were straddling a gate that kept swinging halfway open, only to be yanked closed by squealing hinges. I could look down the road but I couldn't set foot on it. And that was all my fault, because I hadn't had the courage last night to ask Father's permission. What a timid little mouse I was.

The only saving grace was that Mother and Grandmother were so entirely engrossed in curtain installation, requiring another trip to the stores up on Summer Street, that I had most of the morning and all afternoon to satisfy Mr. Stead's other command: Keep studying. That rekindled my fire. I could prove to him, at least, that I was capable. I'd memorize every single disease, treatment, and tonic in my horse care manual—all 652 pages of it. Just watch me. With a newly heaving chest and what certainly had to be a fierce gleam to my eye, I lugged the heavy book off my bedside table, down the stairs past those helpless butterflies, and out to the carriage shed.

It wasn't long before the stable performed its usual magic and I was breathing easier. Musing about the events of yesterday led me once again to the chapter on foaling, and I even read some of those paragraphs out loud. I think the Girl liked the company, because she stood at the front of her stall and leaned her neck over the splintered bar, watching me.

It had been only a few days since the livery fire but her burns were already beginning to scab over, though they wept constantly with a sticky fluid that reminded me of gritty molasses. What was left of Mr. Stead's bandages hung from her body in tatters; she simply wouldn't tolerate them. Unfortunately, they revealed quite grimly how much weight she'd lost. Platter-size hollows marked both flanks, and her ribs resembled a pair of bloody washboards strapped to a protruding backbone. James was purchasing all manner of enticements for her: timothy hay and dried clover, ground oats and a little shelled corn, her daily bran mash and loads of carrots. I'd stuffed nourishment into every pail and dish and crevice so that she hardly needed to take a step in order to eat, but nothing seemed to tempt her.

Closing the manual, I rose and joined her in her stall. Out of habit, I scooped some cold mash into my hands, added oats to it, and cupped the offering under her peeling muzzle. She toyed with the wet mess but refused to eat. Then she lowered her huge head and bumped me hard, nearly knocking me off my feet: She was begging for peppermints. I didn't have any more and reached into my pocket to show her that all I had was half of a sugared doughnut left over from breakfast. To my surprise, she snatched it from my fingers and made a great, messy show of chewing and enjoying it. As soon as she was finished, she bumped me again. I proved that my pockets were empty and patted her neck and offered her some more oats, but she followed me around the stall, stubbornly thudding her head against me.

Should I? There was nothing in the manual about doughnuts, but . . . I raced back to the house. Stealing the last three doughnuts from their covered plate on the sideboard, I returned and fed them one right after the other to her. I munched on one small crescent myself, happily pondering the saying that one's company truly did make a meal.

Then I took up my reading again, glancing toward the doorway at the end of each page in the hope that Mr. Stead would stop by and find me—worthy student—studying. But that whole day the only person who stuck his head through the door was James. On his way home from work, he stopped in to thump down a bag of oats, a different brand this time and one already ground into meal.

"The man at the feed store said this might be easier on her digestion." He looked over his shoulder, then back at me. "Are you waiting for someone?"

My pulse quickened. "No, just reading."

"Out loud, I'll wager." He nodded toward the Girl. "You're not trying to teach her veterinary medicine, are you?"

"She understands a lot more than you think," I countered.

Shaking his head and laughing, he turned to leave. "You two *are* a pair. I'm going to go wash up."

Father didn't come home for dinner that evening, and he sent no word or explanation. On another night Mother might have been perturbed, but she seemed so taken with her new curtains that she positively hurried us through the meal just so she could arrange us in the parlor in front of them. When she had the three of us seated in such a way that passersby could admire our model family through our elegantly curtained window, she brought in jelly cake and coffee. Rarely had I seen her so animated. She perched on the edge of her chair like an exuberant lark and began reciting what she'd learned of the day's events at the International Peace Jubilee here in Boston.

Her tidbits were interesting enough—Johann Strauss himself had conducted an orchestra of one thousand musicians—but I had the chapter on "Diseases of the Heart and Blood" to get through yet, and that wasn't going to be a waltz in the park, so to speak. So as soon as I'd finished my cake, I tried feigning fatigue and gaining an excuse to go to my bedroom. Mother smiled sweetly, almost masking her disapproval. With the flourish and authority of an imaginary baton, however, she pointed toward my embroidery basket. I heaved a pained sigh, eliciting no sympathy whatsoever, and moodily arranged the sampler across my lap. Grandmother opened her Bible and James quickly pulled one of the newspapers from Father's stack and bent over it. Mother admonished him to sit up straight.

The parlor clock played metronome to Mother's informative

jabber, marching us through an evening that could only be described as starched. I embroidered halfheartedly, carelessly even—my mind everywhere but the parlor. I thought about the Girl, her ever-more-noticeable ribs and her terrible burns. I thought about Mr. Stead and his peppermints and, feeling a blush warm my cheeks, redirected my thoughts toward Queenie and her colt. At once my hands got that pleasant tingly feeling. How I longed for the day when I'd have enough skill to lay my hands on a suffering horse and ease his pain. To have enough knowledge to help a colicky horse or a foal stuck inside his mother.

Faster and faster I stitched, the silver needle piercing the linen with a rapid rhythm of faint pops, the drab green thread swooshing through in its wake. A spray of leaves, decidedly ragged, began forming at the sampler's border. Mother would have me ripping out the evening's work for certain.

I shoved my hair behind my ear with mounting impatience. This wasn't important work; this was nothing more than sand trickling through an hourglass, stitches in time for the sake of passing time. Saving horses' *lives* was important work, and I shoved the needle so hard it jumped through the linen and jabbed my thumb. A crimson drop plopped right into the middle of the Garden of Eden.

The sampler was ruined. What was I going to do? I glanced up to see if anyone had noticed, but Grandmother was carefully tracing a verse with her finger and Mother was listening to James read an account of the Jubilee from the newspaper.

In some horror I watched the linen suck up the red liquid like a parched tongue.

Clamping thumb to finger to staunch the bleeding, I racked my brain for a solution. I surveyed the unfinished scene—the leafy garden, Eve modestly cloaked in ivy, the tree of knowledge with its round red apple—and at once it came to me. Hastily, albeit clumsily, I rethreaded the needle, and in a matter of seconds I'd disguised the bloody splotch with some red silk stitches. There, just another shiny apple to tempt Eve.

"Be sure your sin will find you out."

Grandmother's spoken Scripture nearly knocked me off my chair.

"What was that, Mother?"

"Numbers Thirty-two: 'Be sure your sin will find you out.' It's a good reminder to us, isn't it? We're all being watched. We're all accountable."

I blanched, I'm sure, and stuffed the sampler into its basket with such haste that Mother raised an eyebrow. "I'm perfectly used up," I lied, bolting to my feet. Deceit was becoming ever easier. "I really can't keep my eyes open any longer, so I'm going to go to bed." Without waiting for her permission, and folding my bloody thumb inside my fist, I hurried up the stairs.

Guilt needled me all through that night. I'd gone too far this time, it warned. I'd galloped across one too many boundaries.

But I awoke the next morning, Wednesday, determined to put the sampler incident behind me. What was one more apple in the Garden, anyway? Eve was already reaching toward the tree, destined to take a bite. I'd merely provided her a choice of sins.

I dressed as quickly as I could and went down to the kitchen to find Grandmother frying more doughnuts. "I don't know what became of yesterday's doughnuts," she grumbled. "We must have mice." She cast a suspicious glance toward me while scooping golden rings from the bubbling grease.

"We must have," I responded with a grin. I wrapped three of the cooled ones inside a napkin and headed out to the carriage shed.

To my complete and utter chagrin, that's when Mr. Stead chose to make his appearance. And instead of discovering a dedicated student, he caught me feeding freshly made doughnuts to the Girl. I flushed with embarrassment and tentatively offered him one last half. When he shook his head, I stuffed the evidence into my mouth.

In a voice edged with uncharacteristic harshness, he asked, "Does your manual include *doughnuts* on its list of cures?"

I was so near to choking that all I could do was shake my head miserably.

He stepped into the stall and checked the Girl's pulse. Nodding, he examined the silver pin still twisted in her neck. With one quick movement, he pulled it out. A red bead bubbled up, and he pressed his thumb to it. "You can remove what's left of her bandages," he told me. "She's obviously not going to keep them on." He peered into one of the jellylike wounds. "Try dredging these weepy sores with flour. That will help dry them up." He shooed away a fly. "Who's cleaning her stall?"

I swallowed. "I am."

"Why isn't your brother doing it?"

"I told him I would. I want to be the one taking care of her." I hoped that showed how serious I was about learning to be a veterinary, but it only led him to another critical question.

"Have you spoken with your father?"

I looked away, feeling my chance slipping away too. "No," I replied, "but I'm going to soon. I promise."

"It's not to me that you need to make that promise." For some reason, and I was certain then it was my incompetence, newly come to light, Mr. Stead was wasting no time in gathering his things and heading out the door. Still, like a hopeful puppy, I trailed after him all the way to the street and to his buggy.

The weather had turned threatening. Gusts of wind sent leaves clattering across the pavement. Ominous gray storm clouds piled above the city skyline.

"I think she's through the worst of it," Mr. Stead was saying as he climbed into his buggy, "so I won't need to stop by as often." My heart sank. I petted Balder and sneaked him some doughnut crumbs, hoping to keep them both a little longer, but Mr. Stead gathered up the reins. "Have your brother contact me if she takes a turn for the worse." And then he was driving off.

For a heavy, wind-knocked-out-of-me minute, I watched the black silhouette of him and his buggy grow smaller. "Your brother," he'd said. Not me. No "good girl" or "well done." Not even "good-bye."

Underscoring my mood, the iron gray clouds ensnared the sun at that moment, casting a shroud over the entire street. The wild smell of the ocean blew in beneath them. At once miserable and restless, I turned for the house, only to realize that a young woman was standing a little apart from me, staring up at our parlor window. She was dressed stylishly in unbleached linen, though her bodice was cut noticeably looser than those shown in the store windows. Her straw bonnet, set forward over her brow, was trimmed in black, which matched her neck ribbon. I would have thought her one of the Beacon Street ladies if she weren't holding a brick in her hand. The eyes she turned on me were as dark and stormy as those of any bit-soured horse.

"Is that the Selby house?" she asked. "Mr. August Selby's house?"

Wondering if my answer made me a traitor, I nodded. "Is something wrong?"

"Not with me," she said, tossing her head defiantly. A gust of wind rattled the trees. She measured the brick's weight in her hand. "Never mind what *he* says." I knew at once she meant Father. "Are you one of his?"

I nodded again, hoping that didn't qualify me for a crack over the head, though she certainly didn't appear to be a murderess. She looked more like . . . I knew! "You're the woman from his newspaper, aren't you?"

"I used to be with the *Argus*, if that's what you mean. He's mentioned me, has he?"

"Yes."

She tossed the brick expertly and caught it. "Spare me the details or I'll heave this through his window for sure."

There was a desperate bravado in her voice that I somehow found thrilling. "What *are* you going to do with it?"

She looked down at the brick, almost as if seeing it for the first time. "I don't know," she said suddenly and quite solemnly. "I really don't know." A stronger gust whipped down the street. It stirred her into action and she hurled the brick to the ground, which split it into uneven chunks. "It won't get me back what I've lost," she spat, "I know that." She kicked at one chunk, sending it skidding along the pavement.

A boy who was passing with his mother and older sister kicked it farther on. He ran after the fragment, booted it again, and kept up the game until the trio rounded the corner.

The woman followed the skittering rock with her dark eyes. Air seemed to be leaking out of her from an unseen tear. Gradually her shoulders sagged. "It's not that I don't love my children," she mused, "or my husband. I do. But writing gives me something they can't, and seeing my name in type is . . . well, it's like getting a little drunk, you know?" She let out a husky laugh, and at that I began to suspect the source of her black pupils. Grabbing hold of my arm, she spoke with all the urgency of one accused, and I the judge. "I wrote better, my research was better . . . and I worked longer hours. I didn't even ask for a desk; I polished my columns at home, after my family was asleep and before they were awake. But what did that get me? A boot out the door."

Glancing at the remains of the shattered brick, she let go of my arm to pick up a small chunk. She turned it over and over in her hand, pondering something unspoken, then dropped it. A look up at the scudding clouds made her rub her arms vigorously. "It's going to storm like the devil, isn't it?" As if we'd been talking about nothing more than the weather. "I'm getting a chill." And just like that, hugging herself, she wandered on down the street. Only when she got to the corner did she pause to look back. She shook her head sadly and shrugged her shoulders. Before turning and walking off she mouthed something to me. The words carried on the wind were: "It's no use."

A dreadful foreboding squeezed the very air out of me. My future was slipping away. I had to talk with Father that night. No matter how he stormed, I had to stand up to him and I had to gain his approval. And amid the flurry of emotions threatening to sink me, I screwed up my courage.

Solely as if to plague me, it seemed, the wind blew harder, then harder still. All that afternoon it kept up, and by evening it was blasting the house with an unrelenting fury. It whistled round the corners, flapped the shingles on the roof, and hurled leaves and twigs at the windows. I startled at each attack. I tried to school my nerves, but by then I'd become so thoroughly jumpy and skittish that I fumbled everything put into my hands.

"Honestly, Rachel," Mother said, taking the clinking goblets from me. "The way you're trembling, you'd think you'd never heard a storm brewing. Go light the gas in the parlor and the lamp in the hall. James needs to stay at the fire station for a few more hours, but I'm sure your father will be home early tonight."

"It'll be a race between him and the rain," Grandmother said as she methodically arranged the silver on the table.

That evening the acrid odor of the match was especially nauseating and the hissing of the parlor burners, once lit, did nothing to settle my nerves. I hurried into the hall. As the yellow globe of fire grabbed the wick, an earsplitting thunderbolt crashed directly overhead. I jumped, jostling the small table and sending the lamp rocking wildly. I reached out to steady it but—too late—it fell over with a tinkling of broken glass and a sudden bang as the kerosene exploded. I yelped as tall flames lashed over my hands and sleeves.

For a moment . . . and an eternity . . . my arms became the branches that fed the fire. Sensations ran together before shattering. Orange tongues. Hot. Consuming me.

Grandmother appeared. "Rachel, what have you done?" She rushed to bury my arms in my own skirt. Just as fast, she lifted and dragged the hall rug over the table to douse the flames.

"Quick," she said, "let's rub some butter on them."

She pushed me toward the kitchen, but Mother met us with a handful of the pale stuff. With calm efficiency, she picked away the charred fabric of my sleeves with one hand and slathered a greasy coating on my reddened skin with the other. The pain attacked all at once, like thousands of needles.

It was almost unbearable, and I bit my lip and stamped my feet uncontrollably. Mother and Grandmother hugged me between them.

"I'll get some rags," Grandmother said, and before I knew it, she and Mother had me out of my dress, right there in the front hall, and were binding my hands and forearms in white strips of cloth. Tears were streaming down my face, their water useless against the fire imbedded in my skin.

Hurried footsteps sounded outside, followed closely by the jiggling of the door handle. Mother blocked the entry with unusual authority. "Just a moment, please, Mr. Selby." Nodding toward the stairs, she said to me, "Run along to your room. I'll be up as soon as I can to help you."

In a blinding state of shock, I went stumbling upward, though not fast enough to avoid hearing Father shout, "What happened here?" Mother's responses were too soft to carry, so I only caught Father's interrogation. "Is she all right? Is dinner ready, then?"

Gulping shallow breaths, I followed the threadbare runner past the closed doors in the upstairs hall, then climbed the second flight of bare wood to the attic. My reflection in the bureau mirror brought me to a halt. In the blue-black dusk of my unlit room, my chemise and petticoat—and my newly bandaged arms—glowed ghostly white. For an instant I resembled the Girl. Gooseflesh pimpled my exposed skin, and a wave of nausea knocked me to my knees. I stared at the tips of my blistered fingers that poked from their bandages. How was I going to lay *these* hands on horses?

Slowly at first, and then faster, raindrops began pelting the roof. The noise quickly became deafening, drowning my cries from anyone's ears but my own.

❧ SEVENTEEN

ALL THAT NIGHT THE STORM TOSSED WAVE AFTER CRASHING wave onto my room. Screeching winds shook the very nails from the roof's shingles. An unearthly thunder rattled the beams. Twisting with pain—and guilt—I heard the violence as God's anger at me: for reworking the scene in the Garden, for daring to think that I could reach beyond my grasp, for listening to that wild-eyed woman and thrilling to her defiant words. The hour of judgment had come—my hour, anyway—just as Grandmother had foretold. And it had come in both fire and fury. *Rachel, what have you done?*

The torment was nearly unbearable. The bandages that wrapped my hands and forearms only trapped the fire closer to my skin. Holding my arms as still as I could, I kicked and kicked and kicked at the pain. How was I going to survive this? What was going to happen to me?

Sometime during that nightmare the doctor arrived to examine my burns and to spoon a heavy dose of laudanum into me. I remember he looked at Mother and shook his head. I couldn't focus my eyes. Was that a Bible he was holding? Was I dying? Lightning flashed through the room and he was gone, though Mother was still floating in the background. She slipped her hands beneath me and somehow lifted me up and I was as light as a feather. Murmuring words I couldn't understand, she smoothed my pillow and gently laid me back onto it. When she let go, I fell into a sea of bedlam. Raggedy shadows seemed to dance across my ceiling, laughing. Painfully bright lights taunted me, then fled. Even as the medicine dragged me into a stupor, my arms stung like the skin was being stripped from them at that very instant; and I remembered those poor foxes back in Wesleydale, their skins stretched across the barn wall—testament to the awful price paid for crossing boundaries. And I had crossed into Mr. Jude's garden and something about that made me indecent and maybe even evil, too, because I was always galloping headlong down a path of my own making when everyone else was content to travel the one already paved. And I missed Peaches. And I still wanted to heal horses; I didn't care about the cost. I wanted to give them life. *You're not God* boomed a voice in my head at the same instant that thunder boomed above, and I didn't know if it was Father or Mother or God Himself who had spoken. *Rachel, what have you done?*

Gradually the noises scattered, like guests leaving a party and carrying their words and laughter off into the night, leaving me in an empty room with all the doors and windows shut fast, so deaf that there must have been cotton stuffed in my ears. Never had I felt so abandoned.

The laudanum drugged me into a dreamless sleep. As if I was no longer part of my own body, I watched myself floating and flailing and floating again through a hot, airless void, trying to run, but not going anywhere at all.

Hours passed, or maybe it was days, I had no idea, before a disembodied voice pulled me back to life. "Rachel?" I blinked my eyes open. The gloomy light weakly announced morning. Where was I? "Rachel! Are you awake?" A rapid knocking followed.

It was James; I could tell that much now. Groggily I mumbled a lie, "Yes," and struggled to bring myself round as he clambered up to my attic room. I felt drained. Empty. My stomach lay sucked flat against my spine, while my legs sprawled noodle-soft and useless, as if they'd been churning through quicksand. As James neared the top of the stairs, I realized my bedclothes were knotted at the foot of my bed. In my haste to reach for them, I forgot my bandages. Blistering needles of pain shot through to my bones, strangling my breath.

That plastered even more worry across James's already stricken face. "Mother just told me," he said. "Are you all right?"

I managed a nod. I had to, though it was another lie. A hollowness inside told me I might never be all right again. Not like this. Not wrapped in cotton and pinned to a pillow.

"No, you aren't," he challenged, examining my bandages with widening eyes. "It's as bad as Mother said. You're lucky you weren't killed."

Yes, lucky.

He shifted from one foot to the other, uncomfortable. "By the looks of it, you're going to be confined for quite a while." His brow knitted into a serious frown—too serious for James. Something was up, and I waited, watching dully as a sort of gradual awareness transformed his face. "Hey!" he complained in exaggerated protest. "This wasn't all some ploy of yours to have *me* cleaning the Girl's stall again, was it?"

I couldn't help but smile. I ached to the marrow, but I had to. James could, and would, tickle the humor out of a graveside preacher. "How is she?" I croaked.

"About the same. She ate a little of that oat meal this morning. I don't think she fancies me much, though. Nearly took a chunk out of me when I wasn't looking." He pointed to his backside. "Did Mr. Stead stop by yesterday? Did he have anything to say about her?"

That remembrance delivered a different kind of pain, one that was harder to ignore. I took a deep breath, fighting against what felt like irons piled onto my chest. "He said he wouldn't be stopping by as often. He said . . ." I swallowed, sorting through the words I'd heard and the ones I wanted to forget, "He said she was through the worst of it." Unlike me. And why had he abandoned the both of us?

"That's good, then. Well, I'll look after her while you're on the mend. That won't take long, will it?" James smiled mischievously.

I looked into his cornflower eyes and his jaunty grin

and saw that he truly was a creature from a different world. It was always bluebirds and rainbows in James's skies, while lightning storms swept through mine. Maybe I brought them on myself. Nodding mechanically, I cleared my throat and changed the subject. "How long were you at the fire station last night? I didn't hear you come home." Of course I hadn't, drugged as I was.

"It was nearly two," he replied. "Can you believe it? We all had to stay beyond our shifts and decorate for Independence Day, which meant scrubbing the floor—fairly useless with all the muddy boots tracking in and out—washing every one of the windows, and unrolling and hanging miles upon miles of bunting. Plus we had to repolish the engine that I'd just finished polishing, oil all the harnesses, groom the horses within an inch of their lives, and braid ribbons into their manes for the parade today." He nodded toward the dormer window, which showed a blue-gray square of threatening sky. "That's a lot of wasted elbow grease if it gets to raining again."

"There wasn't a fire last night, was there?" It was a sudden thought, but I could swear at that instant that I smelled smoke in my room.

"Not with this weather."

I sniffed the air. Odors of wet potatoes and bleached linen and, yes, a dampened pall of smoke as well.

"You know, Father—"

He read my mind and halted that train on its tracks. "No, Rachel. Even for Father, deliberately setting fires would be too much. And anyway, he's trying to *fight* fires by asking for more men and equipment in his column."

That added up on paper, as they say. But it was still Father's paper. And they were still his words. He had a way of twisting things that left me uneasy. I stared up at the ceiling. Was that a shadowy image left over from last night, or was it just some newly formed water stain? My mind was so fogged, I couldn't think clearly. I felt lost in a crowd of lies, not knowing who or what to believe anymore.

"Was Mr. Lee helping at the station last night?"

James raised an eyebrow. "No, he's still on suspension. Why so many dark thoughts?"

Why, exactly. "I'm not sure." I turned my head toward the window. "I've been thinking about that person that's out there—that firebug—and sometimes I come back to him."

"Well, you're not the only one. I heard some of the men talking. They say he thinks so highly of himself that he'd start a fire just to be seen putting it out."

A cloud-piercing beam of light shot a pain into my left temple, making me wince. Somewhere a horse whinnied. I ached to answer. "Do you believe them?"

"I don't know. I don't know Benton that well. There *was* that warehouse fire Sunday night, after he was here claiming to 'smell' a fire, but I don't think he was seen anywhere near it." He shrugged off the worries. "All I know is he's still on suspension, which means he's out of the parade—and I'm in."

I tried to muster excitement for him. He was my

brother, after all. "*You're* going to be in the Independence Day parade?"

He ducked his head, grinning. "They're even loaning me a uniform, though I'm not legally a fireman. Numbers, I suppose." Feigning nonchalance, he said, "Seems there's a real rivalry with Engine Company Number Five, which is larger. The chief's assembling as many bodies as he can and putting them all into red shirts." His gaze slid from my face to my bandages, turning wistful. "I'd hoped you'd be able to come watch."

I followed his eyes. My arms were burning again like hot embers were packed inside the bandages. I could have cried if I wasn't already cried out and completely empty inside.

"Well," he said, preparing to leave, "never mind what I said about being confined. I know you too well to think you'll be on your back for long." And he winked. "I'll give your regards to the Governor's Girl." Rubbing his backside on the way to the stairs, he said, "You'd better hurry and get better or there'll be nothing left of me."

He wasn't gone ten minutes when I heard Mother making her way up to my room. She entered carrying a tray and wearing her patented smile that tempered gentle concern with stern efficiency. I *was* going to get through this, she insinuated even before she spoke. And the sooner the better.

"How are you, dear?" she asked. "Are you in much pain?" and before I could answer, she announced, "I have some strawberries with fresh cream." She set down the tray, lined in linen and sparkling with Grandmother's good silver. Something flat was hidden beneath the large napkin.

Like a mother bird fussing over a nestling, she fluffed the pillows behind my back, smoothed the bedclothes over my legs and up to my lap, and draped a knitted shawl over my shoulders. "Chilly for a July morning, isn't it?" I hadn't noticed. Then she perched on the edge of the bed. Even that slight movement tugged at my bandages and stippled new pain across my arms. My breath caught. Opening her mouth in that age-old prompt for me to open mine, she spooned a small round strawberry coated in cream onto my tongue. Reluctantly I chewed and swallowed. And tried to smile for her too. I didn't dare say it tasted awful, that the medicine-y residue of the laudanum trounced any flavor. She popped another strawberry into my mouth and it went down just as pulpy and bitter as the first.

"The doctor says time alone will heal the burns and that meanwhile laudanum will dull the pain. Would you like some more now?"

I shook my head. Stinging bees had taken up residence beneath my bandages and my heart was beating faster, but I hated that foggy, confused feeling that the laudanum gave me. I wanted to be able to go see the Girl.

"I know you're going to be bored up here all by yourself. Would you like me to read to you?" she asked. A magazine was pulled from beneath the napkin. "I've brought the newest *Godey's,* and from what I can tell they're predicting lace collars for the fall." She flipped it open and pointed cheerily to an illustration. "They're even showing lace flounces for the wrist. Now what do you think about that?"

Buying *Godey's Lady's Book and Magazine* was a huge extravagance for Mother. I knew she'd done it for me, and I did glance at the illustration of the overdressed woman, lace piled at her throat and bunched around her wrists. But if I was going to have anything read to me I still wanted it to be *The Reliable Horse Care Manual for American Owners.* My eyes left the billowy lace embellishments for the billowy gold manes of the three horses embossed on the book's cover.

She saw what I wanted, though she didn't understand. She couldn't. "Rachel, dear," she said softly, persuasively, resting a hand on my leg, "that won't lead anywhere, and I really think it's time you give it up. I know it's been a fancy of yours, but treating horses is men's work, as it should be. Now, why don't we look through this magazine together and find a new dress style, and I'll talk to your father about getting some money for some fabric and we'll sew up something new for you while you're recuperating." She tested a little laugh. "Goodness knows you've damaged enough since our arrival. A dress really isn't suited for horse care, is it, dear?"

The door that I thought had been opened to me just days ago was being nudged shut. Softly, persuasively. I shook my head and closed my eyes. "I think I'll just rest some more," I said. "I'm really tired."

"All right," she replied. "I'll leave the magazine here and we'll look at it later." I heard it placed on top of my gilt-edged manual and knew the horses' shimmering manes had been snuffed out. "There are some lovely fashions in it, and I know that a project like a new dress will be just the thing to lift your spirits. You'll see." Picking up the tray, she left. I never heard her feet on the stairs. She always moved as silently as a ghost, as if she had no substance, no weight. Was that my future? To fret about fashions and curtains and float around an empty house waiting for someone to notice me?

The attic room fell as quiet as a vault then. I could hear my breath going in and out of my nose. Bound in linen and cotton, I lay motionless, hearing, smelling, breathing, but not moving. In the stillness I noticed how the damp intensified the odors of rotting wood and musty paper in the house. I heard the mice stirring within the walls, behind the bureau at first and then invisibly over the stairwell, but even their scratchings seemed subdued on such a gray day. Far below me, in what seemed like another world, the parlor clock faintly chimed the quarter hour. I counted in my head, waiting for it to chime again, but couldn't concentrate and had to let time tick by unreckoned. The muffled voices of Mother and Grandmother, and sometimes a cabinet's faint squeak or the soft clunk of a mixing bowl on the wood table, rose high enough to disturb the attic air. I felt myself slipping into that void again, and I gave up and let myself go. This time I dreamed of bread baking inside an oven. I was certain I could smell it, doughy and golden. Hot.

EIGHTEEN

A DISTANT BANG AWAKENED ME, STILL ON THE SAME DAY, I was fairly certain. At first I thought the thunder had returned, but there was no advancing rumble, just a sharp pop immediately followed by another and another. Gunfire. It had to mean the Independence Day celebration was beginning.

I blinked my eyes open, tried to focus them. Staring up at the sloping ceiling, I thought about James and the firehorses, and all the other horses that would be in the parade, and wished I could somehow be there to see them. Out on the street, the hurried clatter of a horse and wagon grew loud and then faded. *They* were probably on their way to the parade, I thought enviously.

I'd been to the street that ran along the Common—that's where the parade was passing by—so I could easily imagine how it looked. The expectant crowd would be pushed onto the pavement, necks craning in the same direction. A dog would probably trot across the empty corridor and a child would chase after him, ignoring his mother's calls. But then a commanding whistle would split the air and invigorating drumbeats sound their *rat-a-tat-tat*, and everyone would clear the way and even the sun would obediently scatter the clouds.

That's how I imagined it, and upon the blank slate of my sloping ceiling I made the parade unfold. First would come the grand marshal, a captain in the army, on a handsome bay. Then a commercial entry, perhaps a local coal company driving an enormous pair of black Percherons. In my mind's eye, the horses' massive haunches rippled from blue to black as the harness bells shook. After them I placed a team and wagon entered by a bakery and then one by a candy maker. I imagined the driver tossing wrapped samples to the crowd.

They'd be peppermints, of course, and out of the crowd a hand rose high to grab one; it was Mr. Stead, and he turned and smiled straight at me, and I had to push him out of my mind.

Annoyed, I conjured up the firemen. They burst onto the scene with their shining, hissing steam engine, and the onlookers went wild. James strutted among the other red-shirted men, and they encouraged the crowd to greater noise by whooping and waving their hats.

To my surprise, Mr. Benton Lee charged into view, nearly clipping the fire engine's wheels and—whose parade was this, anyway? I watched in confused horror as the black stallion harnessed to his two-wheeled gig ran backward, squatted, and lifted into a rear. The single seat tipped dangerously, but Mr. Lee—who took the time to give me a sly grin—coolly flicked his beribboned whip and sent the stallion plunging forward and out of the picture.

The parade images evaporated. I became acutely aware of the room's chill and of the unsettling odor of soot in the air. How dare Mr. Lee shove his way into my amusement? And for that matter, how dare Mr. Stead turn up? They did nothing but plague me with their deceptions and then vanish.

Feeling sorry for myself, I kicked against the bed's covers. Mother had them tucked in so tightly I was practically pinned to the sheets. Suddenly I couldn't breathe. I gasped for air like a bluegill heaved onto a pond's bank and abandoned. With my chin brushing the fuzzy rolled edge of the coverlet, I fought to calm my heaving chest. Determinedly I focused my attention on the ceiling again, seeking salvation.

For some time all I saw was the spiderweb of cracks running through the chipped plaster and the brown water stains forming a murky band of clouds across the ceiling's middle. But gradually that murky band became a herd of wild horses thundering across some distant prairie, and recklessly I threw my leg across one, clutched the mane, and galloped. I didn't notice the sunlight slipping away or the clouds returning, the walls fading from ivory to ash to iron gray. As rain began spattering the roof, blending with the drumming of the horses' hooves in my mind, I was lulled into another sleep.

When I awoke, the room was again gloomy, bathed in that thin light that masqueraded as both dawn and dusk. I didn't know what time it was. I did know the laudanum had completely worn off because my arms burned with a relentless fire. And yet there was some air in me. I felt as if I could breathe again, and I sensed the stirrings of something hopeful. The horses had done that. They were better than any tonic.

Out of habit, or maybe unrepentant stubbornness, I gazed toward the spine of my horse care manual. I longed to open its pages and read; but I couldn't light the lamp, let alone lift the book into my hands. Heaving a sigh of frustration, I turned my thoughts to the Girl. If I could just go see her . . . But I knew Mother would never let me past the door, especially now that it was raining again. So I lay there, as helpless as a gasping fish, muddling stupidly about ruffles and samplers, and what made something so right when everyone else thought it was wrong, and wondering with a dull ache just how I was going to fill the long days ahead.

When Mother floated up to my room again, she carried an early dinner and something flat wrapped in tissue. "I have another gift for you," she said in an unusually bright singsong voice. My incapacitation seemed to have breathed new life into her. She set the tray on the bureau to light the lamp, then pulled a rectangular card, about four by six inches, from its tissue sleeve. "It's just now arrived from the gallery, just this very minute." Proudly she held out the photograph that we'd posed for on Saturday.

Three pale faces stared from the gray frame, and it struck me at once that we looked as trapped and lifeless as Father's butterflies. There was Grandmother, grim as ever in her black

widow's weeds, awaiting the world's end. And Mother, neat as a pin in white, her lips pinched together so tightly they'd vanished. With a newly churning stomach, I leaned closer to study my own face. At first glance it seemed just as pale and flat and ordinary as the other two, except—I squinted—what was that beside my ear? A fragment of straw? It was. I quashed a smile. Now I remembered: I'd been cleaning the carriage shed, preparing it for the burned mare. Quickly I examined my hands in the photograph. They were dutifully clasped in my lap as the photographer had directed, but—hardly anyone would notice—that shadow between my thumb and forefinger was actually dirt, rubbed in by the pitchfork's handle. I couldn't hold back my smile then. I was sure I was never going to be the perfect specimen; no camera or glass or bandage was going to contain me.

Mother took my smile as appreciation. "This one is yours. Your father ordered a cabinet card for each of us," she said. "Wasn't that generous of him?"

I nodded, wondering with wry humor if he'd ever notice the flaws in the image that he'd paid to have captured.

After she'd propped the card against my horse care manual, she took up her perch on the bed and began spooning chicken and dumpling stew into me. "It seems I have my baby back," she murmured happily, and I could have choked. When the bowl was scraped clean, she brought out the bottle of laudanum and unscrewed the cap. The skull on its stark label leered.

"Do I *have* to take more of that?" My burned arms

screamed "yes," but I couldn't stay drugged the rest of my life. I had work to do.

"The doctor said it will help you sleep, dear."

"I've been sleeping most of the day," I argued. "Couldn't I just wait a while and take it later?"

She looked at me with some misgiving. "Well, all right. We'll wait another hour or so. Can I bring you anything else?" I shook my head and forced my lips to widen into an agreeable smile, and she left.

I could feel those pale faces staring at me. *This is your future,* they seemed to say. *Your present and your future. Why fight it?* I already was. Gritting my teeth against the pain, I lifted one bandaged arm and knocked the photograph flat.

That revealed my manual and Mother's magazine. My dreams and hers. And that did give me another twinge of guilt. One of the Ten Commandments was "Honor thy father and thy mother." I'd stitched those words onto a sampler when I was just six. But what if your father and your mother were wrong? Just plain wrong. What then?

I did what I'd always done: I galloped.

Mother had loosened my covers enough that now I was able to kick free of them. Keeping my eyes trained on the horse care manual, I gingerly twisted onto my back. Every little movement disturbed the bandages, yanking them across my raw and oozing skin and burning it anew, but I clenched my jaw. Clumsily using my toes for fingers, I wangled the heavy manual toward the edge of the nightstand. Inch by tantalizing inch it came closer.

The *Godey's* was still on top, so when the book finally tumbled onto the bed, the magazine came with it. A very pretty lady corseted into a suffocating S-shape and balanced upon her furled umbrella beckoned me with a smile. I smiled back and kicked the magazine onto the floor.

I hated having to poke my dirty toes under the leather cover, even more to pry apart the gilt-edged pages. But with my hands in bandages, it was the only way. When the manual finally flopped open, my heart quickened. It was like a crack in that door, a door that hadn't been latched quite firmly enough to keep me out. Gathering myself again, I managed to get up onto my knees. The pain almost knocked me back. But like a horse stretching to water, I gradually bent over the book. The words and their knowledge rippled in front of me just as precious as water to the thirsty. It didn't matter that the pages had fallen open to the middle of a chapter, one entitled "A Brief History of the Horse in the Wild." I began drinking them in.

> It's a fallacy, though one widely held, that a stal-
> lion rules the herd. He is there to protect, of
> course, to chase away the wolf and the grizzly
> and the catamount with his superior strength
> and sharp hooves, but it is another individual
> who truly leads the herd. As a Texas Ranger
> with many years' experience studying horses in
> the wild once informed me, there is always one
> wily mare who blazes the way for the others. The

stallion may trumpet his call to run, but it is this one mare who tells them where to go. She knows the safest path to the watering hole and which pastures offer the best grazing. She considers the abilities of those around her and adjusts her speed or her path to accommodate the young, the aged, or the injured. This Texas Ranger said he'd even watched one of these wise mares on a spring evening guide a sister mare to a protected wash to give birth. All that night she stood guard, he said, nickering advice and not leaving even to feed herself. On another occasion she shouldered a colt aside just before a rattlesnake struck. How did she come by such authority? I asked. Did mares fight for supremacy as I knew stallions did? He shook his head. No, he answered, a lead mare always chooses herself. She just seems to know that others need her.

ᴇᵍᵒ NINETEEN

A CLEANSING WIND FILLED MY LUNGS. READING THOSE words was like opening a gate to go at a gallop. I drank them in, gulp after gulp, late into the night. Mother came up to my room twice to insist on more laudanum, but I shook my head. The third time she spooned the awful stuff into me by threat—"I'll take that book away, I promise you"—before turning down the lamp and even pushing my manual out of reach. I lay in the darkness, my heart thudding. Mice skittered behind the walls. I was galloping beyond them.

Over the next several days I read every moment that I could—whenever Mother allowed me a good dose of light and a light dose of laudanum. The pain came and went unpredictably: Some mornings I awoke to terrible, feverish spasms that pinned me to my bed, writhing, for hours. Other days I could block out the waves of nausea by staring at the ceiling and reciting as many as twenty-seven different bones on an imaginary horse skeleton that I saw there.

In one rain-filled week I made more progress through that manual than in the entire six months that I'd owned it. But the more I read, the more I realized that words and drawings were weak replacements for velvet skin and liquid eyes. I needed to be with the Girl. Only I, like her, was a prisoner. Bandaged from fingers to elbows, I couldn't button a dress or lace a shoe or turn a doorknob. All I could do, if my door was left ajar, was hobble down to the upstairs hall and gaze through the dripping pane and across the muddy yard to where I longed to be.

I suppose we all felt confined during the rain, because the first morning that broke to sunshine instead of thunder Mother and Grandmother hurried out of the house. I was determined to do the same. As gingerly as I could, I slipped my bandaged arms into a loose-sleeved robe and negotiated the stairs in my bare feet. Pausing to peek out the window—I could see her!—my heart beat faster. I scrambled down the next set of stairs, ignoring the painful throbbing that brought to my arms. I was almost there. Around the newel post and through the kitchen and right up to the back door and its slippery smooth knob, and I was stuck.

Confound it! What was I going to do now? I tried turning it with my hip. I clasped it between my elbows. Each time the knob began a teasing circuit before slipping back into place. I had no choice, not if I wanted to see the Girl. Clenching my jaw, I plunged into the fire by gripping the knob with both bandaged hands, turning it until I heard that blessed *click*, then opening the door. I sprinted across the yard.

The Girl's nicker helped salve the stinging pain. She seemed genuinely happy to see me. When she stretched her neck out, making little whiffling sounds with her nostrils, her peeling muzzle just kissed my cheek. I noticed the wet stains shadowing her eyes. They couldn't be tears, I told myself; horses didn't cry. They were probably just some aftereffects of her injuries. But the fleeting possibility dampened my own eyes.

Dizzy from my sudden escape, I plopped onto the upturned crate and steadied myself by inhaling the longed-for aromas: warm horse, sweet oats, sun-dried straw. I saw that same spider wave from the pimpled rust of the hoe. And that same brown-capped sparrow, or one of his friends, alight in the window frame and chirp happily. I watched him drop onto the floor and hop over to inspect a crumpled paper sack that hadn't been there a week ago. Curious as well, I went over for a closer look. One nudge from my toe spilled a fragrance of peppermint into the air, and I knew with a sharp pang who had dropped it. Even so, I inhaled deeply and let the aroma stir its own memories.

That healing visit had to hold me for a while, because when Mother returned to find me in the carriage shed she scolded me all the way up to my room. The doctor was coming at any minute to change my bandages, she said, and was I ever a sight!

If I hadn't had that restorative time with the Girl, I don't know how I could have gotten through the next hour. The doctor said he'd proceed slowly and that it wouldn't hurt, but his promises proved meaningless. Having the bandages ripped from my arms was as searingly painful as having the fire consume them in the first place. I couldn't help crying, I simply couldn't, and afterward, when Mother spooned the dreaded laudanum into me, I actually welcomed sleep. That lost me another day with the Girl.

Since the evening of my accident, Grandmother had been making the effort—and it *was* an effort with her bad knees—to climb the attic stairs on a daily basis in order to brush my hair and provide some company. The very next day she happened to carry a greeting from Mr. Stead, along with a newly published pamphlet he'd sent entitled "Vices in Horses: Taming the Stubborn and the Intractable." I recognized it as a sly prod toward my confrontation with Father, but glaring at my bandaged arms, I knew that would have to wait for now. Still, I was pleased with his gift and immeasurably glad that he hadn't forsaken me.

Since finding me in the carriage shed, Mother had forbidden me to return to it. She said that was rightfully James's work. She warned that it was simply too dangerous. She even threatened—"And I mean it, Rachel"—to have the Girl removed to another stable if I didn't obey.

"No!" I begged. "You can't."

"All right, then. See that you stay in your room until you're healed."

I managed two more days. But when Sunday came along and everyone left to attend church, sinner that I was, I scurried right down the stairs and out to the Girl. I figured I had a good three hours or so.

The doctor had left the tips of my fingers free the last time he'd changed my bandages—my palms had taken the brunt of the fire—so the back door posed somewhat less of a problem. I was even able to carry a blank journal clamped to my side. I'd decided I was going to be more methodical about the Girl's treatment. I was going to record all my observations and keep diligent track of the facts of her recovery. Cold facts were Father's currency, I knew. So if I had any hope at all of getting his permission to study with Mr. Stead, I was going to need them.

Settling on the crate again, I gripped a pencil between my thumb and fourth finger and clumsily wrote "The Girl's Progress" on the opening page. That alone filled me with hope. Someday I'd show the journal to Mr. Stead and he'd be impressed too. He'd see me as something more than just a girl feeding doughnuts to a horse and following him around like a stray puppy.

From my horse care manual I'd learned that my first task was to record the Girl's heart rate. And for that I'd borrowed Grandfather's old pocket watch from Grandmother's bedside drawer. Luckily for me, she kept it wound. Cradling the silver disc in my bandaged palm, I stepped in beside the big mare. She nickered. Pressing my ear against her side, right behind her elbow, I found the steady beat of her heart and began counting. Curious, she swung her head around to lightly rest her muzzle on my back. I wondered with a smile if she was taking her own measurement. The manual said that thirty beats per minute, give or take a few, was normal for a horse. For that first entry on July 21 I scrawled "thirty-two."

Next I made a visual examination, nose to tail. A little over three weeks had passed since she'd been burned, yet a gelatinous landscape of red and yellow oozing sores, flecked with black cinders, still covered her neck and back. Behind her withers I could actually peer into a netting of tiny blood vessels and watch them work. While the manual's illustrations had prepared me for such a sight, they had done nothing for the sickly odor. I made some notes and moved on.

A pale, grainy substance clotted some of the wound pockets, along with straw fragments and bits of dirt. Flies waded through the sticky pools. I swished them away, wincing at the pain that caused, but they resettled instantly. James, I knew, had been dredging the sores in flour, and I set down my journal to clumsily scoop a handful from the open bag near the door. As tenderly as I could, I tamped it into her flesh. She tolerated only three handfuls before pinning her ears and shaking her head at me. I stopped at once, recognizing all too well the pain in her black eyes.

The Girl's face wasn't as swollen as it had been. It was still hairless, with a nightmarish mottling of pink and gray that deepened to purple around her muzzle. What little patchy skin remained had curled upon itself like paper ash. I recorded it all.

But registering facts wasn't enough. I had to know more about horse care, and especially burn care, than was in my manual. So on subsequent afternoons, when Mother allowed me down to the parlor, I searched through the newspapers lying around and even tiptoed into Father's study to scan his leather-bound titles. There I found a medical book from the last century that suggested slathering a burn with frothed eggs and salad oil, while another one recommended mixing chalk and hog's lard. How was I supposed to know which one was right? Her care was too important to rely on a guess.

As July's rain was exchanged for August's sweltering heat, I managed to sneak more visits to the Girl. I recorded dozens more facts in my journal and I tore out newspaper advertisements for such cures as B. J. Kendall's Renovating Powders and Royal Equine Cordials—"Used on Her Majesty's own horses"—and pressed them between its pages for future study.

Hungry for knowledge, I even pumped the doctor for facts. The next time he was changing my bandages, I set my jaw against the pain and asked, "How do you treat a burn when bandages won't hold?"

He was at that moment examining a deep, oozing crack in my left wrist, one that threatened to upend my own stomach. "Your bandages are holding just fine," he answered absently, poking at the inflamed edge.

"But would you recommend dredging them in flour?"

"Dredging them—? Certainly not!" he exclaimed, pulling back and blinking as if I'd insulted him.

"Rachel," Mother cautioned.

He turned to her. "Laudanum can sometimes bring on a state of confusion, Mrs. Selby, a light-headedness. Don't worry, it will pass."

But I wasn't at all light-headed. I was as clear and as

lucid as anyone—and determined. "If, for some reason, my burns could *not* be bandaged, how would you treat them?"

That flustered him a moment. But like any good doctor, he came up with an answer. "Well, I suppose applying bicarbonate of soda might bring some relief. But the point is to keep out air, so bandages are best."

Bicarbonate of soda. Another fact for my journal and, since we always had some in the kitchen, another possible healing tool for the Girl. Mother gave me a warning glare, but when she left the house that afternoon on an errand, well . . . I rushed out to the shed and kicked aside the bag of flour. Instead I sprinkled bicarbonate of soda onto the Girl's wounds. I thought she looked more relieved and made just such a note.

A flame was burning inside me that I'd defy anyone to put out. Like that Texas Ranger's wily mare, I'd chosen myself. Mother could faint and God could rumble and Father could puff on his pipe until his lips burned, but no one was going to stop me from learning to heal horses, even if I had to teach myself.

That was akin to shaking my fist at fate, I suppose, because in the following weeks my world wobbled away from order. A terrible storm crashed through the city, spinning carriages off the streets and yanking trees from the ground, and I heard God's rumbling in the thunder. But Grandmother was the one who fainted. She took a spill coming down the stairs one morning and banged her head so badly that she had to be helped back to her bed. Trailing James and Mother up the stairs, I heard her solemnly predict her end and ours. God was close to "seeking his vengeance," she mumbled, and wouldn't you know it, a thunderclap sounded at that very instant and I nearly jumped out of my skin. He was coming, she moaned, "with fire and with fury." My knees twitched an exclamation point to her prophecy.

The part about the fires did prove eerily true. The alarm began jangling two and sometimes three times a week. James spent more and more hours at the station, and even though he wasn't of age, he was being allowed to accompany the firemen, if needed, on some calls. If he saw my lamp still burning when he arrived home at night, he often tiptoed up the stairs to share the goings-on at the station.

"There's a firebug out there for certain," he announced one evening. His eyes signaled a mix of excitement and worry.

My stomach twisted. "How do you know?"

"We've been called out to an unusual number of small fires recently, all of them suspicious—a bakery, a locksmith, even the feed store—but we couldn't find clear proof of arson at any one of them. Today, though, when we got to the scene of a fire behind some dressmakers' shops, we found a half-empty kerosene container. Can you believe it? As plain as day, someone had poured kerosene all over a broken-down delivery wagon left in the alley, hoping the flames would spread. Luckily we knocked it out before it reached the rooftops or it could have taken the whole block." He shook his head. "Philip's going to tell Captain Gilmore—he wasn't there today—what we found. Maybe he'll have a plan."

I hoped so. I couldn't bear the thought of another livery fire and more horses being burned. Only the devil could possess someone to cause such misery.

Father used the increasingly frequent fires to fan his argument for more and better preparation. He wrote in his columns of impending doom, of a conflagration to rival the Great Chicago Fire. He named names and made accusations: misappropriation of funds, conspiracy, arson. "Where are we supposed to acquire the money to purchase new firefighting equipment?" his opponents argued. "Take it from the orphans' homes? Stop treating the sick?" Only their arguments weren't printed in the *Argus*. Father wouldn't allow it. "Let them print their own paper, if they've a mind to, and then they can say whatever they please." But he made certain he read all the other papers, and he slapped his hand across the crackling newsprint and muttered between his teeth, and his pipe glowed a fierce orange.

One sticky evening in the middle of August, when clouds smothered the stars and everyone except Grandmother was sitting in the parlor—Mother was reading aloud from *Nicholas Nickleby*—a brick came crashing through our window. It took one of Mother's potted ivies with it and plunked onto the braided rug amid a spray of dirt and glass. An inflow of hot night air carried the sound of escaping footsteps, and though James and I lunged for the window, the streetlamp's circle of light shone empty. Mother looked past me to Father, laying the blame squarely in his lap, before calmly marking her place and rising. As Father scooped up the paper-wrapped brick, she knelt on the floor, tucked the ivy's root-ball back into its pot, and began methodically pressing the dirt back into place.

James joined Father at the table, and like a pair of blundering deacons they mouthed the threat scrawled on the crumpled paper. Phrases such as "back to the prairies where you belong" and "surely suffer the consequences" poked through my consciousness as I lowered myself into my chair. A chilling sense that a reckoning hour was fast approaching—and that at least two of us had played a part in it—sent me ramrod stiff. Even with the summer air drifting through the room, I shivered.

The doctor returned the next day, as he'd done weekly, to change my bandages. The burns had scarred over, and the bandages' primary purpose now was to keep the salve in place and to aid the healing. He'd come to expect my questions, so the first thing he said after opening his satchel was, "No talking, please. I have to concentrate." This time when my puckered, reddened skin—shiny in places, leathery in others—was exposed, he nodded in moderate satisfaction. "Time alone, I think, will complete whatever healing remains. I'll apply clean bandages this one last time and return in another fifteen days. Then we'll assess the progress."

I was more concerned with the Girl's progress. Something inside me warned that she had to be made whole again, that we were running out of time. Whether it was Grandmother's prophecies or my twitching knees, I didn't know. But before the doctor was even out the door, the fire alarm jangled. He and Mother and I stood on the top step and watched anxiously as the galloping horses pulled the steam engine toward another fire.

TWENTY

THE MONTH ENDED WITH A PLAGUE OF MOSQUITOES THAT had to have rivaled Moses's locusts. Father stamped about the house for days, howling blue murder, after the Massachusetts Republican Party agreed to support women's right to vote. He broke away from his firefighting columns long enough to pen a particularly vehement one predicting doily laws and spittoon abolishment as well as the imminent downfall of the civilization men had fought for and therefore had the right to rule. Grandmother's health had improved enough that one night after dinner she was able to give him a spirited argument. Mother monitored their language with dark looks and the occasional "Now, really!" while I paged through *Scribner's Monthly* and pretended to read. Overcome by heat and each other's company, we retired to our beds earlier than usual.

Sometime in the stillest part of that night I was awakened by the rise and fall of distant voices. I lifted my head off the pillow. The faint conversation—and was that a laugh?—wasn't coming from Grandmother's room; these sounds were farther off. Intruders? I sat up, my heart banging. Had someone gone beyond brick-throwing and actually broken into our house?

Questioning my foolhardiness, I tiptoed down the stairs and along the dark hallway, now cool and damp. The three bedroom doors were closed, as usual, and I heard Father snoring. A peek into the yard below showed nothing moving amid the blackness. I slipped past the butterflies, feeling my way over each stair. At the newel post I paused. The voices—women's voices, I could tell now—were coming from the kitchen. That door was closed too, which *wasn't* usual. Maybe I should wake James. Yet even while I was thinking that, I was sidling closer to the door, holding my breath and prickling with almost numbing fear. I laid an ear to the wood panel.

Mother. And Grandmother. Chatting and giggling—giggling!—as though they were at a noon picnic. When I'd long since heard the clock chime midnight!

The moment I laid my hand on the knob, the creaky mechanism squealed alarm and the voices hushed. I eased the door open to find the two of them sitting in chairs they'd pulled close to the orange glow of the open oven. No lamp was lit. Upside down on the floor between them was the big soup kettle, and on its black bottom I dimly made out a scattering of cracked nuts. Grandmother grinned guiltily and chucked an empty shell into the embers, where it made a small shower of sparks before birthing a new flame. More self-conscious, Mother rested her elbows on her knees, hunching her shoulders. In a subdued voice she asked, "Are you all right, dear?"

Nodding hesitantly, I followed Grandmother's gesture to join them. The atmosphere in the darkened kitchen—unbuttoned, intimate—was so unfamiliar to me that I wondered if I was dreaming. Grandmother, my own grandmother, was sitting spraddle-legged and barefoot. Barefoot! Never in my life had I seen her without shoes, and now I couldn't stop staring at her crooked, rootlike toes. "Did we wake you?" she asked.

I nodded again as Mother wordlessly rose and returned with the stool from the parlor. She set it within their circle and patted the seat. "Here. Sit down."

I sat.

"Are you all right?" she asked again. "Is anything wrong?"

Bubbling with my own questions, I whispered, "What are you doing down here?"

"Talking."

"In the middle of the night?" I sounded like the scolding parent.

She blinked passively. "You wouldn't understand, I'm afraid."

"We were talking about your mother's days as Wesleydale's finest pianist," Grandmother said. "Has anyone ever told you about them?"

I shook my head. Mother modestly turned toward the oven's glow.

"When she was a child," Grandmother chatted on, "all your mother ever talked about was the piano—and about Handel and Bach and . . . and Cho-pin, is that it?"

"*Sho*-pan," Mother enunciated.

"Oh, *Cho*pin. Well, your grandfather and I didn't own a piano—he was just a hog farmer, after all—so every spare minute, even when she was supposed to be doing her chores"— Grandmother nodded pointedly—"your mother raced down the road and over to the church to pound on theirs. Got to be quite good at it too. Good enough to get an invitation to study in Chicago, that's how good."

I think maybe my jaw dropped open, but Grandmother didn't seem to notice and went on happily recounting Mother's youth.

"They hired her to play the church service when she was only fourteen, and I couldn't have been prouder. Wasn't long before people in neighboring towns were leaving their regular churches and traveling to ours just to hear her." Chuckling, she added, "Though to this day I suspect Reverend Lozier thought it was to hear his sermons."

A spontaneous laugh escaped Mother, and she clamped her hand over her mouth in surprise. Speaking from behind it, she said, "Weren't those the longest, dullest sermons in all eternity? God forgive me, but do you know, all week long I'd practice something pretty, like 'Come Thou Fount of Every Blessing,' and then Reverend Lozier would take up with one of his 'begats' sermons—'Abraham begat Isaac and Isaac begat Jacob' and so on—and I'd see half the congregation nodding off and have to switch to 'Mine Eyes Have Seen the Glory' just to stir them awake."

This had to be a dream. These people were strangers to me.

"And wouldn't that congregation go marching down the aisle, still singing it!" Grandmother slapped her knee. "Why, come Monday morning I'd catch some of them still humming it in Milton's Dry Goods. Churches around here could use a little of that Holy Spirit."

Mother smiled and folded her hands in her lap.

I looked at her anew. "Why haven't I ever heard you play the piano?"

Something flickered across her face, a shadow perhaps, there and gone before she spoke. "Because that was a long time ago," she said emotionlessly. "And because I married your father and he had his work."

"Men!" Grandmother grumbled. And when Mother cocked an eyebrow at her, she responded, "I know, I know, he's my own son-in-law, but he's just like the rest of his kind: He can't see beyond his own nose. And if it doesn't concern his newspaper or his belly, he doesn't care a rap about it."

The two of them fell into a contemplative silence, and I felt that I'd become the intruder. But I didn't want to leave. The room pulsed with a warm breath, hugging me to my stool. And so I stayed, the three of us staring into the open mouth of the oven, mute audience to its crackles and sighs.

"What's troubling you, Rachel?" Mother asked at last.

I started. "Pardon me?"

"What's troubling you?"

"Might as well be free of it," Grandmother said, as if she'd been sharing the same thought. "God loves a clean conscience."

I wasn't sure what God thought of my conscience.

Grandmother ventured a guess. "It has something to do with that horse out there, doesn't it?"

I shot a nervous glance at Mother. "Yes," I answered, "partly—or mostly. But . . ." Was this the time to admit to my dreams of becoming a veterinary? The guilt of sneaking around had been weighing ever more heavily on me.

"Are you worried about your hands?" Mother asked gently. "About what they'll look like when the bandages come off for good?"

It was no use. She would never, *ever* understand me. "No," I replied too harshly, and then, schooling myself, "I mean, yes . . . somewhat, but . . ." Looking into the fire, I took a deep breath and tried anyway. "I know you're going to be disappointed in me and I know Father's never going to let me, but . . . I want to learn to be a veterinary."

A chunky ember broke apart with a loud hiss. It sounded like laughter, and that's all it took to break the spell. And when neither of them spoke, I blurted an accusation: "I knew you wouldn't understand."

"Wouldn't understand what it's like to have dreams locked away in a trunk?" Mother replied with some starch.

"Or be packed up and moved halfway across the continent

without so much as an 'if you please'?" Grandmother added.

Mother laid a hand on my knee. "You see, dear, we're quite familiar with grand plans and broken dreams. But we've learned that we can't always be or get what we want."

"Why not?"

"Because we're women, and as women we have other roles, other duties. Now before you say anything, I know times are changing; some women are hiring on in offices and others are enrolling in universities, though why they'd want to push their way into places they're not welcome is beyond my understanding." She shook her head. "I'm not sure it's right. But Rachel, a veterinary? That's men's work."

"What makes it men's work?" I argued.

"Well, for one thing it takes a man's strength to handle horses—"

"I'm stronger than I look," I shot back, my eyes narrowing. "And besides, it doesn't take strength so much as it takes understanding."

"Well then, there so much that's—well, unpleasant about it. That poor animal you're keeping alive out there is hideous to look at."

That struck a nerve. "Like me?" I retorted, holding up a bandaged arm. "Is that what people are going to say about me when my bandages come off? 'She's hideous to look at'?"

Mother was taken aback. She glanced to Grandmother for help but found her intent on picking the meat from a nut. "Of course not, dear," she continued on alone. "Your arms can always be covered up—I mean, I'm sure they'll heal just fine eventually; the scars will fade. But if they don't, you can always wear gloves, and no one—"

I stood, ready to bolt.

"Sit down, Rachel," Grandmother ordered. Mother opened her mouth but was hushed by the upheld hand of her own mother. "Have you truly thought this through? You have a tendency to go rushing into things, you know. Just how badly do you want to be a veterinary?"

The words came gushing out of me with the force of a spring flood. "It's all I ever think about. It's all I read about, all I dream about. I sneak out to see the Girl every time you leave the house." I glanced guiltily in Mother's direction.

She returned a wry smile. "Do you think I don't know that? I've been scrubbing the muddy footprints off the stairs for close to two months now."

"I'm sorry." I blushed even as I charged on. "I know I'd be a good one. I understand horses; I know what they're thinking and what they're feeling. And I've studied hard. Even Mr. Stead told me once that I know more than most horsemen in Boston." Turning to Grandmother, I said, "From the moment I saw that foal being born—you were there, remember?—when it breathed on my hands, I've felt certain that this is what *I* was born to do." Whether from the heat of the oven or the heat from my words, I felt my face flush even hotter. It all sounded so foolish here in the middle of the night. I slumped in frustration.

She continued shelling nuts. "God speaks to us in mysterious ways, even when we're not listening. I felt a little inspired myself that morning. You should have been there, Nora."

Mother took on a wistful air. "I guess I missed quite an event," she said softly, all the while looking at me. "Babies can do that to you." She reached over and shook my knee. "But . . . a veterinary? That's such awfully dirty work!"

"Yes, it is," I answered, remembering Emilyn's horror at my hands. "And yet . . . I simply love it. I love the idea of helping sick horses."

"You always did have a big heart," she mused. "Mother, do you remember when Rachel brought that moth-eaten baby squirrel home, the one that had fallen out of the oak tree?"

"And took it into her bed with her?" Grandmother let out a belt-busting laugh. "I near jumped out of my skin when those beady eyes looked up at me from her pillow. Curled right up in her hair it was! Gracious!"

They revisited their memories awhile, punctuating the silence with chuckles and sighs.

"You'd upset a lot of people," Mother said finally.

I stiffened.

"Oh, Nora," Grandmother began, but it was her turn to be hushed with an upraised hand.

"And it wouldn't be easy, especially with your father's views. But," she eyed me with a steely determination I'd rarely seen, "nothing worth having ever is."

I squealed with utter surprise and delight and threw my bandaged arms around her neck.

"I'm not saying I'm *agreeing* to your being a veterinary," she cautioned. "And I'm not even certain you can do it. But some things that your grandmother and I were discussing earlier tonight have influenced me enough to at least consider it. Now, I assume there's some additional schooling involved." Mother was already working out the details, bless her.

"Mr. Stead told me it's a three-year course. A while back he said he'd teach me some of the basics, but now I think it would be better if I went to a veterinary school and did it on my own. There's one here in Boston, I know. It's where Mr. Stead studied."

"Are you certain you wouldn't rather enroll in some upper-level courses at a high school? I've learned of a very respectable one on Essex." I couldn't blame her, really, for making one last effort.

"I want to attend veterinary school."

She nodded and the three of us fell silent again. We could plot a course readily enough, but that didn't clear the hurdles.

Teetering toward frustration, I said, "I know Father will say no."

Mother pursed her lips in a manner that could only be described as sly. "Get your facts in order first—the cost, the admission requirements, if they'll even admit a young woman—and an argument for how your studies will be to his benefit. Then wait for the right time."

"He's still going to say no."

"Rachel," Grandmother scolded, "your mother was pounding

pianos at fourteen. She knows something about getting her way, so listen to her."

"But how can my studying as a veterinary be to Father's benefit?"

"That is a puzzle," Mother replied, tapping a finger against her cheek. "We'll have to think on it. Now go on back to bed."

"We'll both put our thinking caps on," Grandmother said. "Morning's still a ways off."

⤳ TWENTY-ONE

PUZZLED DIDN'T EVEN BEGIN TO DESCRIBE HOW I FELT. The very next morning, though, I took out paper and pen and as neatly as I could manage wrote to the Boston College of Veterinary Medicine and Surgery. I politely asked when the next set of classes began and if I, a girl nearly sixteen, could enroll. I carried it personally to the post office to drop it in the box. And then I waited, day after day, for my fate to be decided.

Mother and Grandmother said nothing more about our middle-of-the-night conversation, so I could only trust that they were still wearing their invisible thinking caps. At the dinner table Father continued to debate with Grandmother the events of the day, unaware that she and her daughter, his own wife, were sizing him up for another kind of argument. James confided to us that the discovery of the kerosene can, which Father had immediately featured in one of his columns, seemed to have scared off the firebug. There'd been no suspicious fires in weeks. I kept studying.

By early September I could stand beside the big gray mare, lay my hands on various points of her body, and proudly call out the names of underlying bones and organs and ligaments. The manual had given me an almost magical ability to see right inside her: to see her four-chambered heart, as large as a melon, beating deep in her chest; to count each of her upright vertebrae marching like soldiers along her back; to follow her long latissimus dorsi muscles, "essential for galloping and leaping," behind her shoulders. She was so much more complex than I had ever imagined. Everyone around me was. Who would have guessed that Mother had a spine or that Grandmother had so many layers to her?

On the morning of September 12, which just happened to be my sixteenth birthday, I received a wonderful gift: My bandages came off for the final time. I have to admit that while I'd previously brushed aside Mother's concern for my arms' appearance, that morning a certain nervousness poked my insides. I didn't know where to look. At the doctor's serious face, frowning slightly as he tussled with my frayed bandages. At the tatters themselves, grimy with sweat and fuzzed with horse hair. Or at Mother, her hand covering her mouth at first, then propped under her chin, then smoothing her hair—a restless moth that couldn't alight, more worried than anyone, it seemed.

When the air splashed like cold water against my unprotected skin, the doctor cocked his head and nodded approvingly, and mother's face didn't show too much disappointment, and so I looked too. The scars were only slightly faded from the last time, as I had expected. A webbing the color of dried apple peelings spanned both inner arms and thickened into a deeper, mulberry-colored scar on my left wrist. Extralong sleeves, gloves, powder—one glance showed me what was going through Mother's mind. I guess she couldn't help it. What I saw was that I'd be forever twinned with the Girl. And that didn't bother me one bit.

After the doctor left, I had a late birthday breakfast with Mother and Grandmother, who'd fried up some of her wonderful apple fritters especially for the occasion. Everything felt so new against my exposed skin: the silverware cool and hard, the napkin nubby. At first neither one of them would so much as glance at my hands. They each took such pains to look only at my face, in fact, that it became a game of mine to see how many times I could brush back a stray hair with a scarred hand or wipe my lips while exposing a purplish wrist. Grandmother finally caught on and chuckled behind her napkin, but Mother stirred her tea with doubled concentration.

A knock at the door finally rescued her. She returned to the table carrying a fancy, store-bought package in stripes of pale blue and amethyst. Astonishment showed on her face. "Your father has had this sent over from C. F. Hovey's," she said, setting the package in front of me. "I have no idea what it could be."

I licked the sugar off my fingers. Suspicion tempered my curiosity. It just wasn't like Father to spend money in a store as high-flown as C. F. Hovey's.

"Well, aren't you going to open it?" Grandmother urged.

Still growing accustomed to my newly functioning hands, I carefully unknotted the ribbon, laid it flat on the table, and lifted the lid. Perfume wafted out with the rustling of tissue. I folded back the tissue to reveal a pair of fawn-colored gloves.

Mother pounced. "Oh, Rachel," she gasped, "aren't they beautiful?" She draped one across her arm and stroked it as if it were a kitten. Passing its limp mate to Grandmother, she exclaimed, "Six buttons, do you see that?" Grandmother examined it cursorily, nodded, and returned it, looking across the table at me.

I was schooling myself to hold back a flood of ungenerous emotions. I'd never worn gloves back in Wesleydale and I'd resisted wearing them here, giving in only for church. Father knew that. And now, just as if our nighttime conversation had never taken place, Mother smiled at me and said, "You won't have to worry about your hands showing at all."

I tried to be appreciative. I ran my finger over the row of smooth, lustrous buttons. But it was difficult.

She saw my hesitation. "Your father spent a good sum of money on these," she warned. "You know he'll be angry if you don't wear them."

"I'll wear them," I answered quietly. Grandmother raised an eyebrow.

I wore them that very afternoon, in fact. With those gloves cushioning my hands, I could comfortably grip a pitchfork again and happily began a thorough cleaning of the Girl's stall. James would be glad to be relieved of that duty. And stabbing the soiled

bedding, turning it over and out, was its own therapy. The sweat that trickled down my back felt cleansing.

The Girl was freshly attired as well. New skin, pink as a baby mouse, had finally managed to knit a covering across her face and most of her exposed flesh. Snowy hairs dusted the tender sheathing, though the ridge of her neck, where a mane should have been, was still creased and naked.

As I went poking through the straw around her, she stepped sideways and snorted and shook her head almost playfully. She nibbled at the fork's handle. She bumped her big head against my shoulder, seeking attention. When a gust of wind whistled through the window, filling the carriage shed with the invigorating crispness of coming autumn, she let out a squeal and bucked in place. My heart kicked up a little too, in answer to the call. Time we both got some fresh air.

A week ago, James had brought the Girl's halter and lead from the station for just such a moment as this. I knew I was supposed to wait for his permission, or at least his presence, before handling her, but the Girl's eyes were so bright, so eager, that I couldn't keep her confined another minute.

With my heart thumping a little uneasily, I carefully buckled the halter around her head. Her nickers built in excitement. She started prancing in place and even half-reared, which gave me second thoughts. I was certain I could manage her, though; we had an understanding.

The moment the bar was let down, however, I discovered just how lopsided that understanding was. She charged right through me and over me, knocking me aside with her shoulder and yanking the rope clean out of my hands. Straight toward the street she trotted, her ears pricked, her whinny piercing my ears. Panic-stricken, I gave chase. All sorts of terrible thoughts crashed through my head: She was going to run away. She was going to collide with traffic. She was going to injure herself again. And it was all going to be my fault.

A large dog appeared at the other end of our alley. He didn't bark, but his unexpected presence startled her into a backward spin that allowed me to snatch up the trailing rope. I leaned all my weight against it, but she just went trotting off in the other direction, me the flopping tail to a windblown kite.

I ran as fast as I could to keep up with her. Children stopped their play to watch, and the Girl gave them quite a show. Her knees snapped, her nostrils flared wide. She tossed her head and whinnied again and again. I kept tugging on the rope, reminding her to behave, begging her to listen. Gradually she slowed her prancing just enough that we entered into a sort of dance.

The weather could not have been more agreeable. Clear sunlight spangled the street. Cool air filled our lungs. She snorted it out in brassy blasts, and I let it go in uncontrollable laughter. She trotted in circles, and I ran beside her and leaped along with her, throwing back my head and shouting to her joyous whinnies.

As we made our way down the street, more children came pouring out of the neighboring houses. Everyone seemed to know her; they called out her name as if she were a local hero. And maybe she liked being a legend, because when the squeals of joy crescendoed, she came to a majestic standstill and allowed the children to gather around her and touch her and feed her the treats they'd begged from their mothers. Or maybe she was just hungry for sweets, because she bolted everything from apples and pears to jelly cakes and molasses cookies. And licked each small palm just as neatly as any mother could wipe it.

By the time we returned to the carriage shed, I was as tired as I was restored. I'd tasted freedom again, which made the perfect end to the perfect day. Until James met me there.

I expected him to scold me for taking the Girl out on my own, but he hardly seemed surprised. He asked some idle questions, all the while fiddling with the top button on his shirt. That meant something was bothering him.

"What's wrong?" I asked at last.

"It's a couple of the horses at the station," he answered. He seemed relieved to be talking about it. "Chester and Major John are down in their stalls—been that way for two days now."

My euphoria evaporated at the worrisome news. "What's their condition?"

"No appetite, flanks drawn. Chester's coughing a little. Neither will get up."

"Mr. Stead's seen to them, I'm sure."

"He's come by the last two days, but he's not sure what it is. Says it could be distemper." He nodded toward the Girl. "Has she been all right?"

"Yes," I answered cautiously, sensing where he was headed. "This is the first time she's been out, but I can keep her in if it's that serious."

James tugged so hard on his top button that I thought the threads would break. "I think you should. Mr. Stead told us he's seeing lots of other horses in the city suddenly falling ill."

"Distemper *is* a nasty disease." I knew that well enough from my manual. Still, there was a panicked look in James's eyes that suggested more to the story. "What else is worrying you?"

"You don't understand," he said. "Two of the firehorses at our station are down with it, and I heard there's another one at Station Five and possibly another at Station Eleven. If other firehorses get this . . . if *all* of them get it, all over the city . . . do you know what that could mean?"

A sickness stabbed my stomach. Of course. But before I could say anything, James echoed Father's inflammatory words: "With that firebug still out there, this city's a tinderbox. And without the horses, Rachel, we're all at the mercy of the next fire."

✑✐ TWENTY-TWO

I T COULDN'T BE AS BAD AS ALL THAT. I REFUSED TO BELIEVE
it. After such a wonderful day—and having my bandages off
and with the Girl improving, I just didn't want to think of more
horses getting sick.

I could understand James's distress, though. Chester was
his favorite at the station, a prankish white gelding whom he'd
been teaching tricks. For nearly two months I'd been hearing
how Chester could tuck his nose between his knees and bow
on command, how he could search out carrots hidden around
the station, and how he was "this close" to ringing a hand-
bell as long as you first helped him get it in his teeth. He'd
planned on demonstrating Chester's cleverness some upcoming
morning when the firehorses were brought out for public display. Now, slump-shouldered with despair, James returned to the
station.

To add to the gloom infiltrating our house, Grandmother
fell again and broke her spectacles, and then she came down

with such a headache that she took to her bed. She pulled her faded red quilt up to her chin and crossed her wrinkled hands on her chest and lay so still that sometimes I had to stand in the doorway and hold my own breath to see her breathing.

Only Father seemed immune. He kept up his attacks on city officials in his columns. This week the subject was their utter failure to improve the water mains and hydrants in the burgeoning commercial districts. He even went so far as to order a huge box of matches and a thimble filled with water delivered to each of the area's aldermen, with an accompanying note inquiring, "Which is the greater?" That set off the fireworks, so to speak, and for the next several days he devoured his dinner and his newspapers with the same self-indulgent speed and rushed back to his office to create even more combustible columns. I think we all breathed momentary sighs of relief when the door slammed shut behind him.

But in his absence a melancholy air settled over our house. The stair railing sagged, the floorboards felt sticky, and Mother's new curtains slumped under the weighty task of trying to add cheer to such a dismal abode. One afternoon when I came in after examining the Girl, I found Mother sitting alone in the dining room. She was huddled over a steaming cup of ginger tea, looking especially pinched and pale.

"Oh, there you are," she said. A small stack of coins sat beside her saucer and she slid it toward me, creating a ripple in the tablecloth that she didn't bother to smooth. "I need you to go to the optometrist's shop on Boylston Place—you know the one;

it's beside Dr. Safford's office. Your grandmother's spectacles should be ready."

"How is she?"

"Her head's still throbbing with that awful ache, and it seems to be catching." Mother rubbed small circles into her temples, her eyes shut. "I don't know the optometrist's hours; the store may be closing soon, so you'd better take the horsecar."

I gathered up the coins with a smattering of guilt. I was so thrilled to head back outside on such a splendid day, the first day of autumn, that I would have gladly walked the mile-and-a-half distance. But Mother had said to take the horsecar and, well, where horses were involved, who was I to argue?

Sailing through the afternoon shadows that stretched between the brick row houses, I hurried the five blocks over to the stop. All the while I wondered which "grandfather" horse would be ferrying us along this time. I'd always called them grandfather horses because they invariably wore long whiskers and plodded steadily, deaf to the city's distractions. I imagined them settling into their straw beds at night, recalling youthful exploits, complaining of rheumatism and humming tunes from the war.

When I turned the corner, hoping it might be the kind-faced chestnut with the thinning mane, I found more than a dozen impatient people crowding the stop. The horsecar was nowhere to be seen.

A man with a white beard chewed on his pipe, forcing little blasts of smoke from the edge of his mouth. He paused long enough to fish his watch out of his pocket and, cradling it in one hand and his pipe in the other, grumbled, "It's been over twenty minutes."

"We could have walked half the way there by now," his wife complained. "I'll never get all of my shopping done. Don't they have watches of their own?" She surveyed the bystanders for support. In casting her gaze across me she happened to spot my scarred hands. Her mouth fell open ever so slightly. But in the next instant she caught herself and turned away, squinting over her husband's watch. I self-consciously tucked my hands beneath my crossed arms. For a fleeting second I missed Father's gloves.

Two tall, pale gentlemen standing closer to the street exchanged glances. Inclining his head, the one murmured, "I told you something's wrong with the horses," to which his friend returned a sober nod. The worry that I'd tried shoving aside bared its teeth.

We went on waiting, craning our heads time and again down the street. Under my armpits I had both sets of fingers crossed. More than anybody else, probably, I wanted the horsecar to appear, if only to prove that the horses were all right. None showed. The tracks stretched long and empty into the distance.

Muttering an oath, one agitated man with a hawkish bent to him adjusted the overcoat he'd draped over his arm and strode away. That's all it took, and in twos and threes and singly the rest of us, including me, began following in his wake. James's awful news clawed through me like a fever. I scanned the cross streets as we proceeded, hoping to prove him and those two men wrong. But everywhere I looked I sensed a change. It was almost undetectable, like a tide having receded a little ways down the shore when you were busy gathering shells. Eventually I had to admit it was because there were fewer horses than usual clip-clopping along the streets.

A horsecar finally came rumbling along the tracks, but it was loaded almost beyond the poor horse's ability. So many people hung from the leather straps, swaying like smoked hams, that you couldn't even see those that were seated, so of course none of us could get on and we kept walking.

The pavements in Boston had always been crowded, but as we neared the Common, people actually began elbowing others onto the street. A thick-waisted woman clutching the wrists of two children shoved past me so hard I was spun into the path of four surveyors and their arsenal of rolled plans and sharp-edged clipboards. Unfamiliar hands set me right and on my way.

With its rolling carpets of lush green, the Common appeared more than ever as an oasis, a reward for negotiating the city's brick maze. I stowed away my worries long enough to admire its splendor. Golden sunlight slanted between the black arms of bejeweled trees. A playful wind caught up the burgundy and yellow and splotched-orange leaves and swirled them across the carpet like paper fancies. Crows bobbed and called. Squirrels dashed in a game of tag. Only the deer were beyond resuscitation. Inside their meshed cage, they flicked their white tails anxiously and raised their noses to the air, sniffing for something only dimly remembered.

Aware that the afternoon was waning, I hurried on to the optometrist's shop. Grandmother's spectacles were ready, and in minutes I was back outside. Only then did I realize that those horrid, clunky shoes of mine had once again dug painful blisters into my ankles. The walk home was going to be torturous unless the horsecar headed out was less crowded.

The crescendoing clatter of a reckless trot tore through my pondering. It erupted in an awful scrambling—and then a loud crash. People began running toward the Public Garden and I ran with them.

A crowd already ringed the scene. I caught a glimpse of a dark brown horse stretched flat amid a tangle of harness and an overturned buggy. My heart squeezed. Someone shoved in front of me to bob up and down with curiosity, and so I had to search for another view. Sidestepping behind a wall of shoulders, I twisted between jostled packages and pointy elbows and stood on tiptoe myself. At last I could see the driver, staggering, holding a hand to his blood-streaked face. I couldn't see if there was blood on the horse. Was he dead? A young man had left the crowd to straddle the horse's head. "Hurry now!" he shouted to the driver. "Unbuckle the check." But the man was either too dazed or too stupid to help. Others leaped in, and soon there was such a pile of people atop the poor horse that if he wasn't dead already, he certainly risked suffocation.

A burly man in an overcoat reeking of fish guts moved in

front of me, and suddenly I couldn't see a thing again except
his greasy collar and the fringe of untrimmed hair below his hat.
A terrible thwacking sound accompanied a panicked whinny.
The crowd gasped in unison. What was happening to the horse?
Spotting a streetlamp, I grabbed hold of its iron pole and pulled
myself onto the base. A sea of heads and hats rippled around me,
parting at the fallen horse. To my immense surprise Mr. Stead
was kneeling beside the prostrate animal. I couldn't hear what
he was saying over the crowd's din, but I recognized that, in his
calm, confident manner, he'd taken charge of the situation. He
pointed to this person and that one, and buckles were unfastened
in an orderly fashion and the buggy slid away and righted. All
the while he kept a hand flat on the horse's neck, soothing the
convulsive trembling. At least the poor thing was still alive.

Something, I don't know what, made Mr. Stead look up
and drift his gaze across the crowd. As he did so, he caught
sight of me. To my surprise, he smiled and nodded a greeting
before returning to his work. My face flushed warm. A heady
feeling raced through me, the kind you get when bobbing to the
surface of a cold pond or swinging into the sky on the jerking
end of a rope.

When enough of the harness was unfastened, Mr. Stead
rose and ordered the young man to release the horse's head.
Immediately the dark gelding began flailing like some giant
black water bug trapped on its back. As he searched for a hold,
his iron-shod hooves scraped the cobblestones in a frantic staccato. Eventually he got his front end up but then, gasping like a

half-drowned creature, he sank back, his hindquarters still twisted
uselessly on the ground. Sweat slicked his coat. Violent tremors
shook his body. Mr. Stead slapped the horse's flank, urging him
to try again. The gelding swayed, obviously in a state of shock
and exhaustion, but mustered his strength. Grunting with the
effort, he lunged forward. One hind leg found footing beneath
his massive body, and the other one joined in, and together they
pushed him off the street.

Onlookers applauded, relief on their faces. The horse,
on the other hand, a finely bred gelding as dark as polished
mahogany, looked completely emptied. He whinnied anxiously,
and somewhere down the street an unseen horse whinnied understanding. I longed to throw my arms around him and stroke his
neck and tell him everything was going to be all right.

Mr. Stead began helping the same young man refit the
harness, and together they drew the buggy forward. Its folding
canopy tilted and sagged like a sprung umbrella, and the men
had to force it into place. With the crowd thinning, I was able
to hear some of their conversation.

"Have you got it on that side?"

"Almost, just give me a . . . there, that's it."

The driver, meanwhile, was retrieving fallen packages
from the street's windblown debris. He dumped a couple into the
buggy with such a careless clatter that the gelding startled and
leaped forward. Mr. Stead grabbed the reins.

Turning to pick up another package, the driver said irritably,
"I owe you my thanks, I suppose. That blasted animal intended

on lying there the livelong day." It took every ounce of Mother's training for me not to race over and kick him in the shins.

Mr. Stead didn't acknowledge the man's callous words. He was carefully running a hand down each of the horse's shivering legs, murmuring reassurances. When he'd worked his way back to the top, he cupped the horse's jowl in his hand and gazed into the animal's eye. That relaxed the gelding enough that he tried nibbling the brim of Mr. Stead's black bowler hat.

"I'm behind schedule," the driver said, leaping into the buggy and reclaiming his whip, "so if you don't mind?"

Mr. Stead closed his fist on the reins. "I do mind. And I'd advise you to take this horse more slowly until he gets his confidence back." The driver waved away the advice but found the veterinary not as easily dismissed. "He has some bad scrapes the length of his near hip and on his hock, and a nasty cut below this fetlock here." He indicated it with the toe of his boot. "They'll need warm bandages tonight. You'll see to that?"

A silent stare-down ensued. When the driver realized he wasn't going anywhere until he agreed, he said, "Yes, yes, of course. I'll have someone see to it. Now, if you don't mind?" He wriggled like a spoiled child and tugged on the reins. This time Mr. Stead released them. Without even looking for an opening, the man yanked the gelding into traffic, brandished his whip, and went rattling away at a wobbly trot.

Shaking his head, Mr. Stead picked up his satchel and came walking straight toward me. Nonsensically, I froze against the lamp. That put us eye to eye.

"Have you ever seen such reckless driving on a city street?" he asked. "And they'll upend themselves again, no doubt—more's the pity for that nice gelding." Doffing his hat and cocking a sideways smile at my unusual position, he said, "How are you, Miss Selby?"

"Fine," I replied, though the scrolled metalwork was carving into my ribs. "Thank you."

"Good." His single glance at my hands made me want to hide them away again. But there they were, for all the world to see. I expected him to comment; the thought formed on his face, I saw it. Instead he asked, "How's our mare doing today?"

And that one little word "our" gave me another bubbling chill. "I've led her out," I told him. "She trotted as sound as ever and even bucked some. I think she's feeling much better."

He looked impressed. "You took her out all by yourself? She can be quite a handful, you know, even for the men at the station."

"I know," I said, giddy with pride. "We get along splendidly."

I needed to move off the lamp base; the situation bordered on lunacy. Yet I was so eager to sustain the conversation that I clung to that pole as tightly as one of Mother's climbing ivies.

Mr. Stead cleared his throat and shoved his free hand into his pocket. His face lit. "Would you care for a peppermint?"

"Yes," I answered, and decided that was reason enough to hop down. "Thank you."

Another awkward silence ensued as we each rolled the

hard candies in our mouths, clacking them against our teeth, spinning them with our tongues. I watched two boys flinging leaves off the bridge in the Public Garden. I breathed in the smells of marigolds and roasted meats and chimney smoke, all cleansed by the bite of peppermint. As a chill gust of September wind parted around us, I realized the shelter Mr. Stead provided and felt newly warmed.

"I believe I owe you an apology," he began abruptly, "for not . . . well, you see, some of my clients warned that I . . . oh, it's this distemper business as much as anything. It's spreading like smallpox. Everyone has sick horses, it seems." He crunched his candy into nothing and swallowed. "In fact, I'm on my way over to McLaughlin's Livery, where I keep Balder, to see some more right now. I'll be driving on to the fire station near your house afterward and"—he dropped his gaze to his boots and I found myself admiring his sandy-colored eyelashes and the sprinkling of freckles across his eyelids—"and I'd be pleased . . . um . . . to offer you a ride home."

Now *this* could be a day to end all days! "Well, yes, thank you," I sputtered. "I'd like that." And just as easily as that, we headed back up Boylston and past the public library. If there had been storm clouds on that last occasion at our house nearly three months ago, they were gone now. I couldn't be happier walking at his side.

"Are you still reading that manual of yours?"

"Almost finished," I answered.

I expected a look of surprise or maybe a small compliment,

but he walked on without saying anything. The man could be maddeningly close-mouthed. We turned up Tremont Street.

"Your father is certainly making a name for himself with his columns," he said. "I hear everyone talking about them."

Oh, so that was it. I hadn't received Father's permission yet, and he was holding it against me. "Yes, he does like the front page."

"He seems to keep long hours. Just last Wednesday evening I was seeing to a horse over on Atlantic—a case of bog spavin—and as chance would have it, a fire broke out in one of the warehouses, and there he was, already on the scene, furiously scribbling notes."

As chance would have it? At once I could smell the smoke that always seemed to cling to Father like an invisible cloud, and a cold wave of suspicion rolled over me. "Yes," I replied with an involuntary shiver, "he does work hard."

A stamped metal horse head advertised the location of McLaughlin's Livery, though a cloud of blackflies did the same. As we approached its cavernous entry, Mr. Stead stiffened slightly. He seemed to be having second thoughts, and his hand tightened on my arm. "Stay close," he murmured. Day became night as we stepped into the murky stable.

"Ah, the veterinary! Here at last!" An elfin liveryman hobbled from his office to clasp Mr. Stead's hand. His legs bowed wide in parentheses, reserving the space for a missing horse. "My thanks for coming. It's gone from bad to worse for us here. Say, do you want Balder harnessed?"

"Yes, if you will. I have more calls."

The man motioned to a rail-thin stableboy, who hurried away. "And who is *this* angel at your side?" His leer was softened just enough by his grandfatherly age to keep me from bolting. "She's a welcome sight."

"Mr. McLaughlin, allow me to introduce Miss Rachel Selby. I've offered her a ride home—to see to her horse," he added quickly. "She has a wonderful way with them."

I cringed as Mr. McLaughlin examined me as critically as he would an animal up for auction. "Does she now?" he replied. "My granddaughter does too." Maybe I'd pegged him all wrong. "I think the horses come to appreciate a female hand. They're not so dumb as to turn away from a soft pat when they're more used to the whip, eh?" His metallic blue eyes glinted. "Some of my drivers could probably learn a thing or two from you, miss."

"Well, maybe not. I've . . . never actually driven a horse. I'd like to learn, though."

He and Mr. Stead exchanged raised eyebrows and I winced. Too bold.

"Well, we'll just have to see about that now, won't we?" Switching to the subject at hand, he gestured for us to follow. "The first one's this way."

The enormous livery was more like a cave than a barn, and the deeper we traveled into it, the heavier the air became. It was practically dripping with the dank odors of ammonia and manure and mildewed leather. Yet for all its lack of light, the stable was bustling. Horses rattled their tie rings and stamped and nickered. Boys whistled as they mucked stalls, their sidelong glances marking our passage. Others scurried here and there, shouting orders and filling them. Squeaking carriages were rolled out to the vast, planked center of the barn, where horses were led singly or in pairs to have harnesses slapped across their broad backs.

As we passed one of the carriage rooms, I marveled at the beautiful vehicles stored there: oil-black coupés sporting curved glass fronts, emerald-green rockaways accented by carmine or violet seats, a charming basket phaeton awaiting next summer's country excursions. The room even held an ominous-looking hearse, somberly painted in black and silver and ornamented with dusty, drooping plumes. Even without a casket inside, the sight gave me gooseflesh.

"Bartley!" Mr. McLaughlin hollered down one long aisle. "Bring up Firecracker." A smoke-colored cat trotted across his path just then, dangling a limp rodent from her mouth, and in the same breath, though more kindly, he said, "That's a good puss."

During the wait Mr. Stead opened his satchel and donned his apron. The stableboy finally returned from the livery's dark recesses, dragging behind him a lethargic dappled horse who could barely stagger. When the animal caught a hoof on a loose plank and tripped, he very nearly pitched onto his nose. That set off a series of explosive coughs.

"How long has he been like this?" Mr. Stead asked the livery owner.

"About a week."

The man received an exasperated look.

"I know, I know. I should've had you look at him sooner. But there's near three hundred horses here. I can't pay for a veterinary every time one gets a snotty nose." The smallish man tried a defiant glare, but it was shot through with guilt.

Laying an ear to the horse's throat, Mr. Stead asked, "What have you been doing for him in the meantime?"

"I had the boys drench him with some Epsom salts and I've upped his ration, but he's not eating any of it." The man glanced meekly at me and tested a smile.

Mr. Stead examined the horse's crusted nostrils. He felt for heat in the ears and ran his hands down the legs, frowning all the while, then laid his own ear against the horse's throat again. Finally he straightened. "Well, I don't think it's pneumonia—yet. But he's got the distemper for sure."

Mr. McLaughlin groaned.

"How many more like him?"

"Five."

Mr. Stead cocked his head, questioning.

"Well, five for sure. Maybe another ten or twelve on their way."

"That's only the beginning, I assure you."

Poor Firecracker could hardly breathe. Braced on splayed legs, he drooped his head nearly to the floor. Each strangled gasp required a spasmodic wrenching of his neck. Mr. Stead pulled some bottles from his satchel.

"How much is this going to cost me?"

Mr. Stead glanced over his shoulder reprovingly. "My normal charge is fifty cents a horse, but if you don't have it, you can take an equal amount off Balder's bill."

The liveryman nodded, though he didn't agree to anything.

One by one, half-dead horses were dragged to the spot to have a black, oily liquid forced down their throats. They didn't have the strength to struggle and stumbled back to their stalls just as spiritlessly. When Mr. McLaughlin called out for Buddy to be brought up, however, the stableboy returned empty-handed, as pale as if he'd witnessed a ghost.

"He's dead, sir," he told the man. "Dead, right in his stall—stiff as a board."

A crushing sorrow gripped me. Every bone in my body ached to do something to help, but I was ordered to stay in my place while the men went to examine poor Buddy's remains. They returned somberly, the liveryman looking all the more shamed.

"It's not your fault," Mr. Stead reassured him. "This distemper is a nasty piece of work. But move the others up closer to the front of the barn, if you can. They need the fresh air. And try scrubbing their stalls and mangers with a strong decoction of tobacco. That will help keep the disease from spreading."

Mr. McLaughlin nodded humbly as we climbed into the waiting buggy. "Thank you. I'll do it right off, that I will. And Balder'll be getting extra rations this week—on the house."

As if he understood, the bay gelding whinnied exuberantly. It was the only happy note in an otherwise gloomy place, and we drove away in silence.

༄ TWENTY-THREE

WHEN WE WERE OUT OF SIGHT OF THE LIVERY, MR. STEAD pulled Balder to a stop, dropped the reins, and unexpectedly buried his head in his hands. I didn't know what to do. Tentatively, I touched his shoulder.

"They say you get used to losing them," he finally mumbled between his fingers. "But I haven't yet. I still feel like I'm leaving a funeral every time, carrying the shovel in my own two hands." His shoulders rose and fell beneath my hand. Sucking in a deep breath, he straightened. He gathered the reins, pointedly looked away from me, and laughed bitterly. "Now, you don't really want to be a veterinary, do you, after what you just saw?"

What I'd just seen made me more certain than ever. "Absolutely."

The hazel eyes he turned on me lingered so unblinkingly that I shivered again. I got the sense that he was trying to decide something about me, just as the Girl had done. Composing myself, I gazed back just as unblinkingly. Slowly, gradually, a smile lit his face. "Then I suppose you'll need to learn how to drive, won't you?" And before I could open my mouth, the reins were draped across my lap.

My heart bucked. Impulsively I caressed the leather, but . . . what if Balder ran away with us?

"Anytime before dark would be satisfactory."

I laughed nervously. Surely it couldn't be any more difficult or dangerous than jumping Peaches over Mr. Jude's big gate, so I scooped up the reins. They were surprisingly light, and just as alive with messages as telegraph wires. Every movement Balder made was instantly relayed to me. He chewed the bit and the reins danced between my fingers. He stretched his neck and the reins began slipping through my hands. Instinctively I made fists. Balder flicked an ear, confused, then shifted his weight. The buggy began rolling backward. Swallowing a gasp, I looked to Mr. Stead for help.

"Whoa," he said firmly and the gelding came to an obedient halt. Reaching over, he adjusted the tension on each long rein and sat back. "That's it. Keep your hands lifted. Now, give a steady pull on your left rein—not too much. And cluck to him too. That's it. Good girl."

By following his directions, we were soon rolling forward. Late afternoon dusk was settling over the city, and I thanked the Lord for the dim light and the cool air, because my cheeks were burning hot. Driving a horse, rather than riding him, felt like trying to work a long-stringed marionette when you were more used to placing your hand right inside the puppet. Where I might have folded a knuckle on one of Peaches' reins, here I felt as if I had to swing my whole arm.

"That's too much," Mr. Stead corrected. Gently he guided my elbow back into place. "The movement is in the wrists."

That made it clearer. Refining my signals, I kept tugging and releasing. Balder, unaccustomed to my cues, swayed like a drunkard, first in one direction and then the other.

"A little tighter. Your right wheel is almost off the street."

I pulled hard. Balder's head jerked up and we came to a rattling stop. The buggy's wheel made an ominous scraping sound before dropping off the cobblestones with a thud. A gasp escaped me.

"That's all right," Mr. Stead soothed. "You're doing fine." I noticed that he used the same measured monotone he did with nervous horses. "Just give him some slack. Now cluck to him again." It was working. Although my heart still beat doubly fast, my hands shook less. I took a deep breath, let out some rein, and clucked. Balder dropped his head and leaned into the harness. With a lurch, the buggy regained the street. I clucked again and we proceeded in our weird, meandering way.

"You *can* look around."

I didn't take my eyes off Balder's ears. "*You* look around, I'm driving," I answered with exaggerated seriousness. Mr. Stead chuckled.

When we reached the end of the street, I pulled back on the reins and Balder came to a stop. There was more traffic here—people were hurrying to get home before dark—and I waited a long time to find the right moment to plunge into it. Balder shook his head impatiently. The imp even looked over his shoulder at me. Finally, taking the bit in his teeth, he started his way into the chaos, expertly negotiating the opposite paths of a plodding coal wagon and a speeding hack. I sat up tall, feigning control. Whether anyone could tell the difference, I didn't know. The coal man, for one, continued whistling to himself. The driver of the hack was gone in a flash.

Crackling leaves and bits of litter, scattered by late-September gusts, swirled beneath hooves and wheels. Other vehicles hurried past, but we crept along at a walk, keeping to the very edge of the street. The reins felt quite comfortable in my hands now; in fact, I didn't want to give them up. I liked being able to direct our travels.

"How did you come across the name Balder?" I asked.

"Balder the Beautiful? He's a character from Norse mythology. Apparently he owned a horse who broke a leg. By tying a knotted black thread around the fracture and reciting a charm, he cured him. Let's see if I remember how it goes. 'Balder rade' (that means 'rode'), 'his colt slade' (that means 'slipped'). 'He lighted and he righted, set joint to joint and bone to bone. Heal in Odin's name.'" Smiling, he said, "In a way, Balder was the world's first veterinary."

That made me think about his work in the livery. "Aren't you worried about keeping Balder with all those sick horses?"

To my surprise, he chuckled. "Balder? He's built of bricks. Besides, you'll no doubt recall from your manual that if a horse survives distemper he can't get it again. Balder had it when he was a yearling."

The distance to my house was all too short, and well before I was ready, I had to pull Balder to a final halt. He stopped on a dime and Mr. Stead, misplacing the credit, nodded approvingly. "A fine job. I should hire you as my private driver."

I swelled with pride and glanced toward the parlor window to see if Mother or Grandmother was watching. The lamp shone yellow behind the new glass. But silhouetted above it was Father's glowering face.

Mr. Stead didn't see him. "I'll just wait here for you to help me down," he joked until, noticing my stricken look, he turned toward the house.

Reluctantly I handed him the reins. He wrapped them around the whip post and hurriedly climbed out of the buggy to help me down with the utmost propriety. Father came out of the house to meet us at the bottom of the stairs. Extending his hand, he said, "Mr. Stead, isn't it? The veterinary?"

"Yes, sir. How are you this evening, Mr. Selby?"

"Fine. Just fine. Lovely autumn weather, isn't it?" A particularly chilling gust of wind raked the street, but Father stood by his words. He waited, rocking back and forth slightly, enjoying our discomfort. "Are you here to attend to that horse in my stable . . . or to something else?"

My face burned like a flame was being held to it.

"Oh, she's made remarkable progress, sir," Mr. Stead replied. "The Girl, I mean. The Governor's Girl."

"Yes . . . well then, I'll have my son, James, return her to the fire station and to her duties."

My heart plummeted. *No!*

"Begging your pardon, she's better off here for the meanwhile. You see, there's this nasty business of distemper—"

"I'd heard that," Father interrupted. His newspaperman's instincts for a story were aroused. "Is that why a man can't get a horsecar these days?"

"Well, yes, and—"

"And a lot of the other workhorses around the city are absent with it?"

"Yes, but—"

"And"—he was just like a cat, I thought, a smug one that toys overlong with a mouse before whomping it flat with a decisive paw—"and you don't want that burned horse back at the fire station because this distemper's flared up there. Is that true?"

"Yes, I suppose it is," Mr. Stead answered innocently.

Oh, no.

"Wait until the populace learns about this!" Father crowed. "Take me over there. Now."

Mr. Stead didn't know what to say. He glanced toward me, but I was no help: Father was already brushing past us and climbing right into the buggy. His brash behavior came as no surprise. What did put me on my toes, however, was the sharp odor of kerosene on his clothes. That made my mind spin wildly.

With guarded generosity, Mr. Stead climbed into the buggy as well and unwrapped the reins. Just as they started to drive away, though, the fire alarm jangled. Balder was pulled to the side of the street and, out of habit, we all paused to listen for the response. Around the corner and down the street, men could be heard shouting orders. The dalmatian was barking, as were other dogs in the neighborhood, but there was no clatter of hooves. We looked at one another in wonderment and waited.

Time took a strange turn and everyone sensed it. Up and down the street people came to a stop and waited. They ceased their sweeping, their chatting, their hurrying. They cocked their heads and listened for the reassuring response of the horses galloping forth to quench yet another upstart fire. But it didn't happen.

At long last, hooves were heard and three horses did round the corner. But at the sight of them my hand flew to my mouth: These creatures were mere ghosts! Although they were the engine team, chosen for their combined strength and speed, this trio was struggling to go at a shaky trot. While the steam engine hissed menacingly, the horses stumbled, coughed, and gamely struggled forward. A whitish phlegm seeped from their nostrils. I looked past them. No hose cart, no ladder wagon.

"Oh, that's murderous!" Mr. Stead protested. "Those horses are sick. They shouldn't be made to work!"

"Let's follow them," Father urged.

Out of the dusk, James came running up the street, easily besting the sickly animals dragging the engine. He gasped for breath. "It's your newspaper building," he called to Father. "It's on fire!"

Time took another strange turn and, again, everything happened too slowly. I watched Father cock an apparently interested ear to James's words. He digested them with a composed face. And then, as if his cue had been whispered to him offstage, he suddenly responded, "It is? No, it can't be." Leaning forward on the edge of his seat, he motioned to Mr. Stead. "Hurry!" he shouted. "You have to drive me there. I have to save my newspaper."

⁓ TWENTY-FOUR

THE WORDS KEPT RINGING IN MY EARS: "THEY SHALL hunger no more, neither thirst anymore; the sun shall not strike them, nor any scorching heat."

It was the reverend's graveside farewell to the two young men killed in the newspaper building fire. They were brothers, valiantly trying to carry out the trays of type when a wall collapsed on them. Father called them heroes. A sickening feeling inside me moaned that they were sacrifices.

A fretful wind swirled leaves around our feet. Grandmother coughed and leaned more heavily on my arm. Ironically, the widow's weeds she'd worn ever since Grandfather passed away were finally appropriate. As the reverend droned on, bandaging the few mourners with his Scriptures, she stared into the two holes with such a wistful gaze that I worried she was going to leap in before the caskets were lowered.

I sneaked a glance at Father. He was standing a little apart from the circle, an equal distance from his surviving employees and their families and from Mother and the rest of us. A journalist might describe him as pensive, but he didn't seem sad.

Maybe that was my own misinterpretation, based solely on something I'd overheard last night. It was late and I was on my way to bed after checking on the Girl one more time. I was so worried she'd somehow catch the distemper that was spreading like wildfire that I'd gone out to see her between each one of my chores. A basket with my neatly folded laundry sat at the bottom of my stairs, and as I bent to pick it up, I heard Father and Mother talking in their bedroom. Their words were as starched as the laundry, the pauses between them heavy with meaning. I didn't want to listen, and yet I did.

Mother was opening and closing the dresser drawers, putting away their laundry. "I found a large stain of kerosene on your gray trousers," she said matter-of-factly.

With knee-jerk speed, Father had replied, "I spilled some when I was refilling a lamp."

There was a pause.

"It was a lot of kerosene," Mother said.

"I spilled a lot."

Another, longer pause.

"Yes, you did."

A blue jay shrieked from a tree limb right above my head, scolding me back to the service. "Yea, Lord God, the Almighty," the reverend beseeched before setting off on another long verse.

A pair of squirrels, unmindful of the solemnity in their midst, came dashing around and between the weathered headstones, across the twin piles of fresh dirt, and over by the two black horses waiting patiently in front of their hearses. I was sure that the nearer vehicle was the one I'd seen at the livery, only the black plumes had been freshened and the silver polished to a gleam.

The two horses stood as still as stone, with their heads slightly bowed. It occurred to me that the reverend's words could just as easily mark the passing of the brave firehorses. Only this morning James told me that Chester and Major John, who had risen to their feet to pull the steam engine one last time, were dead. The third horse, the gray gelding who had replaced the Girl, was down in his stall.

"It's as quiet as midnight inside the station," he'd said. And the men, not normally of a religious bent, were muttering uneasy prayers that no more fires start before they could get some healthy horses brought in and properly trained.

I cast an eye over the street running beside the cemetery. The fire station was not alone in its silence. With so many horses absent from the streets, a funereal pall had settled over the entire city. I'd heard it rumored that four thousand horses had died already. My stomach ached every time I heard someone talk about it; but it was all anyone could talk about, because the horses' services affected everyone's lives. Without healthy horses to pull the wagons, stores couldn't get their merchandise, and goods were piling up at the wharves and railway stations, and clogging warehouses and alleyways. Without healthy horses, homes couldn't get their regular deliveries of milk and ice and coal.

Yesterday, a man with a weasel's face came hollering his way down our street, prodding a team of oxen ahead of him. Oxen! He had coal for sale, but at triple the usual price. Mother told him she'd go without a fire in the stove before she'd kneel to such blatant extortion, and Grandmother had shouted after him that he was a miserable sinner on his way to meet the devil. He'd only let out a brassy, gap-toothed laugh and called back that he'd made enough money off this horse sickness to buy out the devil himself.

Having stood so long in the cemetery, I began to shiver. Grandmother squeezed my arm. Almost overnight, the air had turned frosty. A gust of wind riffled the drying leaves, making them rustle and quaver, turning them inside out so that they flickered orange and yellow. *Just like flames,* I thought, and shivered again. When would the next fire start? I wondered. More important, who would fight it?

For the next seven days Father had the excuse of resuscitating his newspaper to miss our evening meals, but on the following Monday he arrived home early. He was bursting with pride that the *Argus* hadn't missed a single edition all week—even with the fire—and allowed himself a small beer to celebrate. While Mother rummaged through the cellar, he stood at the top of the stairs and explained to her again how he'd rented office space in a neighboring building and made arrangements to borrow the presses of another newspaper, a morning one. Then, as Mother and I carried the small plates and saucers of pickled and preserved foods to the table—foods that didn't require ice—

Father took his place at its head, still talking. James rushed in through the back door just before we sat down, stirring the air with the intoxicating aromas of harness oil and fresh straw. He made a face at our meager spread: pickled beans and asparagus, applesauce, hard-boiled eggs, and bread. Mother added a bowl of dusty dates to the table. Grandmother remained in her room with another sick headache.

"We've struck a spark tonight," Father stated happily as soon as we finished saying grace and before the first plate was passed. He leaned back, beaming.

"How is that?" Mother responded politely. She was trying hard not to look at the half-empty glass of beer in front of him and therefore drawing all the more attention to it.

"This horse sickness, this distemper. It's wider spread than anyone thinks, which makes for a wonderful column. Listen to what I have to say in this evening's edition." With a great show of snapping the paper to attention, Father began reading select passages from his column.

"'Further illustrating the fact that this city is teetering on the brink of a fiery disaster, this newspaper has uncovered a terrible secret. That secret relates to the sickness invading Boston's working horse population. The presence of this disease will come as no surprise to those of you with blisters on your feet, as the dearth of horsecars has made walking the new fashion.'"

Grandmother surprised us by lumbering wordlessly into the room as he read. She looked mothy white and tired. Muttering something akin to an apology, she pulled out her chair with a reckless scrape and plopped into it. Father looked momentarily irritated, but once he had our attention again, recovered.

"Now," he told us, "here's the meat of the article. By the way, Mrs. Selby, that's something we could use a little more of here."

"There's no meat for the icebox because there's no ice for the icebox," Mother explained. "We're having to make do."

"Yes, well," he grumbled, "that's going to have to change. Now," he snapped the paper again and read on, "'What the general populace may be surprised to learn is that this horse disease has crept into the city's own fire stations, and while we don't wish to alarm you unnecessarily . . .'"

Grandmother snorted.

"'. . . we feel it only right to inform you that most, if not all, of Boston's firehorses are currently lying dead or dying in their stalls.'"

My stomach flipped. I laid my fork across my plate.

"It goes on here," he said, "with some facts and figures that my men assembled. Seems this sickness goes from Boston all the way to New York and back. And," he scanned further, "they're estimating that as many as thirty thousand animals will be afflicted before we're through with this business."

Nausea scratched a finger up my throat.

"Let's see . . . here it is: 'Our valued readers are urgently warned that the horses may not be the only victims of this disease. While its stealth cannot take human lives directly, one careless spark—and one alarm gone unanswered—will certainly result in the loss of property, of valuables and—quite likely—of human life itself.

"'As we have stated before, the city of Boston is ill-prepared to defend itself against any major fire. Our situation has only become more dire now that the firehorses are dead. And so, dear readers, the stage is set. We, like you, await the play with bated breath and hope the third act isn't a fiery finale.'"

He looked over his newspaper, grinning smugly. "How do you like that? That will have them talking, I tell you."

Them, maybe, but not us. No one said a word.

"Come now. James, what do you think?" He held his knife in midair.

"I think Captain Gilmore will have my head on a platter," James replied. "He didn't want anyone to know about the sick firehorses, and he'll think I told you."

"Nonsense." Father dismissed James's concern with a brandish of his knife. "The health of the firehorses is a topic for public knowledge. It must be. We depend on them too much not to be made aware of their illness. Besides, it was Captain Gilmore's own veterinary, Mr. Stead, who informed me."

Though he'd done so innocently.

"And as long as we're on *that* topic . . . Mrs. Selby, are you aware that your daughter has been accompanying this Mr. Stead all over the city?" He didn't so much as glance in my direction while he spoke. I watched his eyelids flutter behind his spectacles like trapped butterflies. "I have it on good authority that he's taken her inside liveries, and you know the sorts of scoundrels one finds there. It's not seemly by any means, and it's liable to harm my reputation, so from now on please confine her to this house unless she's in your company."

That jolted me into speech. "You can't do that!"

He calmly transferred some asparagus to his plate, ignoring me completely. "Pass the salt, please," he said to James. "Honestly, Mrs. Selby, you have to put some meat on this table. Do you hear me? A man can't sustain himself on these weeds."

Mother folded her napkin and laid it on the table. She pushed back her chair and stood. "Do you hear *yourself*, Mr. Selby?"

"What? What is this? Sit down."

"I am not a dog, Mr. Selby, to be ordered to speak or stay quiet at your command. Nor is your daughter. Her mind is every bit as capable as yours, and you must stop dismissing her as if she didn't exist."

Mother was surprising me again, surprising us all. With Grandmother murmuring a mutinous "Amen," Father looked as if someone had thrown a bucket of cold water in his face. His mouth opened and closed, but for an instant, no words came out.

He leaned toward James, rolling his eyes exaggeratedly. "They've all taken leave of their senses," he whispered in a loud, conspiratorial voice that was meant to be heard. "Yes, the Selby women have gone mad. Berserk. They've—"

Grandmother lunged to her feet, jostling the table. "*I'm* not a Selby," she proclaimed, "but I've spent enough time with this family to understand who has their senses and who wouldn't recognize good sense if it bit him in the leg. If you'd ask your daughter why she's accompanying the veterinary, you'd learn it's because she wants to *become* a veterinary."

"Ridiculous!" Father thundered. "She's a girl. Girls don't become veterinaries."

"Why not?" I demanded, rising to my feet as well. I braced my calves against the chair to keep from shaking.

Behind his spectacles, his eyes narrowed. On the table, his fingers closed into a fist. "Well, for one thing," he said, "you can't even light a lamp without trying to burn down my house."

"Mr. Selby, that's—"

"Good Lord, I don't—"

My chair flew backward, hitting the floor with a horrific clatter and silencing both Mother and Grandmother. "That's not fair and you know it!"

"But it's true, isn't it? It's a *fact*." How could anyone look at his own daughter with such cold disfavor?

My fingers clenched into fists. But rash emotion wasn't going to help anything. Father was like a vicious horse, a thoroughly stubborn one, and you had to hold your temper with them. You had to hold your temper and you had to hold your ground, too, or they'd trample you. I sucked in a deep breath. "I *can* light a lamp," I said evenly, "and I have, countless times—you know that. And I can wash and iron and put up peaches and weave mats for the table." I took another deep, calming breath. "I can also write letters—good letters. In fact, I've written a letter to the Boston College of Veterinary Medicine and Surgery inquiring about enrollment. I'm certain they've received it by now."

"Well, if they're idiots enough to accept you," he retorted, "you'll not be attending at any rate. Educating a girl is a waste of my hard-earned money. I might as well educate that horse of yours."

He was striking at me but I wasn't backing down. "Then I'll find the money elsewhere. I'm going to be a veterinary, Father." There. Finally I'd said it to him. Mother and Grandmother had paved the way, but I'd finally stood up to Father.

"Not while you're living under my roof, you aren't."

I swallowed. "Then I'll live elsewhere."

"Fine!" Whisking his napkin from his lap, Father tossed it on the table. "I don't have to suffer this insolence," he shouted. "I'll go where I'm welcome—somewhere where they serve men decent food." Scowling like a madman, he bolted from his chair, stormed through the parlor, and left the house with a thunderous bang of the front door.

James slid a bemused look across our faces, ending at mine. "I think the stall in the carriage shed will sleep two."

"Oh, James," Mother said as she dropped into her seat. "Your sister can keep her own bed. Mr. Selby just needs time to grow accustomed to the idea."

"How much time do you have?" he teased. "Rachel's not getting any younger."

She squared her thin shoulders. "Well, the Bible tells us

there's a time to keep silence and a time to speak. And whether Mr. Selby likes it or not, I believe it was time to speak." Her words were brave enough, but her fingers smoothed the linen with white-knuckled intensity.

"It certainly was," Grandmother agreed, having already lowered herself into her chair. "And since it also tells us there's a time to plant and a time to pluck up what was planted, I believe I'll have some more of these weeds." She stabbed a pair of the pickled asparagus spears, and we all resumed eating in an uncomfortable silence.

TWENTY-FIVE ❧

HE BATTLE LINES HAD BEEN DRAWN WITHIN OUR HOUSE
and I, for one, fully expected Father to have my trunk
carried out to the street the very next day. But to my utter
surprise and some suspicion, Father didn't even mention our
argument or my supposed quarantine. He just went on ignoring
me as he had since we'd moved to Boston. Then it occurred to
me that he considered himself victorious. He'd forbidden me to
become a veterinary and, well, I hadn't become one, had I? That
rankled me no end, and I longed for the day when I could wave
that acceptance letter under his nose.

Oblivious to my resolve, Father rode off to another battle.
He'd recently pulled his attention from Boston's firefighting
abilities, or lack thereof, and had thrown it into supporting the
reelection of President Grant. Shoving aside public accusations of
a dishonest administration, he wrote that he'd rather see a cor-
rupt U. S. Grant in office than that "lily-livered socialist lunatic"
Mr. Horace Greeley, editor of the *New York Tribune*, who was

running against him. Or, even worse, that Mrs. Victoria Claflin Woodhull, a woman of questionable morals who'd formed her own party to declare herself a presidential candidate. What was this world coming to? he asked his readers. Better to stick with the tried and true, even though imperfect, than go galloping off into uncharted territory.

As October unfolded, I grew more and more anxious that my acceptance letter had not arrived. Had it been lost? Had it fallen under the dean's desk? Should I pen another one, or would that appear too insistent? I reread the chapters on anatomy, guessing they'd be of prime importance, and drew diagrams from memory and quizzed myself over and over. Why didn't that letter arrive?

The cool days and foggy nights seemed to dampen the city's fires at least, which gave James and the other men—and the firehorses—a much-needed rest. At the first signs of fever, Duke and Black Jack, the horses that pulled the ladder, had been sent to a stable outside the city to recover, if possible. The owner there promised to exchange two well-trained harness horses who'd already survived the plague of distemper, though they'd not yet arrived. Ned, the chief's buggy horse, and Brownie, who pulled the hose wagon, were all right so far, James told me, and the gray gelding they called Freckles seemed to have nothing more than a cold and was back on his feet. Engine Company Number Eight could probably deliver their steamer if absolutely necessary, he said, but for the present they were keeping their fingers crossed and were grateful for the quiet.

Best of all, the Girl continued to escape the plague. I regretted now having taken her out—what was I thinking?—and scolded myself for putting her in such danger. For several weeks after James's announcement I'd approached the carriage shed with a thumping heart, certain I'd find her down in her stall. But each morning she nickered a welcome and pricked her ears happily. I ran my fingers along them anyway, searching for fever, though none flared up. Her overall health continued to improve, in fact. She put on weight and her dappled coat grew in almost completely. The fire's scars left leathery patches near her withers and across one cheek, and it appeared that her mane might never grow back, but no one could look at her and say she wasn't a beautiful mare.

Her improvement made her continued confinement doubly cruel. Every time I cleaned her stall she sprayed me with restless, snorting gusts. She tossed her head madly and even bucked in place. With her black eyes she begged me to trot her up the street again. *Please.* But I couldn't do it; I couldn't risk losing her to that invisible predator that was devouring so many others.

I wanted to tell her that she was one of the lucky ones. And if it weren't too awful for anyone's eyes, including hers, I would have shown her the wagons piled with stiff-legged carcasses that rumbled up and down the streets by day and squealed through my anxious dreams by night.

Mr. Stead was forced to view those carcasses and those fragile, wheezing creatures on their way to becoming carcasses. He told me that, with the spreading contagion, he was examining sixty, seventy, or even eighty horses a day, many just hours away from death. He'd begun stopping by again whenever he could, not bothering to knock on our front door but coming straight around to the carriage shed because he knew he'd find me there.

It pained me to see him wrestle through such exhaustion. At each visit his eyes were more rimmed with red. His jaw hung slack and his skin took on a pasty hue. I didn't know when or if he slept, though one morning when he appeared in the doorway, a growth of brown hair fuzzed his chin. I brought him a cup of hot tea from the house and imagined it a tonic as he drank. I knew that if he'd been an overworked horse I'd have returned him to condition by grating some ginger into a quart of warm, spiced ale and by wrapping him in warm blankets and by bedding him thickly in clean straw. But as he was human, all I could do, really, was listen to his weary complaints.

"There are just too many sick horses," he moaned, pressing the small of his back into the door frame. "I can't help them all, though Lord knows I'm trying. And so many of the ones that have died were such nice horses, Rachel, such nice horses. That's the added shame." He finished the tea and cradled the empty cup in his hands, warming them. Staring into it, his voice quieter, he said, "Yesterday I went to see a little girl's pony, one she's had all her young life, and"—he cleared his throat—"she'd made her bed in the straw right at his side. I could barely examine the little fellow the way she had her arms clasped round his neck. And today . . . today I learned that he's died." His broad shoulders stooped with defeat.

All I could do was listen and pray. Each evening, as soon as the Girl was safely tucked in, I got down on my knees and begged God to send the plague away; I begged him to stop horses from dying. And I begged him, if it was his will, to please let the veterinary college accept me. I didn't know if he listened to me anymore or if he cared, but surely he had to take notice of my cause. He'd created horses before Man.

Each evening Father dumped his newspapers and magazines on the hall entry table and I pounced on them to see if there was a letter from the Boston College of Veterinary Medicine and Surgery. Weeks crawled by with no response, and I nearly succumbed to nervous prostration until one evening a slim envelope with my name on it did fall from the mess of publications. My hands trembled as I picked it up. Inside that envelope lay my fate, and I wanted to rip it open at that very instant; at the same time I hesitated because of what that fate might be.

"Rachel," Mother called from the kitchen, "will you set the table, please? Dinner is almost ready."

"I'll be right there," I answered. Taking a deep breath, I slid my finger beneath the flap and removed one sheet of heavy paper the color of spring honey and unfolded it. After the salutation, inked in bold penmanship, I read a single curt sentence: *It is not advisable in our collective opinion to offer educational courses in the field of veterinary medicine to women, as we find they are not suited to such rigorous studies.*

Somewhere a door slammed.

I expected I might cry. Or at least grow teary. But neither happened. I just stood there, numb, not even able to think of what I should do next. Because there was no "next." Father had, indeed, won.

"Rachel?"

"I'm coming." Stuffing the letter back in its envelope, I shoved it into my pocket.

Dinner had no taste for me. Conversation held little interest. James, I think, told about a new leather hose the station had received, and Father looked up from his newspaper long enough to question him about it. He went on to say something about Brownie and Ned having runny noses. "Mr. Stead has treated them," he told me, to which I only nodded. Two more empty stalls at the station. I knew their fate well enough.

Father informed us of some events relating to the upcoming election. He seemed fairly certain that President Grant would be reelected, at least if men voted with their minds. And he read from his column: "'It is patently unnatural for a woman to want to do a man's work, and we suggest that a medical professional perform a complete and thorough mental examination upon Mrs. Woodhull. And one on Mr. Woodhull, too, for having the poor sense to marry her.'"

I knew some of his comments were directed at me and I burned with humiliation, especially with that letter in my pocket trumpeting his victory.

"Will you have some more beans, Mr. Selby?" was Mother's

only response. Grandmother, who might have raised her sword to him, had stayed in her room.

Afterward, Mother and I bumped about wordlessly in the kitchen. Not until we started washing dishes did she ask, "Is anything wrong?"

I didn't want to tell her about the letter. Not yet. And so I took my time putting on my apron and digging out a clean dish-towel and finally sidestepped her question by asking, "Why are the newspapers saying such awful things about Mrs. Woodhull?"

"I'm afraid that's the price you pay for thinking or acting differently."

"Did people ever call you names?"

She smiled grimly. "No, playing church services at fourteen wasn't quite as threatening as a woman running for president. Although one older lady in our congregation, Mrs. Wendelsdorf, did do me the 'favor,' as she said, of reminding me that 'pride goeth before destruction and an haughty spirit before a fall.'" She handed me a wet plate.

"Oh." I wiped it dry and set it on the table. Glancing over, I noticed the fine wrinkles radiating from her lips and the crease across her forehead. I saw, as if for the first time, the ever-weary wistfulness in her eyes. "I'm sorry."

That got me a quizzical look. "There's nothing to be sorry about. Mrs. Wendelsdorf could believe whatever she wanted. I knew there was no 'haughty spirit' behind my piano playing. It was something for which I had a talent and something that I enjoyed. That's all."

Nodding absently, I finished drying the dishes and the glasses and then carried them to the sideboard. "If you don't need me for anything else, may I go to my room?"

"I've borrowed a book of Robert Collyer's sermons from the library. I thought I'd read from them while you put in some time on your sampler. It's been weeks since you've threaded a needle." She must have heard my inward groan because as she wiped her hands, she cautioned, "Never mind your Father's words, dear. The battle isn't over yet."

That's what she thought.

I couldn't help it; I felt the tears coming, and she saw them, and before I could say anything at all she excused me with, "All right, tomorrow night, then. Will you please look in on your grandmother on your way up, ask her if she feels like eating anything?"

"Yes."

Sand seemed to fill my shoes as I climbed the stairs. Or maybe it was the iron weight in my pocket. The butterflies taunted me from behind their glass prisons: *Hah! Thought you could escape, did you?* Even my confounded corset, which I'd had to start wearing again now that my fingers were healed, gripped me with an unusual ferocity. *Hold straight now. No bending or reaching or running. Stay in one place.*

Grandmother heard me coming. "Rachel, is that you?" she called from her darkened room. "Could you light the lamp, please? My hands are shaking like a jelly and I don't trust them to do it."

"Of course." I felt around her bedside table for the matches. Striking one, I removed the glass chimney and carefully held the flame to the wick. I always lit lamps carefully now. Carefully and cautiously: Those were the watchwords for my future. Using both hands, I replaced the chimney.

The yellow light illuminated her blinking face. With her spectacles missing and her mussed gray hair fanning across her pillow, she could have been a stranger. "Can you reach my spectacles?" she asked, stretching a trembling hand toward the table. I picked them up and gently fitted them across her face, tucking each wire arm behind a fleshy, misshapen ear. "There, that's better," she said, blinking some more. "Now I can see . . . why, my gracious, Rachel, what's wrong?"

Not only had Grandmother always been able to read my emotions, she had always addressed them directly. But I just wasn't ready to tell her about my disappointment. So it surprised me when the words jumped out unbidden: "They won't accept me."

"Won't accept you?" she said. "Who won't?"

"The veterinary college that I wrote to." I pulled the letter from my pocket and held it up. "They said women aren't suited to their 'rigorous studies.'"

The news seemed to hit her almost as hard as it had me. She snorted once and adjusted her position and then became pensive. "It's our fault, your mother's and mine. We shouldn't have raised your hopes that night in the kitchen. 'Dreams born beside the hearth die too easily on the streets.' That's what *my* mother used to say." Her trembling fingers twisted the rolled edge of her quilt. She heaved a sigh that ended in a rattly cough. "You'll need their help," she said at last.

"Whose help?"

"The men. Your father, Mr. Stead, maybe James. Your mother and I were supposed to put on our thinking caps for you, weren't we? I don't believe we came up with much." Her eyes surveyed the small room. "That night seems like a long time ago. Seems like Wesleydale was a long time ago."

No use thinking about that. "Mother wants to know if you're hungry," I said. "Can I bring you anything to eat? We had boiled fish and cabbage."

She moved her head ever so slightly. "No, dear. I'm not very hungry tonight. But thank you."

"All right. I'm going up to my room. Call me if you need me."

I gave the carriage shed a last check through the hall windows, then climbed the attic stairs. The first thing I did when I got to my bedroom was unfasten that horrid corset and kick it under the bed. I crumpled the letter and threw it after. Then I lit my own lamp, opened the horse care manual, and tried to lose myself in a sea of healing words. Below me, Grandmother began reciting her Scriptures in a shaky voice that was still loud enough for the neighbors to hear. "They shall go out from one fire," she intoned, "and another fire shall devour them." I shivered.

TWENTY-SIX

ER PROPHECY RANG TRUE, BECAUSE THE CITY'S REPRIEVE from fires came to an end. The very first week in November, Engine Company Number Eight was called out to three fires in the space of just forty-eight hours. "A house fire on Appleton Street," James recounted at dinner on Friday, "a devil of a blaze in a furniture factory, and another one in a bakery. I'm perfectly used up." He ran stained fingers through his hair.

"How are the horses?" I asked under my breath. I was starting to get back to my old self as well; there were other colleges, other avenues of learning.

I could see that James still missed Chester; the evidence was right there in his faded blue eyes. "Well . . ." he began, and hesitated for so long that even Mother looked up from her plate, "the answer isn't good. The replacements we got for Duke and Black Jack are terrified of fires, and we can barely get them within a block of the flames. Obviously, the man who lent them lied about their training. Captain Gilmore's sending them back tomorrow morning and hoping to have Duke and Black Jack returned at once." He heaved a long sigh. "But to tell you the truth, Brownie's now taken a turn for the worse and Ned's stopped eating."

That dampened my appetite.

Father lowered his paper. "Any more sign of that firebug? Any suspicions with these recent fires?"

"The men thought the bakery and house fires were likely human carelessness," James replied, "but the cause of the one at the furniture factory was harder to identify. I think Captain Gilmore is going to look into it further."

"Is that so?" Father folded his newspaper. Rising abruptly, he said, "If you'll excuse me, I have some work waiting for me at the office."

"What time will you be home?" Mother asked.

It was an innocent question, but he bristled visibly. Oddly out of character, he then masked his irritation with a smooth answer and a polite nod. "I'll need at least two more hours," he answered. "You needn't wait on me. Some of the work that has crossed my desk of late hasn't been up to my standards. Good evening." Grabbing his hat and his coat, he hurried out the door.

James poured himself another goblet of milk and was noisily draining it when the parlor clock chimed. That appeared to set off an internal alarm, because he set the goblet down with a *clunk*, pushed back his chair, and stood awkwardly. "I have some business to attend to as well. Will you excuse me?"

"Surely you're not heading back to the station again," Mother exclaimed. "They're working you too hard."

He'd been claiming fatigue, but all of a sudden there was a certain jumpiness about him, a sort of happy energy that I'd not seen since Wesleydale when . . . I knew. "I'll bet he's off to *fan* a fire, rather than put one out," I teased. "What's her name?"

"You think I'd tell you?" He kissed Mother's cheek, paused in front of the hall glass to run his fingers through his hair one more time, and went out.

"Well, the Selby women are alone again," she said, "and with more dishes to wash."

We worked side by side with little more than small talk, and when the table was cleared and the dishes washed and dried and stacked, Mother took up her own embroidery in the parlor. Since she didn't invite me to join her, I tiptoed toward an escape up the stairs. As usual, she took notice of everything, and just as I was rounding the newel post, her voice captured me. "Please look in on your grandmother on your way up."

"I will," I answered, though I already knew what she'd be doing: reading her Bible. That's all she did anymore. She seemed to be surviving on air and Scripture. As I gained the top step I heard that tonight's menu was yet another of the bitter plates offered up by the prophets. I shook my head as I paused to glance out the hall windows. Moonlight shone faintly in the backyard, silhouetting the fence and the carriage shed and . . .

A yellow light flickered inside it. Was that . . . ? It was. Fire!

I grabbed up my skirts and went sprinting down the stairs,

past Mother and out the back door and across the yard and into the shed.

"Hello! Hold on there!" Mr. Benton Lee, of all people, caught me up short. One hand gripped my shoulder as he lifted a lantern out of the way.

"What are you doing here?" I demanded, jerking myself free.

"I'm sorry to have startled you, Miss Selby. Really I am. I just had to come see my girl." He hung the lantern on its nail and ducked under the bar of the Girl's stall, casually draping an arm over her withers. The way she curved her head around to nuzzle him filled me with an unchristian jealousy. "So many of the others have died," he told me, "that I had to be certain she, at least, was still alive." His fingers gently passed over her mottled face, tracing the patchy scars of pink and gray. He seemed sincere enough, though something about him always stirred the hairs on my neck. "I can't believe she looks so good. You and your brother have performed wonderful work." The Girl nibbled at his hand and I saw him slip her something. It was probably a peppermint, the way her teeth crunched noisily. What a traitor! She was too easily swayed by a piece of candy.

He smiled at me broadly, ingratiatingly, and sneaked a glance toward our house. "Would your father, by chance, be at home?"

So he hadn't come here solely to see the Girl. He was looking for Father, the editor. He wanted his name in the paper. But why hadn't he just knocked on our front door, then—at a more civilized hour?

"No, he's not," I answered. "Why?"

"I have some information he might want to put in the *Argus*."

The fire chief's accusations of self-promotion were proven true. "You'll have to talk with him tomorrow."

"This can't wait." He seemed awfully pleased with himself. "You see, there was a fire at a furniture factory this past Tuesday, and I know it was a case of arson."

"James already told us that. He said—"

"I also know who started it."

"You do?" An image of Father's kerosene-stained trousers loomed large in my mind. I guessed what was coming, and yet I didn't want to hear the words.

Mr. Lee dragged out the moment. He left the stall to examine the doorway with a rather theatrical flair, apparently to ensure that no one was eavesdropping. Satisfied, he took me by the arm, guided me to the crate, and sat me down on it as if I were a small child. Only then did he whisper his suspicions on a moist rush of tobacco and garlic. "It was Captain Gilmore."

I leaped to my feet in surprise. "Captain Gilmore? But . . . but that's nonsense. Why would a *fire chief*—someone who's *paid to put out fires*—be starting them?"

"I don't know," he said, digging his hand into his pocket, "but have a look at what I found." He opened his palm to reveal a small glob of brass. The Girl, thinking it was another candy, stretched her neck over the bar and nickered.

"What is it?" I asked.

"A button, mostly melted. I found it in the ashes of the furniture fire."

"So how does that prove Captain Gilmore started it?"

"Just look! It's from his uniform. That proves he was there."

Oh, this was lunacy. He was grasping at straws. "But of course Captain Gilmore was there. There *was* a fire."

"No, no, no. You don't understand. He *wasn't* there during that fire; he left before we got the alarm. He told us he had business down in Dorchester that day and wouldn't return until Tuesday night."

"So what does this button prove?"

"That he *was* there—at some time." He turned the button around, encouraging me to take a closer look. "See? You can still make out the number eight—for Engine Company Number Eight. The chief's the only one who wears buttons like this. So it had to have fallen from his jacket, which means he had to have been on the scene before the fire began."

It sounded logical. But was it truthful? Could Mr. Lee have manufactured this evidence as revenge on the man who'd suspended him? Was he now seeking Father's assistance to publicly, and perhaps wrongly, accuse Captain Gilmore of arson?

My mind was spinning. At least Father wasn't starting the fires. Or at least he wasn't starting them by himself. But what if he'd been conspiring with Captain Gilmore? Such a plot seemed absurd, except for what I'd overheard in the hallway of our very own home: Father leaning into Captain Gilmore and murmuring, "We'll both get what we want." His abrupt exit after dinner, immediately upon the mention of Captain Gilmore's name, suddenly seemed all the more suspicious.

"Have you mentioned this to James?"

"James?" He shoved the button back into his pocket and began pacing the narrow confines of the shed in that black cat manner of his. "As much as I like your brother, he's been asking too many questions at the station. And we've caught *him* sneaking off a time or two, so he's not above suspicion."

James, I knew in my heart of hearts, was above suspicion in all matters. He had nothing to do with the fires. But question marks hung over so many others, including the agitated Mr. Lee. "Why are you telling *me* all this?" I demanded.

He looked like he'd had his tail pulled. "You? Because I thought you cared about *her*." He jerked his head in the direction of the Girl, who was at that moment watching us so intently she seemed to understand the topic. "I thought you cared about all those horses that died in the livery fire, the one where *she* almost died. That wasn't the first act of arson by this deceitful scoundrel, and it won't be the last. That's why I came to talk with your father. Captain Gilmore's missing again. He's supposed to be at the station and he's not. I have a sense he's up to something."

All at once I felt a little twitchy myself. "Well, my father's not here."

"What's he doing at this hour?"

The awful possibilities made my stomach flip. "I don't know."

◈ TWENTY-SEVEN

HAT NIGHT I LAY AWAKE IN A COLD AND MOST UNFRIENDLY darkness. Even two quilts, the madder brown one with the yellow stars and the heavier nine-patch, brought no comfort. I was adrift, confused. Was Father guilty? Or was the firebug truly Captain Gilmore? And if either were true, why was I still so suspicious of Mr. Lee's late-night appearance? What was his motive?

I desperately needed to talk with James, but he still hadn't come home. Where was *he*?

Shivering from head to toe, I couldn't tell if it was the cold or an awful foreboding that kept my knees twitching and jerking. I began to believe that the fire alarm was going to jangle at any moment, and as the parlor clock chimed the quarter hours I startled at every distant bang or whistle. But they were false calls, every one of them. That was fitting because nothing, anymore, was as it seemed. People wore masks and talked over your head or behind your back. No one was as they appeared. I was scared to close my eyes.

Some time during that long night Grandmother closed hers.

As I passed her open door the next morning, I noticed her lumpy body silhouetted under the bedclothes. That sight alone gave me another chill. Rising with the sun was religion for her. "Are you all right?" I whispered into the curtain-darkened room. An unseen fly droned and banged against the windowpane. I didn't hear anything else. "Grandmother?"

Having moved so far from home, we had no friends to tell. No one came to sit in the parlor and share remembrances of church picnics and blue-ribbon fudge, of first love and first steps. No one came at all except for the undertaker, and when he and his assistant carried Grandmother out of the house, the narrow brick building felt so empty.

Mother began cooking. It was what she knew how to do. She penciled a list and put on her wrapper and went out the door. I ran out to the Girl and buried my face in her warm neck and cried and cried. The muzzle she rested on my shoulder was as comforting as any hand.

Later, as I stirred a fire in the stove, I found myself stirring memories. Each crackling orange spark lit a photographic image in my mind: of Grandmother's floured finger touching my nose; of her brown, well-worn Bible opened across her lap (to the Psalms, meaning she was happy); of the three of us huddled in this very kitchen, shyly sharing dreams. Tears continued trickling down my cheeks.

Mother finally returned with a precious slab of corned beef and a basket full of all the fixings for chicken and dumpling stew. How were we going to eat it all? There was no ice to keep leftovers. Oblivious to the practicalities, she silently began chopping and measuring. I did the washing and the drying and, when asked, set about ironing Grandmother's favorite tablecloth, the one she'd embroidered with tulips in all four corners. That task alone took nearly an hour, during which time neither of us spoke of our ache.

Not wanting to pull Father or James from their work, Mother decided to hold the news of Grandmother's passing until evening. She ordered the front steps swept and the hall rug shaken out and the parlor dusted. For whose eyes? I wondered. Still, I dampened a rag and began running it across the mantel. As for herself, with the beef boiling and the stew simmering, Mother began rolling out platoons of biscuits.

When I slid her potted ivies over to wipe their crusted water rings off the windowsill, I paused to glance outside. A pleasant enough fall afternoon: hazy blue sky, yellow leaves skating down an empty street. But without any horses, all too quiet.

I didn't know how many more hundreds had died. I'd given up walking the pavement because I couldn't bear to see the wheezing, snotty-nosed horses cruelly harnessed to their wagons, or far worse, the stiff carcasses, piled with legs akimbo like so much firewood. Maybe I wasn't suited for the rigors of veterinary medicine.

As I stepped away from the window, I tripped over my sewing basket. The unfinished sampler, with its two apples sinfully stitched in bold red, fell open on the floor. I stuffed it back in the basket with a flush of guilt, then gathered up the newspapers Father had left strewn around his chair. A small headline in one caught my eye: FIRE CHIEF REASSURES PUBLIC: HORSES STAND AT THE READY AT ENGINE COMPANY NO. 8.

My jaw dropped. A quick scan of the interview showed it chock-full of falsehoods. "'I've personally supervised every one of the fires,'" Captain Gilmore claimed, "'that my company has been called out to fight.'" Farther down he stated, "'On several occasions, when the cause of a fire has aroused suspicion, I've personally and thoroughly examined the aftermath. In most cases I've found that simple neglect, along with Man's capacity for error, has proved to be at fault, so I don't believe the public need worry itself about some soulless hooligan skulking around our city and purposefully striking sparks.'" Asked about the distemper epidemic, he had the brass to respond, "'I don't know the situation at other companies, but the horses at Engine Company Number Eight are all in fine fettle. They're standing at the ready, just as my men are.'"

Such lies! At least two of his horses were dead, I knew that for a fact, and he wasn't at the furniture factory fire. Mr. Lee had to be right. And I had to tell James.

Folding the newspaper along with the others beside Father's chair, I hurried into the kitchen. Flour speckled both the table and floor and coated Mother's arms in white. She shook the hair out of her face and kept rolling dough steadily.

"It's almost five," I said. "Do you want me to walk over to the station to get James?"

"No, we can wait until he gets home."

"But I need to talk to him. I didn't get a chance to last night."

"We can *wait*," she snapped. "Now please fetch some potatoes from the cellar. Six or eight will do."

I brought up the potatoes and, at her bidding, hastily and sloppily mopped the hall and kitchen floor. Under her critical gaze I was forced to get a bucket of clean water and mop them again. I was ready to explode. Only after I'd set the table to her satisfaction was I excused to my room. Angrily, I took the stairs two at a time, ignoring her hollered command to walk like a *lady*. I whipped past the pinned butterflies and Grandmother's empty room. Everything was wrong. Firemen were setting fires and journalists were printing lies and Mother was cooking for people who would never arrive. And even though this was the quietest of November evenings, with stars just beginning to poke through the graying sky, I knew a storm was brewing. I just knew it.

I paced my room for an hour like a horse trapped in a too-small pen—from the bed to the bureau to the window and a glance down the dark street. The lamps were lit, but it still lay empty. Why didn't James come? And where was Father at this very minute?

Flopping onto my bed, I opened my horse care manual. I'd always found solace in its detailed descriptions of illnesses and, more importantly, its cures for them, so I tried leafing through the pages. But I couldn't concentrate. Voices in my head drowned the words on the page. First Mr. Lee's, which had been echoing in my ears since last night: "I thought you cared about those horses." And then Grandmother's, repeating a verse of a few weeks ago, "They shall go out from one fire, and another fire shall devour them."

Two floors below, the parlor clock chimed. I jumped off the bed, ready to run—to where? This was unbearable.

A loud crack sounded outside: the Girl kicking the carriage shed's wall. I cocked an ear, though I hardly needed to decipher the code. She kicked again. I pictured her pacing just as fretfully as I had been. A loud, urgent whinny split the air and that was the final dot after the dash: She was calling for me. I began tiptoeing down the stairs with the plan of sneaking out of the house. Mother caught me at the bottom.

"That horse of yours is making an awful racket."

To my way of thinking, that was as good as an official leave. "I'll go have a look at her," I said, and before she could second-guess herself, I darted past her and through the kitchen. The odor of burned stew trailed me out the door.

The instant I entered the shed, the Girl spun to face me. In the darkness I saw her ears prick. Eagerly she began weaving from side to side like an athlete anticipating the ball. She knew something was going to happen too, even with that cotton stuffed in her ears she knew it. Did she sense a fire somewhere? The alarm hadn't yet rung. I decided to go after James. "I'll be right back," I promised, and gave her a pat on the neck. She nickered anxiously. Gathering my skirts, I tore down the alley.

Running through the dark and drinking in the cold air

was a wonderful tonic for worry. I almost imagined myself a firehorse, dashing to the blaze with utmost speed, pouring every ounce of energy into a lifesaving effort. Even with those awful shoes cutting into my ankles, with pain stabbing my side, I kept running. I pounded the pavement until my chest was near to exploding, until, gasping for air, I clattered to a stop in front of the silent fire station.

Its lower level was completely dark, though lamps glowed in the second-story windows. The big main doors were closed. For the first time I noticed the small sign beside them that read PUBLIC NOT PERMITTED. I wondered if that overzealous dalmatian was waiting inside to enforce the rule. With my heart still thudding in my ears, I tugged the door ajar.

No dog—yet. Stepping inside the station was like entering a grand hotel lobby, though a strangely empty one. I hadn't remembered the floor being so polished or the ironwork dividing the seven stalls at the back so ornamental. Moonlight spilled through barred windows onto six piles of empty golden straw. Only the seventh appeared occupied. Mesmerized for the moment, I tiptoed across the room to solemnly read the names engraved on marble and brass plaques above each stall: Chester, Major John. They were long dead. The stalls of Duke and Black Jack stood empty. As did those belonging to Brownie and Ned. Only the stall reserved for the Governor's Girl had an occupant, and the rangy gray imposter slumped inside it looked deathly ill.

I heard the firemen upstairs, their talk interspersed with laughter. I imagined them playing cards, telling jokes. How was I going to get James's attention? And where was that sneaky dog?

I felt the nation's founding fathers glaring at me from their portraitures on the wall: *trespassing girl!* I turned my back. No point in arguing that. On the adjoining wall, an alarm box and an oversize clock hung above a lone desk and chair. A logbook lay open on the desk, pen at the ready.

The firefighting vehicles had been backed into place in orderly fashion, their corresponding harnesses suspended in odd fashion above them. The web of pulleys made them look like giant leather spiders waiting to ensnare hapless victims. I shook off a shiver, screwed up my courage, and started up the stairs.

At my first footfall the alarm jangled. I jumped out of my skin. The men scrambled above, and the rope barriers to all the stalls automatically fell open with simultaneous thuds. The gray gelding grunted in surprise. Valiantly he struggled to his feet and stumbled toward the engine as the men came spilling down the stairs. I ducked inside an empty stall.

"Where is it?" someone shouted.

A man in red darted toward the alarm box to peer at the telegraph tape. "Summer Street," he called back.

"Summer Street? All the way up there? Are you sure?"

The man checked the tape again. "Yep. Box Fifty-two. Summer and Kingston. Must be a big one for them to call us out." He glanced up at the clock. The pointy black hands were inching toward eight o'clock.

The gelding had made his way to the steam engine,

stopped, and obediently backed himself into place under the suspended harness. His legs quivered and his head drooped below any bridle's reach. No one moved to fasten the harness.

"Where's the chief?"

Attention swung toward the office. The door was closed; no strip of light shone beneath it.

"What are we going to do? Freckles can't pull the steamer all by himself."

"Put him back in his stall," a vaguely familiar voice ordered. "He's too sick to pull a flower cart." I peeked over the half wall to see Mr. Benton Lee giving orders. What was his role in this? "There ought to be enough of us to drag it. Shall we give it a try, men?"

"All the way to Summer Street?"

"If you're afraid of some blisters, Holmes, then stay behind. The rest of you, tie some ropes to the front of this contraption. My father's always telling me how *real* firemen used to pull their own engines; we can do the same."

"Your father's engines didn't weigh two tons," someone grumbled. But his complaint was drowned by cheers and the loud creaks of the opening doors. The sick gelding was chased back to his stall, two long ropes were knotted into a makeshift harness, and the men themselves began rolling the shimmering apparatus into the night. James left with them, pushing from behind.

As the heavy rumbling and rousing calls faded away, I heard my heart pounding its own alarm: Summer and Kingston!

Kingston was the street we'd walked down to get to McLaughlin's Livery. That's where Balder was. If the stable was on fire . . . !

I dashed outside. I thought I could smell it: the sharp odor of fresh smoke. Looking up, I gasped. An orange glow already silhouetted the city's skyline. How big was this fire? That set me to running, retracing my steps. Playing the part of a firehorse was fancy no longer. Balder and hundreds of other horses were in danger. Or already . . . no! I wasn't going to think of that. Chasing images of charred bodies from my mind, I prayed to God to spare their lives.

I received some sort of answer in an ominous rumble that shook the ground, as if a giant dragon were shaking himself awake. The whole world vibrated. *This is the end,* I thought. *Judgment Day.* Up and down the street, the gas lamps went dark, snuffed by some unseen hand. Now only the fire lit the sky. Gooseflesh prickled my skin. Did it matter anymore? Fighting my aching lungs, I kicked up my speed through the inky blackness. God forgive me, but I was saving some horses before I died.

TWENTY-EIGHT

THE CARRIAGE SHED WAS EVEN DARKER THAN THE STREETS.
And so silent I thought the Girl must have kicked through
the wooden bar and galloped off by herself. But as shapes con-
gealed into various shades of black, I saw her outline. She was
standing stone still now, her dark eyes burning. Only her nostrils flared slightly with each breath. We looked at each other,
appraising one another. Did she deign to let me climb onto her
back? Did I dare to do so? Leading her was one thing, but galloping a horse as powerful as she was with no saddle and only a
halter for guidance was nothing short of lunacy.

But there was no other way to get to the livery in a hurry.
With my heart crowding my throat, I pulled the halter from its
hook. I buckled it on her head, looped the rope around her neck
for makeshift reins, and knotted the end under her halter. She
began prancing in place, her big hooves thudding the straw and
her shoulder jostling against me. "Whoa!" I ordered. Keeping
one eye on her, I carefully lowered the bar. She lunged through

before it hit the ground, yanking me off my feet. "Whoa!" I cried again. It was no use. In her fervor she went caroming off one wall and into another. A bucket upended, a rake clattered to the floor. Her shrill whinny split my ears. Aware that I could be crushed in her frenzy, I nonetheless rushed toward her and grabbed hold of the rope again. I yanked as hard as I could and she came to a tense halt, eyeing me with momentary surrender. Forcing her head toward her stall and away from escape, I managed to push open the sagging carriage shed door. The rush of night air spun her round and she charged the opening. With all my strength, I pulled her back. In one smooth motion I kicked a crate into place, then lightly stepped onto it and onto her broad back. There was no mane to grasp. We were already moving, and I remembered to duck my head a split second before she shot through the doorway.

In all my life I'd never felt such raw power. I was terrified and thrilled at once. The Girl's huge shoulders lifted and sank, building speed, eating up the ground in great, rolling strides. She headed out to the street and instinctively veered toward the fire station—which was the wrong way. Desperately trying to maintain my balance, I pulled on the rope and kicked her in the opposite direction. In a couple of thundering heartbeats we were turned around and galloping toward the Common. When the street opened up in front of her, the Girl lengthened her stride. I looked straight through her ears, concentrating. The sharp clang of her iron shoes hitting the cobblestones told me any fall would be fatal.

Up and down the street, people began calling out to their neighbors and pounding on doors. Some stared at the fierce orange skyline in mute stupidity, while others began sprinting toward it. Like a runaway locomotive, we galloped past them all.

The commotion at the south end of the Common slowed our careening enough to let me catch my breath. To my astonishment, the green expanse was already jumbled with furniture and merchandise of every description. Trunks and cabinets and crates teetered in massive piles; animals were leashed to trees; people ran hysterically toward the flames and back, filling their arms and carts with salvaged goods, filling the night with their panicked cries. Like a fine gray snow, ash coated the battleground.

The Girl shook her head and reared, sliding me backward. She was impatient to be moving and I pulled her in circles, trying to remember which street Mr. Stead and I had turned down to get to McLaughlin's Livery.

A pathetic clanging sounded above the tumult. The tinny ring moved closer and closer until, prodded by shouts, the crowd parted. Here came a lone steam engine, dragged by half a dozen weary firemen whom I didn't recognize. They paused just long enough to push their helmets off their sweat-glazed foreheads and gaze at the hellish scene. Joined by a few bystanders, they leaned into their work and struggled on, like so many Davids coming to fight an awesome Goliath.

The Girl kicked out at someone who'd come too near. She pinned her ears at another and began pushing through the crowd on her own, ignoring the otherworldly screeching that ripped the night's fabric. All faces, including mine, lifted to watch a huge granite building crumble in slow motion. Blocks fell through the sky like playthings; splintered molding stitched orange threads that frayed before our eyes. The final, violent explosion shot red sparks high into the air.

In the brief silence that followed, I heard horses screaming. The Girl pricked her ears. Eyeing a likely-looking street leading off the Common, I nudged her in that direction. I half expected her to resist charging toward another fire, but she bravely broke into a canter, scattering people right and left as we proceeded.

There was the corner florist's shop that I'd remembered, and we raced down that street and then onto Washington. We were making progress until we found ourselves behind another throng. Like a tenuous dam, a line of policemen held back a flood of frantic, crying onlookers. Over their heads I saw a desolate street heavily shrouded in a haze of smoke. Snapping flames licked windowpanes like fiery serpents, and right before my eyes I saw them dart out and entwine themselves around the next building, devouring its contents at will. A huge glass pane plummeted to the street with a nerve-shattering crash.

"Please!" a man shouted at an official, "just let me get my tools. They're my livelihood."

"No!" came the adamant reply. "It's not safe."

Somewhere in the night another horse screamed, and the Girl whinnied an answer. She bucked once and spun to the left, and I barely held on. Another official came running up to the barricade, waving his arms and shouting, "Get these people away from here. The fire's spreading by the second." Joining arms, the police began pushing us backward. At first the mare was a solid white rock in the stream, but then the crush of people began forcing her to move, little by little, along with them. Bumping her with my legs and tugging on the rope, I managed to edge her out of the retreating mass and into a store's recessed entry. She tossed her head impatiently, flicking foam onto my face.

To my surprise, the lady journalist who'd worked at the *Argus* was hunched next to the store's window, madly scribbling away in her notebook. She kept glancing out at the disaster, then back at her page, not even noticing the restive horse and rider almost climbing on top of her. "Pardon me." She couldn't hear me over the din. "Pardon me!" I yelled.

"What?" She looked up with that same wild-eyed expression she'd worn outside our house.

"I have to get to McLaughlin's Livery on Kingston Street. Is there another way around?"

"Are you mad?" she exclaimed. "The entire business district is on fire."

"I have to get there."

She squinted, considering. "I know you," she said. She gripped my knee to study my face. "We've met. When?"

"I'm Rachel Selby," I replied loudly, feeling my cheeks flush with guilt. "My father was your—"

"Matchstick!" she shouted in a voice so shrill that I wondered if she was the one who was slightly mad. "Now I remember."

"Matchstick?"

She tossed aside the question. "Some other time. What are you doing here?" And then, as if it had suddenly struck her, "Do you know where your father is?"

It gave me a start that she sounded as if she already knew where he was. And that I ought to know as well. I shook my head. At the moment I had other worries. "Please," I begged, "can you tell me if there's another way to get to Kingston?"

"Why?"

"I told you: I have to get to McLaughlin's Livery. The fire started near there and the horses might be trapped. I don't know the city well. Is there another way around?"

"Not tonight," she shouted. "Take a look for yourself." She nodded toward the chaos of smoke and flames, of people screaming and whistles shrieking. "It's Dante's Inferno come to life. Why . . . granite buildings are crumbling like . . . like sandcastles . . . like sandcastles beneath the tide of a fiery ocean. Wait a minute!" She flipped open her notebook to scribble the words. "That's good."

"But I *have* to get there. Some of the horses are sick. One of them belongs to a veterinary friend of mine."

"Really?" Her pencil paused, then waggled furiously. "'Veterinary's Own Horse Burned in Livery Fire.' That *might* be another interesting story. Is it one of the sick horses?"

A scare gripped me. "I hope not. But I know there are a lot of sick ones there. Please, just tell me which street to take."

She peeked out toward the policemen and back at me—sizing me up, it seemed—then motioned me to follow her into the crowd. We obediently retreated with the others a ways until, without warning, she darted down a narrow alley. I reined the Girl after her.

The passage was barely wide enough for a person, let alone a big horse with a rider, and the rough-edged bricks clawed at my skirt. The outline of the woman hurrying ahead of me quickly melted into the inky blackness, and I wondered if I should be following her with such trust. Before we'd gone twenty steps, another ominous rumble vibrated the air. It ratcheted louder and louder until it exploded in a nearby *boom!* that rocked the very walls pressing on us. The Girl flinched. A hot wind blasted my face, lifted my hair, and vanished. In its wake, luminous specks of orange spiraled downward like dying fireflies. I brushed them from my sleeve with a growing panic that we were walking *into* the fire rather than around it. And what would we do when it descended on us? There was no easy escape from this suffocating chasm. Sweat began prickling my neck, my underarms, the backs of my legs. Oddly enough, the Girl waded forward with renewed spirit.

An orange light beckoned us; whether it was heaven or hell, I wasn't sure, but by then I was ready to welcome either. When we stepped out onto the desolate street I saw cobblestones glowing red beneath swirling embers. A sucking heat snaked down my throat and parched it raw. It burned my eyeballs in their sockets. Deafened by the fire's howling, I recalled the words of Ezekiel, one of Grandmother's recent favorites: *An end is come, the end is come. It watcheth for thee. Behold, it is come.* Choking and blinded, I let the Girl carry me on.

The suffocating confines of the next alley seemed a haven after the firestorm. Again we were moving through a narrow black chasm with no end in sight, but this time I didn't care. As my eyes adjusted to the sooty walls and the scattered debris, I noticed shadows flickering across the cobblestones. I thought they must be rivulets of water and wondered if a pipe had broken somewhere, although I didn't hear hooves splashing. As my eyes cleared even more, I saw that the shadows were rats, legions of them, swarming in the opposite direction, desperate to reach safety. They came poking through vents and squeezing out of cracks and pouring down rainspouts. One leaped onto my shoulder, trailing its naked tail along my neck and then my arm before clawing its way down my skirt. My throat was too dry to scream.

When we came into the open again, smoke churned all around us. I heard more glass shattering. The journalist turned to say something, but the fire's roar ate up her words. Chunks of ash and cinders pelted our shoulders with increasing fury. A live ember burned right through my sleeve, and the flashing memory of flames consuming my arms nearly knocked me off the Girl. My heart banged against my tightening chest.

I knew we were on Summer Street because I could make out C. F. Hovey's store through the smoke. We weren't alone this time. Men and women and even a few children ran the length of the street, many pushing wheelbarrows loaded with papers and books and files, and anything else that could be grabbed from the jaws of the flames. Others smashed through windows and emerged with bulging sacks. Some had only their arms to measure what they could carry. A desperate-looking man, blackened with soot, came running toward us, kicking a rat out of his way. He hugged a wrapped bundle close to his stomach.

Another explosion shook the ground. The journalist pointed, and I followed her down a winding, smoke-filled street. She was running now, and the Girl picked up a trot. We rounded a corner, kept going as fast as we could through the haze, and rounded another corner.

There was the metal horse head, shimmering an eerie orange. We'd arrived at the livery from the opposite direction!

"Here you are," she said while gasping for breath. "Now give me a story worth writing about." She ducked beneath an overhang and opened her notebook.

TWENTY-NINE

THE CHAOTIC SCENE BEFORE US HAD BEEN RIPPED STRAIGHT from the onionskin pages of Revelation, the last book in the Bible. Judgment Day truly had arrived—at night. Through the livery's partially collapsed roof, an unseen red dragon spewed his smoky breath. Orange flames snapped and hissed at every opening. Pinned against the shrouded sky above, winged creatures glowed with an unholy fire. A closer look proved them to be wild geese reflecting the blaze on their pale underfeathers, but in the shifting haze they could easily have been the seven angels, robed in white, trumpeting our doom.

That trumpeting was echoed in horses' screams. Hundreds whinnied from inside the burning livery. Tied to the walls of their stalls, they cried and kicked in growing panic. Men were in there too. I heard their shouts above the crackling flames and the ominous groans of burning timbers.

From out of the mayhem, hooves clattered on cobblestone, and four horses with ropes dangling from their halters rushed past. The Girl tensed, poised between her instinct to flee with the herd and her calling to save lives. Her entire body vibrated with a piercing whinny as she lunged forward, carrying me toward the burning livery.

At its smoky doorway we ran smack into a stableboy leading out a pair of frightened horses. A boy behind him led two more horses. They dropped the ropes and waved their arms, shooing the horses away. The Girl shied sideways, nearly unseating me. Scared out of their wits, the horses hurled themselves mindlessly at each other. They spun and reared and trotted in circles until one, a hammer-headed bay, bolted back inside the livery. The herd scrambled after him. The Girl shook her head, fighting my hold. She reared, too, and whinnied again. For a chilling second I thought she was going to carry me into the burning building.

Our path was blocked when one of the stableboys returned. He was leading out another frenzied horse and Mr. Stead was with him, leading two more.

"Rachel! Thank God!" Mr. Stead shouted. "Here! Take these horses to the depot yard. It's down that street there. Just turn them loose and come back." He tossed the ropes to the three horses across the Girl's withers and I barely had time to grab hold of them all before he disappeared.

The Girl pranced fretfully, ready to bolt. To make things worse, the three excited horses were straining in opposite directions. They bucked and spun and tangled their ropes until I became the Maypole in an impending disaster.

"This way," someone called. Risking a glance over my shoulder, I saw one of the stableboys running back toward the livery. He was waving his arms. "Take them to the depot. Someone there will help you." He pointed, too, then dived into the smoky cavern.

The three crazed horses began tugging us after him, but the Girl, more sensible finally than them, braced her legs. I added my own weight, and though it seemed my arms were being yanked from their sockets and new burns were being branded into my palms, I wrestled them to a stop. Thumping the Girl's shoulder with my heel, I turned her around. With open space ahead, she struck up a powerful trot. The anxious horses, satisfied to be moving anywhere, followed.

Somewhere in the city a thunderous boom rattled the ground. It sounded like battle. More than anything I wanted to gallop—I needed to gallop—and I leaned over the Girl's neck. She hardly needed the urging. Her withers rose and she powered into a rolling gallop that soon ate up the ground.

The four horses and I moved as one. Shoulders banged my knees. Heat poured from body into body. My breathing joined theirs and I allowed instinct to overtake me. I became a galloping horse too, charging recklessly into the night, fleeing death.

Several blocks ahead a man waved for attention with one arm and pointed down another street with the other. We rounded his corner like racehorses. I saw the finish line straight ahead: the gate to the freight depot yard. A few horses already milled behind it, and as we thundered closer, a boy shooed them away and swung the gate open. We rushed through it like an undammed river. The Girl slid to a halt and I dropped the ropes, allowing the horses to join their frightened stablemates. With the grace of a dancer and no signal from me, the Girl wheeled about and bolted back through the gate and toward the burning livery. Her gallop, I noticed, was amazingly smooth and, now that she had her work, amazingly calm.

This time I was handed the ropes to four horses. A mounted stableboy joined me, tugging along a small herd of his own. The Girl insisted on leading the way. She pinned her ears and shook her head, and not one of the galloping horses dared to nose past her. A shrieking wind hurled burning cinders at our heels. It rained ash on our shoulders and flanks. The night sky was a sheet of luminous orange and it seemed the entire world was aflame.

When we'd safely delivered those horses to the depot yard, the Girl wheeled around again and went racing straight back through the smoke and popping sparks and gagging fumes. We were handed more ropes, and more horses banged against my knees and ripped fresh sores into my oozing palms. I swallowed their sweat and saw my own panicked reflection in their panicked eyes, and we galloped flat out like the devil himself was chasing us.

Again and again we sped toward the livery, grabbed the ropes to frantic horses, and sped away from it. With each trip I hoped to find Balder at the end of a lead rope, but the horses I rescued were all strangers to me. The Girl never slowed until a dozen or so trips later, when we found ourselves dragging some of the sick horses to safety. The distemper had dulled them beyond caring. I think they would have stood in the livery doorway and been burned to a crisp if I hadn't jerked on their ropes and yelled and made them stumble all the way to the depot yard.

By that time sweat drenched my body and stung my eyes. Some eighty or a hundred horses wheeled and whinnied in the yard, a far cry from Mr. McLaughlin's original three hundred, but all that had survived the plague of distemper, I supposed. Or the fire. As I released the sick horses I was so relieved to see Balder's gentlemanly bay face among the other survivors. Someone else must have delivered him to safety. He was a welcome sight in an otherwise ghastly night.

When we returned to the livery, no more horses awaited us. The back of the building had completely collapsed, and splintered timbers jutted upward like broken bones. The fire's roar was deafening, and I couldn't hear any whinnies at all. I hoped all the horses had been freed. Some firemen had finally arrived, pulling an antiquated hand pump. They were spraying a weak stream of water on the front of the livery. It was just enough to hold the flames at bay while the more expensive carriages, piled high with harnesses, were wheeled out. I was thankful for the break, because I was trembling with exhaustion. Even the Girl seemed willing to stand and blow. Under my legs her sides expanded and compressed like a bellows.

The wind had shifted, pushing the massive fire away from us. At least the horses in the depot yard would be safe. But as I scanned the city skyline, the extent of the unfolding catastrophe struck me dumb. In all directions flames licked the heavens. They ran unchecked from one building to another. Beneath the din, steam whistles screeched their puny protest. I imagined other firemen aiming their hoses at the inferno, and I hoped James was safe. Somewhere deeper in the business district, two cannonlike booms shot a mass of fresh sparks into the night. A rumble and crash shook the ground. It sounded as if the firemen had resorted to dynamiting buildings, to snatching fuel from the jaws of the flames in a desperate attempt to starve it into submission. Two more booms produced a prolonged earth-shaking. I worried that the fire-soaked walls of the livery would collapse with the next explosion. Where was Mr. Stead?

Wiping the smoke from my stinging eyes, I watched the men dragging out the carriages and searched each face. From inside the livery someone shouted, and I thought it might be him, but before I could be sure, a chestnut colt, no more than a yearling, burst through the doorway with an extralong lead rope trailing between his legs. He seemed to be the fire's own wild creation as he bolted straight out of the flames. Dazedly he trotted left and right, whinnying for help. Home was inside the livery, and he stretched his legs and ran for it. Mr. Stead spread his arms to block entry. The leggy creature spun away and wildly went bounding over and through the maze of carriages and heaps of harnesses. He leaped over a wheelbarrow and cleared the two shafts of a buggy and, finding himself boxed between carts, twisted and tried to scramble over the enmeshed wheels. No man-made barrier was going to hold *him*. In midair, his head snapped around like a weathervane in a summer storm, and he was yanked to the ground with a wicked thud. Instinct made him fight. With fierce, high-pitched whinnies he kicked blindly at his attacker. Gaining his feet only to find that the rope had his head snared tight, he flailed all the more. I was off the Girl and running.

He was a cyclone, a little red cyclone with tiny hooves and stumpy tail flinging every which way, and I loved him instantly. Looking for an opening, I found my opportunity and jumped in at his shoulder. I grabbed hold of his halter with one hand and his tail with the other and pulled him in close, buffering his panic with my body.

Mr. Stead hurried through the mess to untangle the rope that had the colt caught. "Good girl," he said to me. "Hold him there now. I've almost got it."

I took the music of his words and hummed it to the squirming colt. I rocked against him and hushed his whinnies and drew his head into my chest. "Easy there, little one. Easy now."

The damaged livery gave out an eerie groan, like that of a dying animal. We all turned our heads to watch the far wall waggle dizzily and cave inward in slow motion. That brought the rest of the roof with it, and bricks and rafters and moldings piled one on top of the other in a thunderous crash. A rush of heat and a shower of snapping sparks shot over us, frightening the colt into another panicked scramble. I cradled him tighter.

Ducking his head, Mr. McLaughlin came running through

the sparks with a pair of thrashing cats in his arms. "We got everyone, I think." He opened his arms and the two felines dashed beneath the shelter of a carriage. They swished their puffed tails angrily and surveyed the scene with glinting green eyes.

"There!" Mr. Stead rose, triumphantly displaying the disentangled end of the rope. "Now, let's have a look at this little rapscallion. Are you all right?"

I nodded. I could barely take a breath with trying to hold the fractious colt to my chest, but I wasn't letting go. There was something special about him, something that had drawn me like a magnet.

Then I noticed the dangling leg. The colt was so restless he pranced airily in place, but his off foreleg didn't move. As Mr. Stead began his examination Mr. McLaughlin bent down beside him. "Is it broke?"

"Most likely," came the awful answer, and then I couldn't get a breath at all. Mr. Stead began moving his hand down the leg. At each probing pause I mentally named the unseen bone: radius, carpus, metacarpus. "It's so hard to tell in these young horses."

"Aw, that's a right shame." The liveryman patted his bulging pockets and felt about his coat and finally pulled out a palm-size pistol. He checked the barrel, nodded, and stood. Reaching for the colt's halter, he said, "Miss, you'd better step out of the way. Just close your eyes now and cover your ears and let the veterinary and myself handle this."

I hunched my shoulder to block his reach. "You're *not* going to shoot him."

"It's for the best, Rachel." This was a nightmare. Unbelievably, Mr. Stead was trying to ease the halter from my grip. "You can't save them all. Besides, this little fellow's in a lot of pain. That's why he's struggling so hard, but soon he won't feel a thing."

They were blind, both of them. Couldn't they see how special this horse was? Couldn't they see that his heart more than compensated for his injured leg?

Quite as if he understood the men's words, the colt gave up his fight at once and sank his damp, trembling body against me. His nostrils fluttered. Smallishly built, he had the same narrow face and almond-shaped eyes as Peaches. He even had her copper-colored coat. No wonder he'd kindled me.

While Mr. Stead had been examining the colt, some of the stableboys had gathered. They ringed us like a hungry pack, exchanging cold glances, shaking a head here, scoffing there. Deciding our fate. Well, I'd fight them all if I had to. Hugging the colt to me, I glared at each of the men in turn. "You aren't going to shoot him," I said. And to Mr. Stead I pleaded, "You aren't even sure that his leg's broken. And if it is, we could put him in a sling until the bone mends."

"That's impossible," Mr. McLaughlin interrupted. "Where would I hang a sling when I don't even have a barn?" He waved his pistol at the livery's smoldering remains. "Now step out of the way and let us men do our job."

Mr. Stead hesitated. A flicker, just a flicker, of agreement showed on his face. But it vanished. "Do you know the commitment required in keeping a horse in a sling," he questioned, "especially one as young and wild as this? Do you know how much time and labor are involved?"

"Two to three hours to construct the framework," I recited promptly from Chapter Eleven, giving it all I had. "If it's a simple fracture, a month or so in the sling, which can be cut from either bagging or sailcloth; if it's a compound fracture, as many as three months. Cotton padding and starched bandages to wrap the limb; the affected area to be made wet with warm saltwater at least five times daily." That last sentence came rushing out on one triumphant breath.

He only smiled sadly. "You're well up on your reading, I see, but it's just not—"

"Here now," Mr. McLaughlin said, clamping hold of my wrist and giving it a jerk, "no milksoppy girl gets to decide the fate of *my* horse."

"Ow!"

Mr. Stead lunged. "Henry!"

"Stop that at once!" A booming voice that I recognized too well froze everyone in place. Father, of all people, strode onto the scene like the exasperated director of a stage play. "What's going on here?"

The liveryman released his grip. I tried to soothe the startled colt by pulling him close to me again, though what comfort he'd find next to my pounding heart I didn't know.

"Begging your pardon, sir," he said, "but we've got a horse with a broken leg here and we're trying to put him out of his misery, but this girl—"

"Mr. Stead?" Father interrupted. "What do you have to say about this?"

"The colt's badly injured, that's a fact—"

"But he's not beyond saving," I argued. Father's scowl only grazed me.

"She is right," Mr. Stead admitted.

"Then why aren't you saving it? Aren't you a veterinary?"

That led into a contentious debate of capabilities and responsibilities and probabilities that flared into a shouting match. I sank my chin onto the colt's thick, short mane, murmuring a prayer, and when I opened my eyes, I noticed the Girl standing a little apart from us. Her ears pricked toward the flames that marched away to devour other buildings. She looked more contented than I'd ever seen her, and I realized that this was where she belonged: in the thick of disaster, fighting to save lives.

In the shadows behind her, something else caught my eye: a familiar flash of white about the size and shape of a dalmatian. And was that a fireman scurrying along beside the dog? A fire chief, perhaps? No, it couldn't be. Fatigue was playing tricks on me. It was probably just another looter. The city's disaster seemed to have attracted its share of vultures.

The lady journalist—I still didn't know her name—left her shelter to join the circle of men. Boldly she stood right beside

Father, studiously flipping through her notebook. That irritated him into bellowing, "What are you doing out here at this time of night?"

"I could ask the same of you," she replied with confident raciness. "What have *you* been doing these past few hours?"

In all my days, I'd never seen him look so flustered. "Are you daring to accuse me of something?" he challenged.

"Are you guilty of something?"

"Of course not!"

"What about your friend?"

"What friend?"

She flipped back a few pages. "The friend I've been following most of the evening," she explained, "thanks to woman's intuition . . . and a tip from someone familiar with fires." She paused, allowing us to wonder just who that someone was, then went on. "Let's see, I watched you and your friend— accompanied by a dog—carry something that resembled a kerosene can down the alley behind Tebbetts, Baldwin & Davis. You loitered there from seven twelve until seven thirty-nine. Then you went separate ways. I followed your 'friend,' who was no longer carrying anything, over to a jeweler's, where he broke the glass at seven forty-eight, let himself in, and emerged at seven fifty-two."

"You're drunk!"

She shook her head and raised one hand. "Sober as a judge, Mr. Selby."

"Well, you can't prove any of your fabrications," he said.

"And if you try to sully my name with them, I'll have you brought up on charges of slander."

"No one's looking to slander you, Mr. Selby. We don't need to."

A weakened timber screeched painfully as it broke in two. Its thunderous collapse yanked one last rafter along after it, and a spray of orange sparks shot toward us. "We'd better move," Mr. Stead suggested. "What are we going to do with this fellow?"

"I don't give a rap," Father exclaimed. He looked ready to bolt.

Mr. Stead turned to Mr. McLaughlin. "Since you're willing to shoot him, I assume you'd surrender claim to him, is that correct?"

The man shrugged. "I suppose so."

I shook nearly as hard as the colt, realizing what was going to happen. Mr. Stead turned to me. He tried in vain to hide his smile. "Is this another hapless creature you want to take on?"

Of course I nodded.

"Does she have your permission, sir?" he asked Father.

I looked in his direction, and the lady journalist did too. Father drew himself up. "She does not!" he bellowed. "She doesn't even have my permission to be here."

"I'm taking him home anyway," I stated firmly.

He settled one of his withering looks on me. "Your days of playing veterinary are over."

"I'm not playing, Father; this is work. Yours may be to burn down and to tear down, but mine is to heal."

Father vibrated like an overheated teakettle on the verge of exploding. Even Mr. McLaughlin took a step back, his eyes bulging, as Father roared, "I don't have to put up with this!"

The lady journalist calmly raised the ante. "Unless you want to read in Monday's *Pilot* what I witnessed tonight, maybe you do."

"You can't blackmail me."

"It's not blackmail, Mr. Selby. It's fact. And I know how you love your facts."

Father ground his teeth. He looked at Mr. McLaughlin and Mr. Stead and the ring of stableboys. He even looked at me. "There was a time when women knew their place," he growled. "Keep the colt, for all I care. But you," he stuck his finger in the journalist's face, "had better keep out of my sight. Because I'm more dangerous than you know."

"Then we're well matched," she replied.

THIRTY

THE FOLLOWING TUESDAY I ATTENDED MY SECOND funeral in two months. Turning sixteen seemed to have introduced death into my life, but I refused it more than a sideways glance.

Mother had found a small Episcopalian chapel in Lower Mills, south of Boston, that had a suitable graveyard behind it. As we stood shivering inside its iron fence, listening to the minister glorify the life of a woman he'd never met, my thoughts and eyes wandered. Rosebushes had been planted at regular intervals along the fence, and someone had tied their leafless arms to the uprights. I wondered what color the blossoms would be next spring. A stone angel larger than me smiled from above a neighboring grave. She stood darkly silhouetted against the thin light of a November sky. Looking past her to the rolling hills and listening to the soft rush of a nearby river, I knew Grandmother would have loved it here.

Few people marked her burial. Huddled in front of the minister were only Father and Mother and James and myself, and for some reason Mr. Benton Lee, who'd asked to come along at the last minute. He sort of hovered behind and between Father and James, shifting his weight from foot to foot, restless as always. Mr. Stead had promised to join us, but although I kept an ear open for Balder's familiar *clip-clop*, the road leading up to the church remained silent.

Even this far outside the city, the odor of smoke still hung in the air. It seemed to have permeated our clothes and our hair and our very skin, and I wondered if we'd ever be cleansed of that dreadful night.

The cataclysmic fire had burned for twenty-four hours, all through the next day and into Sunday evening. Even with the flames finally cornered and extinguished, acres and acres of rubble that had once been Boston's business district still sent up white clouds of smoke. The newspapers that had managed to print editions on Monday stacked their headlines with exclamations: BOSTON IN FLAMES! THE HEART OF THE CITY BURNED OUT! LABYRINTHINE STREETS CHOKED WITH A HORROR-STRICKEN MULTITUDE! Notably absent was the popular and widely read *Boston Pilot*. Its offices on Franklin Street had burned to the ground. What was to become of the lady journalist now?

Yesterday I'd raced through every article I could find to see if investigators had discovered the cause of the fire. One witness claimed to have seen a disreputable character near Summer and Kingston Streets on Saturday evening but gave police only a vague description. Hooligans caught up in the frenzy of the presidential election had been setting small fires in the past weeks to garner attention, and one newspaper laid the blame in their corner. But again, there were no faces and no names.

Father donned his coat of humility and wrote that he bemoaned the disaster, truly he did. Poor Boston! But before he reached the end of his column, he'd flung off that coat and was crowing. Hadn't he warned his readers that this was bound to happen? Hadn't he been saying all summer long that Boston wasn't prepared? Maybe people would listen next time. I squirmed at his vainglory, wondering if he'd boast so bravely if the lady journalist had been able to publish her findings in the *Pilot*.

While the journalists across the city scrambled to report the fire's epic devastation, the preachers went to great lengths to make sense of it. Summaries of their sermons were printed in the newspapers, and after reading them I believed every preacher in Boston saw the fire as neither arson nor accident, but as a direct message from God. Most said it was clear evidence of His wrath, a visitation on Boston for its sins, and how easily I pictured Grandmother nodding her head to just such a sermon. But the famous Reverend Henry Ward Beecher, preaching from his New York pulpit, said that if that were truly the case, then what city in the nation would deserve to stand?

"Fire," the minister intoned, and I jumped to attention, "is a test of strength. Man can construct great buildings—four, five, and even six stories high—which Nature, in the form of fire, can destroy in an hour. Does that mean that we should stop building? That we, as humans, should give up hope? No. Because fire, like death, is God's way of reminding us that our lives are temporary. All things material, He tells us, including our bodies, can be lost. But the soul—the soul that truly believes—will live on. Let us pray."

The minister—Reverend Biggs, his name was—and his wife, Clara, as well as Mr. Lee, returned to our house for some cold lunch, followed by tea and cake. In hanging their coats on the hall tree I saw that more newspapers and some letters had been set on the table. One of them was addressed to me in Mary Grace's elegant hand, and I warmed at the thought of a piece of Wesleydale finding me here in Boston. I could almost hear her chatting on about her upcoming wedding, could almost see her curls bobbing as she eagerly detailed her dress and the flowers and the foods they'd serve at the church reception. I slipped it into my pocket to enjoy later.

Then I joined Mother to make small talk with Mrs. Biggs, who, ever since arriving, had been glancing from my scarred hands to my face and silently offering her most sincere pity. She and her husband, who was talking with Father, reminded me of a pair of salt and pepper shakers: identically stout bodies of average height, bland faces, he with a close-cropped head of white hair and she with a froth of curly black. They were even relating the same story, taking turns giving a lengthy account of the misfortunes of a son of one of their congregation's members who had lost his entire inventory of carpets in the fire, to which Mother nodded her head and murmured, "Such a shame" several times over. I'd never been more relieved to hear a knock on the door, and I bolted to answer it before Mother could rise.

To my astonishment, the lady journalist stood there, her collar turned up against the cold. She leaned close with eagerness. "Just the person I was hoping to see," she began, then, catching a glimpse behind me, "Oh, I'm sorry. You have guests. Perhaps—"

"No, it's fine." I was happy to get outside, away from the formalities and artificialities. Away from the pity. I closed the door, having to hug myself to ward off the chill.

"The matchstick," she said abruptly.

I couldn't help noticing how the harsh wintry light aged her features. She looked as if she hadn't slept in days. "Pardon me?"

"I didn't explain about the matchstick, about your father being a matchstick."

My stomach plummeted. So he *was* guilty.

In that wild, unchecked way of hers, she grabbed my arm. "What you have to understand is that a matchstick can destroy—and it can kindle. It all depends on how you look at the fire it creates."

"I don't understand. Did my father start the fire?"

Her eyes shot toward the parlor window. "Is he at home?"

"Yes."

That appeared to give her pause. She released my arm to tuck a strand of hair behind her ear, though the gusting wind pulled it loose. When she went on, her voice was still urgent but lowered. "That's not what I came to talk about. What I want to tell you is more important—much more important. You see, when your father discharged me I thought he'd destroyed me, and for a while, I let him. That day when I spoke to you, right there," she nodded toward the pavement at the bottom of the stairs, "was one of my lowest. But then I decided that being a journalist meant too much. So I pulled myself together and wrote some more stories, and I sold them to other newspapers, and one, the *Boston Pilot*, hired me on at an even better salary. That's when I began to see your father as a matchstick that had kindled a stronger flame in me rather than a matchstick that nearly destroyed me."

"But the *Pilot* burned down. What will you do now?"

Her grin tipped sideways. "The building alone burned, sweetie, not the work." Echoes of the minister's graveside sermon, delivered again.

"Are you going to print that my father started the fire?"

"I'm not completely convinced that he did."

"But you said that night—"

"I said that I'd been following him and his friend, whom I believe to be Captain Gilmore, throughout the area where the fire began. I think their actions were quite suspicious, and I'm determined to learn more about what they were doing that night. But did I see either of them actually set match to kerosene? No. I did, however, see Captain Gilmore break the glass of and let himself into a jewelry store—that was after your father had left—so if Mrs. Gilmore comes parading by in a new diamond necklace in the next few weeks, I'll alert the store's owners."

Behind us the door opened, and James and Mr. Lee, in mid-conversation, crowded us on the top step. Trading apologies amid the jostling, we all four descended to the pavement. I felt it my duty to perform the introductions and even had my mouth open until it occurred to me that, although I'd spoken to her more than once, I still didn't know the woman's name. With a perceptive nod she extended her hand. "Mrs. Sarah Cornwell," she said. "I already know Mr. Lee here, though not this other young man." She gave James a flirtatious smile.

"James Selby," he said, returning the smile.

That had the effect of squelching hers. "Oh . . . so you're another one of *his*." Wrinkling her face, she gazed up at the house. "Are there more?"

James shot a quizzical look at me.

"No, just James and myself," I responded. "And our mother." Why did she always come as an afterthought?

The door opened again and this time Reverend Biggs and his wife emerged, waving their good-byes. They cast suspicious glances at the four of us as they passed by, though they made an effort to nod politely. Hurriedly they climbed into their buggy and drove away.

Mrs. Cornwell spoke to James and Mr. Lee. "I was just about to leave myself, although I wouldn't mind talking with you some more about the fire. I'd like to get a few more details about how you and your men were able to drag the steam engine all the way to the scene. Would you mind walking with me a ways?"

"Of course not," Mr. Lee replied and gallantly offered his arm. James raised an eyebrow in my direction before the three of them set off along the pavement. I watched them go, feeling vaguely as if they all knew something that I didn't, something that was so plain to see that it needn't even be spoken about. Rubbing my arms, I climbed the stairs.

The parlor was empty. Teacups sat abandoned on table and mantel and bookcase. Their matching bone china dessert plates lay freckled with cake crumbs. I didn't hear Mother in the kitchen, so she must have gone upstairs. The house seemed so lifeless without Grandmother, so empty.

Through the doorway to the study I saw Father seated at his desk, writing. Packing materials had been neatly refolded beside a small opened box that cradled a fragment of a rainbow. I craned my neck to see a butterfly sandwiched between cotton and glass. Even in death it shimmered with the colors of a summer forest: violet blue, dusky brown, and sunlit orange. When was the last time it had flown free?

My throat clamped in disgust. Father was still trying to pin me under glass. Perhaps he thought he already had. But even without that letter of acceptance, I needed to show him where I stood. And I needed to know exactly where he stood. Just how far had he gone to win his battle?

Tentatively I rapped a knuckle on his door. "Pardon me." Too whispery. Clearing my throat, I tried again. "Pardon me."

He looked up with a scowl.

"I need to ask you something." I took a deep breath. "Did you start the fire?" I'm sure I said it quietly enough, politely enough, even, for accusing one's own father of such a heinous act as arson. Yet the words slammed off the walls of the small room as if they'd been shouted.

His pen stopped moving. Peering over his spectacles, he examined me with that critical stare that had always made it so hard to breathe. "Do you have facts to support such a brazen accusation?"

"Mrs. Cornwell said she saw you and Captain Gilmore there. With a kerosene can."

Carefully he laid his pen in its brown marble tray. Lacing his fingers, he rested his forearms on the edge of his desk. "She's correct—in this instance."

I was asking the questions, yet I felt as if I was undergoing some sort of graduation examination, expected to come up with the right answers as well. Terrified as I was, I had to keep going. Inching inside the study, I asked, "What were you doing?"

He blinked passively, awaiting my misstep. "Captain Gilmore and I had been evaluating the insufficient water hydrants in the business district when we discovered an empty kerosene can near the Tebbetts, Baldwin & Davis building. The fact that it had been haphazardly abandoned beside an open back door aroused our suspicions. While Captain Gilmore went inside looking for an arsonist, I went in search of a policeman."

"What happened then?"

Irritation edged his voice. "You know what happened then. The catastrophe I've been predicting for the past four months came true." He picked up a letter opener and began tapping its blunt end on the blotter. "You wouldn't be troubled with such concerns if you hadn't come galloping in where you didn't belong."

"I saved horses' lives! How could I not belong?"

"Because you're a girl, and saving horses' lives is the work of men. And because you didn't have my permission to leave this house. Your behavior continues to be willful and indecent."

There was that word again: indecent. Kaleidoscopic images flashed through my mind: of Peaches and the locomotive and the orchard, of the fire station and the Girl, of Mr. McLaughlin leering inside his livery, of Mother and Grandmother huddled in the kitchen, sharing dreams beside a dying fire. It was all indecent in someone's eyes. And then I remembered Mrs. Cornwell, the wild-eyed journalist. She'd laughed at tradition's shackles. She'd shaken them off and galloped down her own path. And she'd said Father was her matchstick. Backed against the door frame, I trimmed my wick and took his words—his facts—and as calmly as I could, turned them back on him.

"If saving horses' lives is the work of men, why are so many thousands ill? Why are thousands of horses already dead? Why aren't the men saving them, Father?"

His eyes narrowed. "If you're onto that veterinary idea again, you can forget it. You'll never receive my permission."

"I'm not waiting for your permission." My fists clenched,

and I could feel my chest heaving. "If I waited for your permission . . . to do anything at all with my life . . . I'd end up one of your horrid little butterflies." I eyed the one on his desk. *Stay calm,* I told myself. *Stay calm. Keep breathing.* "One way or another," I went on when I'd settled some, "I'm going to become a veterinary. And even if the veterinary college here in Boston won't accept me, I'll apply to another college. And then another. Because somewhere, somehow, someone will accept me."

"You've been talking to that hysterical harpy Mrs. Cornwell, I imagine. It's all 'want, want, want' with her kind, with no thought as to who works to pay for those wants. Let me remind you of this fact: I'm not paying for any more schooling. I'll pay for your dresses. I'll pay for your wedding when the time comes and if any man wishes to be saddled with you. But I'll not pay for schooling of any kind. No Selby woman is going to humiliate me by taking a job that rightfully belongs to a man."

"She's not *all* Selby, you realize." Mother appeared out of nowhere and clasped my shoulder. She gave Father a defiant glare, the likes of which I'd rarely seen. "I've found a few things in my mother's room to remind me that the Boon women have some strength of their own." She handed me a worn leather wallet thick with bills. "Here's your money, Rachel. It's more than enough, I'll wager, to persuade a college to overlook your gender and judge you on your abilities."

Father's eyes narrowed. "Where did that money come from?"

"I don't know. Maybe from the sale of my parents' hog

farm. I thought it had all gone to Father's brother years ago."
Giving my shoulder a squeeze, she said to me, "I know she'd
have wanted you to have it. You'll find a fairly recent newspaper
clipping tucked inside about Cornell University; they're considering opening their doors to women next year."

I could hardly comprehend the possibilities. I think my jaw
hung open. I looked from Mother, beaming, to Father, where-
upon my smile vanished.

"I won't allow it," he said, settling back in his chair and
crossing his arms.

"Yes, you will," Mother replied just as calmly and coolly
as if she were coaxing medicine into a stubborn child. "You've
always been the first person to jump in and demand a change or
an improvement when the situation calls for such. That's one of
the things I first admired in you. Now—"

"No," he declared.

She sighed and took a different tack. "August," she began,
and I started. I could count on one hand the number of times
she'd used Father's Christian name. "Men haven't been able
to cure this horse epidemic, now, have they? So why not let
your daughter lend her good sense and good mind to the cause?
Healthy horses can only bode well for Boston—and for Boston's
safety, wouldn't you agree?"

"I'll not agree to her attending veterinary school. It's not
right."

"Who's to say what is right? Ever since we moved here
you've been telling Rachel that time's overdue for some changes.

Well, times are changing, August. And your daughter—*our* daughter—is well equipped to lead some of these changes."

He silently stared at the two of us for what felt like an eternity, blinking solemnly behind his spectacles. At last his shoulders dropped a notch and he exhaled a blast of contempt, admitting temporary defeat. "I don't know the source of this stubbornness."

He could have been referring to Mother . . . but I accepted the compliment. "I do," I said, giving him a broad smile, then transferring it to Mother. "And thank you."

~ THIRTY-ONE

A KNOCK SOUNDED ON THE DOOR, AND WHEN MOTHER opened it, Mr. Stead was standing there holding his hat.

"I'm sorry I missed your mother's funeral, Mrs. Selby," he said. "I was treating the Crowningshield stable of horses for this distemper plague when I was called out to two emergencies in a row—a colic and a founder—and just now finished up. I came straightaway to pay my respects."

"Thank you, Mr. Stead. Won't you come in?"

"Hello, Rachel," he said.

"Hello," I answered with a smile, taking his hat.

Seeing Father in his study, Mr. Stead nodded a greeting, which prompted Father to rise and close his door. "I have a lot of work to do," he said gruffly, "so . . . forgive me."

Mother rolled her eyes and headed for the kitchen. "I think I'll brew another pot of tea. Rachel, please make Mr. Stead comfortable in the parlor."

In our too-small entry, shoulder brushed shoulder and I

blushed. Mr. Stead allowed me to lead the way, and then I stepped aside so that he could lower himself onto the settee. His long legs and arms folded into odd angles. I perched on the edge of a chair. The room suddenly seemed awfully warm to have a fire going.

"How long is this plague going to continue?" I asked.

He gave a weary shrug. "I don't know. At last count some twenty-eight thousand horses have taken ill between here and New York. It's still spreading, though some of the earliest to be affected are back in harness." Stretching his shoulders, he said, "I don't know which is going to give out first, the distemper or me. I'm exhausted."

He needed a good tonic, but with none at hand, I changed the subject. "How bad was the founder?"

"Rather bad," he replied. "The gelding's aged and his front feet were so feverish that he couldn't put any weight on them at all. He was nearly sitting on his haunches from the pain."

"Did you bleed him?"

"Yes and drenched him with warm saltwater."

"Did you soak his feet in the saltwater too?"

"Yes, Madam Veterinary, I did." He cocked his head in mock deference but grinned. "And I left instructions with the owner to continue soaking his horse's feet every hour. Now, did I forget anything?"

His smile lit mine. "No, you did a fine job, as usual."

When Mother returned with our tea, she found us engaged

in a spirited debate about shoeing a foundered horse. Mr. Stead firmly believed shoeing had no effect on the condition, while I maintained that letting the horse go barefoot—a more natural state—could at least make him more comfortable while he recovered. She shook her head in bemusement and left us to our quarrel.

I ached to tell him about the money, but the time didn't seem quite right, so when our conversation lulled, I asked, "Would you like some cake?"

"No, thank you," he replied, setting down his empty cup and standing. "It's warm in here and with me being so tired I'm starting to nod off. How about if we go call on our other patient?"

"All right." In short order we were heading out to the carriage shed.

The moment we stepped inside, the chestnut colt whinnied shrilly. It still seemed odd to see him in the Girl's stall, suspended in his sling. He looked so small and bony after her meaty presence. A pain stabbed my heart. I missed her, but I knew how much she'd missed her work. James had moved Freckles to a different stall and scrubbed hers with soap and scalding hot water, then again with a decoction of tobacco, before returning the Girl to the station on Sunday morning. He said he could hardly hold her back the last block, and that when she got inside the station, she'd rushed right into her stall, sniffed all around it, and given the wall a resounding kick that claimed ownership.

The colt whinnied another plea for freedom, and I ducked under the bar to stroke his neck. As usual he scrambled, three good legs and one bandaged leg flailing. "Easy there," I soothed. "You're going to be just fine. And don't you worry, I haven't lost a patient yet."

Mr. Stead joined me in the stall. He felt along the length of the bandage, then wiggled two fingers inside the top wrap to check for swelling. "How's he taking to the soaking? Are you managing it at least three times a day?"

"Five," I answered proudly. "And we're getting along wonderfully. I think we have a promising future together."

He stood up, looking at me in a funny way. "Is there room for one more in that future?" He cleared his throat and my pulse raced as he moved closer. He was going to . . . No! I was going to. I rose up on my toes and kissed him full on the lips. His eyes widened and he seemed momentarily taken aback. Thank goodness he chuckled. "You don't wait for anyone or anything, do you?"

"Not anymore," I half-croaked. I felt my face flush. "I'm going to become a veterinary. I'm determined to do it. The veterinary college here in Boston, the one where you went, turned me down, but Grandmother left me money, and I'm going to apply to some other colleges and . . . and I want to thank you for everything you've done. I promise I won't let you down."

Gentle humor lit his eyes. "I hope I don't let *you* down." Affectionately he brushed the tip of my nose just the way Grandmother had, and I got another pang at that. He ducked under the bar, all business again. "I'm completely used up, so I'm heading home for a long nap—I hope. I'll stop by tomorrow to check on him—and you," he added, smiling, "but send for me sooner if you need me."

"I will." I didn't want him to go; I wanted the three of us to stand ankle deep in the sweet-smelling straw and savor all that had happened, but I also needed time to think. And the carriage shed, even on a cold November afternoon, was the perfect place for contemplating the future.

When Mr. Stead's footsteps had faded, I turned back to the colt. He stopped his fretting long enough to nose my pocket inquisitively. He was a smart one; he'd already learned about the peppermints. I laughed and ran my fingers through his short, fluffy mane. He bumped me again. "All right, all right," I said. Reaching into my pocket, I discovered Mary Grace's letter. I'd almost forgotten it. Quickly I handed the colt his peppermint. He nodded his head up and down with enthusiasm, and I took that opportunity to duck out of the stall.

The packing quilt was folded on an empty barrel. I shook it free of dust and spiders, wrapped its heaviness around my shoulders, and settled onto the crate. Already smiling at what I expected to be Mary Grace's dramatics, I tore open the envelope.

When I unfolded the letter, a small coil of reddish horsehair fell onto my lap. I knew at once it was from Peaches, and my heart gave an anxious thud. The heading was dated October 5,

1872—over a month ago. What could have delayed its delivery?

"Dear Rachel," Mary Grace began.

I'm terribly sorry it's taken me so long to write. You know me, always tackling too many tasks in one day, correspondence rarely being one of them. I've been so busy planning my wedding that I've hardly had time to eat, which I've found is beneficial to the waistline and fainting spells. Mother says I'll be marching down the aisle in my underdrawers if I don't hurry up and decide on fabric for a dress, but did you ever realize how many different shades of white there are?

The real reason I'm writing is to tell you about your horse, Peaches. Why didn't you tell me that you were planning on selling her? I was so shocked to see her offered for sale at that old Mr. Cox's livery, and I said to myself, "They can't sell Rachel's horse to just anybody; it's not right." So I made my father go right down there and buy her for my sister Lucy. She's moony for horses like you were—are you still?—and I knew that your mare would take good care of her. Anyway, she lives in our carriage house now with Father's other horses and I think you would say that she's happy here. Lucy combs her mane so much that it rivals my hair for shine, and I don't think that horse goes to sleep at night until she's bedded knee-deep in clean straw. I've even caught Lucy trying to sleep in her stall with her. Honestly, she's just like you.

And that's the other reason I wanted her to have your horse, Rachel. You see, I've always admired you. I know we're different—I like clothes and shoes and fine china and you like horses, horses, and horses! Ha! But I like the fact that you never cared what people thought of you. I probably care too much, and that's its own kind of misery. I hope my sister grows up to be like you: strong and able to stand on her own two feet and on her own terms.

I was going to close this letter, but Lucy just came in and dropped this awful hank of hair on my writing desk. She says it's to remind you of Peaches and to let you know that she's happy. I hope you are too.

With all my best wishes,
Mary Grace.

Brimming with emotion, I refolded the letter and cradled it in my hands. The chestnut colt—I'd have to think of a name for him—was watching me with an impish look that promised adventure, and I smiled back at him with complete and utter satisfaction. Now *this* was a day to end all days . . . or to begin them.

AUTHOR'S NOTE

The Great Boston Fire of 1872 occurred only one year after Chicago's devastation. This historic blaze ate through Boston, destroying 775 buildings and causing millions of dollars in damage. The first sparks came from an empty hoopskirt factory, but how they ignited is still a mystery.

What made this fire unlike any of the other "great fires" of the time, though, is that half of Boston's firefighting strength—the horses—were sick or dead in their stalls when the alarm rang out. A huge epidemic, variously called "distemper" or "influenza" or "epizootic," was storming across the country that year. The disease had struck some thirty thousand horses in New York alone, and in Boston, commerce was at a virtual standstill. The city became a tinderbox, unprotected, and on the evening of November 9, everyone learned the value of the missing firehorses.

As I began to collect research materials on this unique event, and as a story began to form in my mind, I came across the diary of a fourteen-year-old girl who'd lived in Boston in

1872. Her writings became a prime resource, not only for the daily weather, but for household activities, meal preparation, and, most importantly, characteristic hopes and dreams of a Victorian teenager. Rachel's drive and her often intense emotions are modeled on the spirit of that diary.

But was the diary's author typical? Just what could girls achieve in 1872? Outside the home, I discovered, not much. This was an era when women couldn't vote, couldn't own property and, if they managed to enroll in university courses, often found that the boys in those courses refused to share the classroom with them. A retired Harvard medical professor even published a book warning that women who strived for such higher levels of learning risked the atrophy of their reproductive organs.

And yet there were stirrings—maybe corsets weren't necessary, maybe skating or hiking wasn't overly dangerous, maybe employment outside the home wasn't completely impossible. Independent spirits such as Elizabeth Cady Stanton and Susan B. Anthony were tirelessly demanding that women receive the same legal rights as men. In New York City, Dr. Emily Blackwell was overseeing the Women's Medical College founded by her sister and fellow physician, Elizabeth. Out west, Calamity Jane (born Martha Jane Cannary) was dressing in soldier's clothes and serving as a scout for George Custer. She rode, shot, and drank with the men. (Back East, though, it would take another thirty years for riding "cross-saddle" like a man to lose its scandal.)

So . . . what would happen if a girl who simply loved horses, who required their presence as much as she required oxygen, decided to become a veterinarian? In 1872 she'd have to fight against so many institutions: social convention, scientific "fact," familial beliefs, and even religious constraints. Could an adolescent have the strength to strike out on her own path, relying only on an instinct that said "this is what I was born to do"?

With the framework of my story in place, I set out to fill in the details. I read several novels from the period to better understand Victorian language and customs, as well as such conveniences as horsecars, kerosene lamps, and iceboxes. I consulted books on firefighting history to learn about firehorses and their training. Amazing. These specially chosen horses had to be brave enough to gallop *toward* a blazing fire rather than away from it. They had to be strong enough to pull a steam engine weighing two tons or more, yet agile enough to negotiate narrow streets and tight corners. On top of that, they had to be smart enough to dart from their stalls at the sound of the alarm and back into position in front of the engine or ladder or hose cart, waiting to be harnessed. It's no wonder these talented horses became neighborhood heroes.

As I was working my way through this novel, a serendipitous but calamitous event occurred: strangles (an equine disease also known as distemper) infected a stable run by a good friend of mine. I saw firsthand how the firehorses must have suffered: fever, lethargy, respiratory distress, a chokingly thick nasal discharge (horses can't breathe through their mouths.) Week upon week of stall rest was the only safe treatment agreed upon by local veterinarians, though antibiotics and surgical drainage were advised for the more severe cases. One horse died.

What did veterinarians of 1872 do for this disease? Research showed that veterinary medicine was still in its infancy at the time. While a few reputable veterinary schools existed, a diploma could easily be purchased through the mail. Antique veterinary manuals from my own collection advised noxious tonics and/or bloodletting for almost every illness.

I'd visited Boston once, but as I neared the climax of my story, I decided to travel there again. I arrived in late October, just two weeks before the anniversary of the fire. I walked the Common and the historic neighborhoods surrounding it, taking lots of photographs. I spent one fascinating morning in the city's library reading archived newspaper accounts of the fire, and discovering how the front pages of newspapers in 1872 featured stories little different from those of today. From those accounts I also tried to acquire an ear for the more florid language of the time so that Mr. Selby's columns would sound authentic.

Back home, one detail was still missing. I've ridden all my life, so I could draw on personal experience for much of Rachel's interaction with Peaches, and later, the Girl. I've often assisted equine veterinarians (and my father is a retired veterinarian), so I've seen much of what Rachel experiences. But one thing I'd not done is ridden—let alone galloped—a large, draft-type horse. A friend arranged for me to experience the power of a magnificent Friesian on a wide-open trail. Though I wasn't bareback, I was thus able to imagine Rachel's first breathtaking gallop astride the Governor's Girl.

As a woman living in the twenty-first century, I'm lucky

to have had spirited women pave the way for me. Yet even in these times of "equal rights" I've been told on more than one occasion that women can't or shouldn't venture into certain areas reserved for men. I don't believe that. This story is for all those girls who have been told "you can't" and still decide for themselves that "I *can*."